# Praise for

# VICKI HINZE

Dear Reader,

We're new, we're thrilling, and we're back with another explosive lineup of four Silhouette Bombshell titles especially for you. This month's stories are filled with twists and turns to keep you guessing to the end. But don't stop there—write and tell us what you think! Our goal is to create stories with action, emotion and a touch of romance, featuring strong, sexy heroines who speak to the women of today.

Critically acclaimed author Maureen Tan's *A Perfect Cover* delivers just that. Meet Lacie Reed. She'll put her life on the line to bring down a serial killer, even though it means hiding her identity from the local police—including one determined detective.

Temperatures rise in the latest Athena Force continuity story as an up-and-coming TV reporter travels to Central America for an exclusive interview with a Navy SEAL, only to find her leads drying up almost before her arrival. That won't deter the heroine of Katherine Garbera's *Exposed*....

They say you can't go home again, but the heroine of Doranna Durgin's first Bombshell novel proves the *Exception to the Rule*. Don't miss a moment as this P.I.'s assignment to guard government secrets clashes with the plans of one unofficial bodyguard.

Finally, truth and lies merge in *Body Double,* by Vicki Hinze. When a special forces captain loses three months of her memories, her search to get them back forces her to rely on a man she can't trust to uncover a secret so shocking, you won't believe your eyes....

We'll leave you breathless! Please send me your comments c/o Silhouette Books, 233 Broadway, Suite 1001, New York, NY 10279.

Best wishes,

Natashya Wilson
Associate Senior Editor

Please address questions and book requests to:
Silhouette Reader Service
U.S.: 3010 Walden Ave., P.O. Box 1325, Buffalo, NY 14269
Canadian: P.O. Box 609, Fort Erie, Ont. L2A 5X3

# VICKI HINZE

# BODY DOUBLE

*Silhouette*®

**BOMBSHELL**™

Published by Silhouette Books

America's Publisher of Contemporary Romance

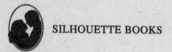

**SILHOUETTE BOOKS**

ISBN 0-373-51326-7

BODY DOUBLE

www.SilhouetteBombshell.com

**Printed in U.S.A.**

**VICKI HINZE**

is the author of fourteen novels, one nonfiction book and hundreds of articles published in more than forty countries. Her books have received many prestigious awards and nominations, including her selection for *Who's Who in America* (as a writer and educator) and nominations for *Romantic Times BOOKclub*'s Career Achievement and Reviewer's Choice Awards for Best Series Storyteller of the Year, Best Romantic Suspense Storyteller of the Year and Best Romantic Intrigue Novel of the Year. She cocreated an innovative, open-ended continuity series of single-title romance novels and has helped to establish subgenres in military women's fiction (suspense and intrigue) and military romantic-thriller novels.

To my beloved granddaughter:
Kaylin Elizabeth

You are my sun and joy, little one,
And I pray I prove worthy of the love for me
I see in your eyes.
Love,
Gran

# Chapter 1

They were going to kill her.

The odds of her leaving the Middle Eastern desert compound under her own steam grew slimmer by the minute. Her instincts hummed it. And if there was one thing Amanda knew she could count on, it was her instincts.

From the age of three, her instincts had warned her to hide when her dad got tanked up at home in New Orleans and came looking for her to use as a punching bag and then locked her in a wooden box until her bruises faded so looking at her didn't offend his eyes. Instinct had warned her to protect herself through a year of grueling CIA training at the nine thousand wooded-acre, barbed-wire-fenced hell known as "the farm" and four years of subsequent covert operations. Instinct had warned her it was time to get out of the CIA or wake up dead, and when the U.S. Air Force had recruited her out, instinct had told her to go.

Shortly thereafter, she had been assigned to S.A.S.S., Secret Assignment Security Specialists. On paper, they were a division of the Office of Special Investigations buried in the Office of Personnel Management along with all the other air force members assigned to paramilitary or covert operations, and had an official name so secret it changed every six months. Keeping up with the changes had everyone in the need-to-know loop dubbing the unit S.A.S.S. for convenience and consistency.

Her instincts had been on target all those times, and a million others, and they were on target now. She had used up her nine lives.

Today, Amanda West had run out of last chances.

"If she moves, shoot her," the beefy guard whose nose she'd broken told the other guards.

A certain satisfaction rippled through her. He had quickly developed a healthy respect for her and the damage she could inflict, but seriously. *Move?* Absurd. The ropes binding her to the chair cut deeply into her wrists and ankles, scraping her chafed skin, rubbing it raw. Her spine tingled, her ass and legs had been numb for hours. Her shoulders ached, head throbbed, and never in her life had she been more thirsty or tired.

She'd given up illusions. She had no idea what country they'd dragged her to, and during the last two days of intense interrogation by GRID's second-in-command, Paul Reese, she'd lost any hope that her identity had remained secret. GRID—Group Resources for Individual Development—was the largest intelligence broker in the world on U.S. resources, assets and personnel. Its operatives were experts at gathering and selling information, and masters at torturing to obtain it.

In the worst cases, evil is about ideology shaped by greed. GRID wasn't just shaped; it was twisted. That elevated GRID's ranking to worst of the worst. Its leader, Thomas Kunz, resented Germany's reliance on the U.S. military presence in his country. In his convoluted logic, Germany's economic woes were the U.S.'s fault, and he hated Americans for it. Of course, if the U.S. military pulled out of his country and Germany's economy suffered, Kunz would hate the U.S. for that, too.

Bottom line, Kunz hated the U.S. and what he hated, GRID hated.

Weak sunlight streaked into the cavernous metal building through dirt-smudged windows high overhead. Whether it was dawn or twilight, Amanda couldn't say. She'd been in and out of consciousness, and had lost track of time. All time. Sweat beaded at her temples, pooled between her breasts. Her once-white blouse clung limp, damp and dirty against her body, and her navy slacks were covered with a thin layer of dust. Her bare feet against the sandy dirt floor were crusted and itched.

They'd taken her shoes.

That had been her first warning that Reese knew who she really was, knew that her hands and feet were lethal weapons.

Through slitted eyelids, she looked over at him, standing with his hip hitched against a folding table, smoking a pungent cigarette that smelled of cloves. Tall, dark and, some would say, gorgeous with black hair and come-hither eyes, Reese was a lady-killer. Figuratively and, she feared, literally.

He exhaled, and smoke rose into obscuring plumes between them. Tossing the butt to the floor, he crushed it under his loafer-shod foot and glanced at the dozen guards circling her, as if reassuring himself of their presence and protection.

Wise move. Amanda wanted to kill him. Given the opportunity, she would kill him. And Reese knew it. He assumed professional necessity drove her, but it didn't. Her reasons were damn personal. Amanda's dad had been the last man to hit her and live. That was a record she intended to keep intact.

The guards stood ready, dressed in camouflage gear, looking like the skilled mercenaries they had proven to be during her capture. She had only disabled three of them. Only three.

They were professional warriors, and for all they had known, she was merely a small, fragile woman. They hadn't yet contended with Captain Amanda West, former CIA operative and current U.S. Air Force paramilitary S.A.S.S. operative—the real her. Now they'd gotten a taste.

Because she'd downed three of them, they hungered for revenge the way starving dogs covet bones: standing at the ready, just hoping she'd give them the slightest excuse to cut loose. All twelve of the men carried M-16s, all twelve aimed directly at her chest.

"Amanda." Reese sounded exasperated. He stepped over to her but stayed out of striking distance, in case the ropes didn't hold. "You're being totally unreasonable."

Unreasonable was denying her water and sleep. She should feel grateful the bastards hadn't resorted to rape, but in a sense they had. They hadn't molested her body, but Reese had done all he could to rape her soul. Fortunately—though it was hard for her to imagine "fortunate" and "her father" in the same breath—she'd been raised by the devil himself. Reese wasn't nearly so formidable.

She wasn't a kid anymore. And she damn sure was not helpless, not anymore.

"I wished to avoid this, but you've given me no choice." Reese sighed heavily, a tinge of regret touching his voice. "I've called Thomas."

*Thomas Kunz.* Her heart slammed against her chest wall, hammered hard. Reese was dangerous, but Kunz was lethal. The GRID mastermind had united henchmen of all nationalities and from all walks of life with a single, driving goal: to destroy the United States. Under his leadership, GRID had proven so capable at infiltrating U.S. assets, and so elusive at being pinned down long enough to be captured, that Secretary of Defense Reynolds had deemed the situation critical and issued a by-name request through Colonel Sally Drake, action officer and commander of S.A.S.S., to gather desperately needed insight on GRID and devise a containment plan.

That by-name request had been for Amanda.

"Answer me, Amanda." Reese shoved a hand into the pocket of his black slacks. "What have you reported? To whom do you report?"

Reese's yellow shirt looked fresh and crisp, his tanned skin hydrated, and no dark, exhausted circles marred the skin beneath his eyes. Hating him for that, she stared at him from under her lashes. "I don't know what you're talking about."

Reese slapped her.

Her face stinging, she glared into his eyes, smiled, then feigned hurt, preying on his vanity—a tactic that had consistently proven effective with him. "I guess chivalry is dead."

Unable to hold her gaze, he looked away.

It was a small victory, but at the moment, she'd take any she could get. Paul Reese was clever but shallow, into money and power, with a fondness—and weakness—for pretty women, and an ego the State of Texas couldn't hold. He had described himself to her as a gallant white knight, chivalrous to women, and she'd come to realize that the deluded fool believed it. Blowing his image by torturing her had gotten to him. He didn't have the guts to kill her.

That, Reese would leave to Kunz.

Never in her life had she heard of anyone quite as cold-blooded and ruthless as Thomas Kunz. Or as suspicious. Grudgingly, she admitted that those were the very attributes that had kept him alive.

"He's coming, Amanda." Reese switched tactics, his voice and expression concerned and urgent. "I don't want him to hurt you."

"Hurt me?" Kunz would kill her, and only an idiot wouldn't

know it. She swallowed a grunt and taunted Reese. "After all we've meant to each other, you're going to allow him to do that?"

Exasperated, Reese forgot caution, grabbed her face and squeezed until her teeth cut into her flesh. "Do you want to die, woman?"

She didn't. She wanted to live—God, how she wanted to live—and to bring GRID down. When the pressure on her cheeks eased and settled to a dull ache, she softened her voice. "Will you let him kill me, Paul?"

"Let him?" Reese let his head loll back, blew out a sigh. "Don't you understand? I can't stop Thomas. No one can stop him." Reese dropped his voice. "He likes inflicting pain. He *likes* it, Amanda. You won't die easily."

In her premission briefing, she'd been warned that Kunz took a sadistic pleasure in torture. If any of his victims ever survived to act as witnesses, he'd be prosecuted for war crimes as a hostile combatant in the war on terror. So far none had made it.

That knotted the muscles in her stomach. Fear and bitterness flooded her throat. "I'm not afraid to die." It was true. Her fear had always been in living, not dying. In death, there was safety; there was peace. In life, there was brutality and pain. You had to be clever, sly, cunning, always on guard and able to defend yourself. And she had been. Yet in some situations, defeat was inevitable. The realist in her warned that this was one of them.

Stiffening her spine, she watched for an opening. She was going to die, and she wouldn't get Kunz. But she would take Paul Reese with her.

"You'd better fear it." Frustration reddened his face, had the veins in his neck sticking out like thumbs. He bent to her. "You'd better fear him."

"Reese." Leaning forward, she brushed her lips close to his

ear. "I'll tell you a secret." She sank her teeth into him, doing her damnedest to rip the jugular right out of his throat.

He howled, jerked, and she lost her grip, scraped his throat, then clenched her jaw and latched on to his face. Backing away, he dragged her, chair and all, until finally his flesh gave way. Her chair tipped over and her shoulder slammed into the dirt.

Screaming curses, he held the side of his face. Blood streamed between his fingers, over his hand and down his arm. He kicked her in the ribs, then again in the thigh. His guards stood stunned, too surprised to react.

"There's your secret, darling." She glared up at him, feeling his wet blood soak her face. "You'd better fear me."

He took a white handkerchief from one of the guards and pressed it to his face. "Shoot that bitch right between the eyes."

"Come on, Reese. Be a sport." She smiled. "I missed your jugular."

He kicked her again. "Give me a gun!"

Her ribs ached like hell. Still she laughed, hard and deep. So she wouldn't die with the pleasure of having killed him. Maybe to Reese, screwing up his face was worse than death. There was solace in that.

A guard passed him an M-16. He took aim at her. Adrenaline rocketed through her veins, but she knew how to die. She'd been prepared for this moment since she was three years old and her father first beat her. *No fear. Not from me, you bastard. Never from me. "Ich dien."*

"What did she say?" Reese looked at the guards, wild-eyed.

The response came from the door. "I serve."

*Kunz.* Blinded by the sunlight streaming in around him, she could only see his silhouette.

He walked over to where she lay on the floor, still tied to

the chair. "Captain West. How good of you to visit," Kunz said. "I wasn't aware you spoke German. Hmm, I wonder how we missed that. Please note it, Paul."

Kunz was acting as if he'd missed the fact that she was taunting Paul, letting him know—letting them all know—that they hadn't broken her and never would. Kunz was younger than she had thought. Forty, tall, blond-haired and blue-eyed. Amazingly, he looked like a good-natured, sunny kind of guy. Certainly not like the devil incarnate that would do his reputation justice. This man didn't inspire fear, or even alert the senses that danger was near, and Intel had it all wrong on his photos. She didn't know who was actually in the pictures but it was not the Thomas Kunz standing before her now. "Mr. Kunz." She nodded, grinding her ear into the dirt. "I would say it's a pleasure, but at the moment your hospitality lacks a certain, shall we say, charm."

"Ah, your southern roots are showing. Finally." His smile didn't touch his eyes. "Put the gun down, Paul." He glimpsed toward Reese. "I've decided the good captain doesn't need killing, only burying. But not in a grave. Captain West prefers tombs to graves. They're more in keeping with her New Orleans heritage."

Reese's eyes stretched wide. "You're going to seal her in there alive?"

"Of course." Kunz walked over to the table and opened a metal box that had been sitting there untouched for two days. "It's only civilized to give her time to make her peace, hmm?"

Amanda tried not to shudder, but it was obvious that the real torture was only now to begin.

"I said to put down the gun, Paul. Hostility doesn't become you." He nodded toward the door. "Get someone to see to your face."

Reese walked to the door still cupping the blood-soaked

handkerchief over his wound. "I'm glad you're going to die a slow death, you bitch."

"Do think of me, Paul." She smiled. "Every time you look in the mirror."

He slammed the door shut. The windows above rattled.

Kunz took her measure. "You're very astute, Captain. Few things could upset Paul as much as damaging his face." Kunz's eyes sparkled respect. "And you're clearly not a coward." That seemed to intrigue him. "Few men have refused to respond to Paul's inquiries, knowing they would next face mine. You're the first woman to do so, actually."

She hiked an eyebrow. "What shall we do to celebrate?"

He looked back over his shoulder, saw her defiance, smiled, and filled a syringe. When he tapped it, a small amount of fluid spurted and soaked into the floor. "I have a special treat for you," he said, walking over and then injecting her. "In honor of the occasion."

The stick in her arm burned. There were other needle tracks on her inner arm. How had they gotten there? She couldn't remember. Stark terror shot through her. This would kill her or cost her everything.

Kunz smiled.

The bastard knew. He knew, and it amused him. Her temper exploded, and it took everything she had to restrain herself. He had taken everything else, she would not give him that, too. Panic seized her, contorted her muscles. *No. No fear. No fear. You will find a way around this, Princess. You will not show this scum fear.*

"There you go." He pulled out the needle, and then backed away. "Contrary to what you might believe, in your time with us, you've been very cooperative. We've learned all we need to know from you, Captain. For now."

He wasn't bluffing. And if he wasn't bluffing, she'd definitely breached security. What had she told him? *When* had she told him anything? She'd never seen the man until today. He was bluffing—had to be—and he was damn good at it, making her doubt herself. "So now I die," she said. "I suppose it doesn't matter, but what did you give me?"

"Peace." He brushed her cheek with a feathery-light fingertip.

It sent icy chills down her neck and through her chest.

When she didn't cringe as he obviously expected, respect lighted in his eyes. "I'd love to stay and enjoy the day with you, but you've caught me at an inopportune time. I'm very sorry to say that this will be clean and quick. You would have been intriguing, I'm sure." He let his gaze roll over her, prone on the floor. "But my loss is your gain. You really should thank me for it."

"Thank you," she said and meant it. He loved torture and she'd seen file photos of what was left of some of his victims. She was truly grateful to be spared.

He picked up on her sincerity. "You're welcome, Captain West." Walking back to the table, he put the syringe into a box. "The miracles of modern medicine amuse me." He waved a loose hand. "Incidentally, that injection won't kill you. It'll just make you sleep for a while so you don't injure any more of my men. You'll wake up, and then—well, you'll see. No need to make peace with your God just yet. You'll have a few days to decide your fate."

"My fate?"

"Yes. Your reaction to it will be most amusing to watch."

Puzzled by his cryptic comments, she shot him a questioning look. "My reaction to my fate will be amusing?" What the hell could he mean by that?

"You've got a dilemma before you, Captain. The dilemma is entertaining, but your reaction to your fate will be by far the most intriguing aspect of your—shall we say, situation."

She opened her mouth to snap at him, to inform him with

unwavering certainty that her fate was her own and none of his business, but her tongue was too thick; she couldn't speak. He droned on, but she couldn't make out his words. His voice faded, as if echoing from deep in the belly of a cave. Amanda strained to keep watch, but her eyelids wouldn't stay open.

"She's safe," he eventually told the guards. "Bury her—remember, a tomb, not a grave. The good captain has a fondness for aboveground boxes."

*The box.* She might have groaned, though she couldn't be certain the sound was hers and not the guards laughing. The box was the thing she hated most—and the thing people like Kunz would imagine she feared most.

She did fear it. But she also had learned young to hide in the damn thing to avoid being found and beaten. Inside the box was the *last* place her father ever would have thought to look for her. And *that* Kunz didn't know.

Yet he did know about the box. But how? The only other person in the world who knew about it was her father, and she had avoided him for years. Even today she didn't trust herself to see him and not kill him. And never in her adult life had she given *anyone* the means to connect them. So how had Thomas Kunz known about the box?

Even beaten to within an inch of her life, she would shield that information. She had never admitted it to another human being—often, not even to herself.

But if her father hadn't told Kunz about the box, and she hadn't told him, then how did he know about it? As the blackness overcame her, all she could think was, *How?*

Amanda awakened in pitch-black darkness.

Her mouth felt like cotton, her head throbbed. She lay wedged in a box, but this one wasn't wood, it was brick, and the mortar was still wet.

*The son of a bitch actually* had *bricked her into a tomb.*

That was her first thought. Which son of a bitch? was her second. Somehow she knew it had been Kunz, knew he'd told her he was going to do so. But for some reason, she couldn't remember the actual telling.

They'd taken her out of the chair; it wouldn't fit with her in the small area. But her hands were still tied. She worked the ropes loose with her teeth. Finally, they fell free.

Sliding her hand along the wall, over the rough brick, she felt the wet mortar stick to her fingers. "Where's a good spiked heel when you need one?"

She felt all along the perimeter of the sealed tomb, dragging her fingers through the dirt. Nearly through working the grid, she felt a bump, backed up, and felt—a stick? No, spear-tipped. Feather. An arrow. It was an arrow.

Reese collected arrows. He'd buried it with her as a final dig, proof that he had won.

But he hadn't won. *Not yet. Not…yet.*

Seeking the wettest mortar, she hoped that it was away from whomever was watching her, if anyone, and dared to hope, too, that they didn't hear the noise. "You will dig yourself out of this tomb, Princess," she whispered to herself, using the hated name her father had called her. "You will live. You will kill Paul Reese for hitting you. And you will capture Thomas Kunz and steal his life for stealing yours."

It took forever. She slept, worked, slept and worked and worried about what to do. Her knuckles were raw, her stomach turning over on itself, and she was so thirsty she thought she might die from that alone. Finally, she punched through the wall. Bracing, she drew up her knees, got leverage, and then kicked. Before long, she'd kicked out a hole large enough to crawl through.

Wary, expecting to be leveled or shot by a guard as soon as her feet touched the ground, she dived through the opening, rolled over the crumbled brick and concrete. A chunk dug into her hip and pain shot through her side.

"An actual cemetery." She looked around at row upon row of graves and tombs, reflecting in the full moonlight. Seeing no one, she hurriedly stacked the loose bricks back into the opening, hoping to lessen the odds of her escape being quickly noticed, then crept from tombstone to tombstone to get a fix on her location.

James St. Claire. 1926–1959.
Jacob Charles Anderson. Beloved Father and Husband.
Alison Hayes. Age: 3 Blessed Days. "Safely into the arms of Angels."

American, Amanda thought. Definitely American. The smell of ash trees and wildflowers filled her nose. Somewhere in the south, but not Georgia. In the Carolinas, maybe. She eased out of the cemetery and into the woods, her left arm throbbing.

Pausing, she twisted it in the moonlight. Dark bruises muddied her arm, wrist to elbow. It was swollen and caked with blood near the thumb side of her wrist. It was a wound. An IV wound.

Baffled, she just stared at her arm. When had she had an intravenous tube?

Her stomach soured. She frantically looked around. She'd been in the desert. Now she was in the woods. *Where was she?*

A road stretched out up ahead. Deserted, no buildings—nothing but woods and empty road in all directions. She walked down it until she reached a crossroad and saw a sign. *Freedom Lane* and *Liberty Way?*

Amanda came to a dead stop. This couldn't be. She'd been somewhere in the Middle East. Somewhere in the desert. How had she gotten to a North Carolina cemetery? To a CIA extraction point, for God's sake?

Kunz was rubbing her nose in it. He was betting she would hide the truth about this lapse in her memory to save her job. He knew she was a loner, that her job was all she had, and if she reported the memory lapse, she'd lose her security clearance. A S.A.S.S. operative without a security clearance was worthless. She'd have nothing.

Dread dragged at her belly. Thomas Kunz knew far more than S.A.S.S. or the CIA believed—about her, and obviously about U.S. clandestine operations.

Stunned, reeling from the implications of all this, she checked the moon. Dawn would come in about two hours. She walked off the road into the open clearing. A chopper would be by before daybreak. This was a daily drop zone she and other intelligence sources used often. There was an artesian well here. *Water!*

She ran to it, drank thirstily, then drowned her face and washed in the cool water. As it sluiced over her, she sighed. Sex had rarely felt this good.

The chopper arrived before she stopped dripping water. She wrung out the edge of her shirt, signaled, and it set down in the clearing.

What had Kunz done to her? That she didn't know roused demons of being violated and abused and her hatred for not being in control. Her skin went clammy cold and her heart raced, thumping like a jackhammer in her head.

*What are you going to do about this?*

She should report it immediately to her boss, Colonel Drake.

*You'll be fired on the spot.*

But if she didn't report it, S.A.S.S. missions and operatives could be vulnerable. Kunz had gotten her from the Middle East to Carolina without her knowing it. Was it so hard to imagine him getting her to talk, to breach security and identify and compromise other agents and missions?

*There's no easy way out.*

There didn't seem to be even a reasonable way out.

*There isn't. You're screwed.*

Totally.

*Kunz took a huge risk, leaving you at a CIA drop zone. He had to be extremely confident you'd hide the truth. How could he be so confident?*

She didn't have a clue. At the moment, she didn't know herself what she was going to do.

When she boarded the chopper, a stranger sat in the pilot's seat. "Who are you? Where's Harry?"

"I'm Jim." The pilot blinked hard and fast. "Harry's dead, ma'am."

She plopped down in her seat and buckled in. *"Dead?"*

"Yes, ma'am. He crashed in Iraq about two months ago."

The man had lost his mind. "What the hell are you pulling here? Harry was alive and well less than a week ago."

He reeled off his security-clearance code and then asked, "Would you verify your identity, ma'am?"

"Captain Amanda West," she said. "Alpha Tango 135812."

"I was sure by your pictures, but—but—" he sputtered, stalled, and then finally went on. "You can't be Captain West, ma'am. It's not possible."

Oh, for God's sake. She was exhausted, starved, soaked and out of patience. "It's possible. I'm here, aren't I?"

"No—I mean, yes, ma'am. But you can't be here. I mean, how did you get here, ma'am? You've been MIA."

"Yeah, well. This jerk bricked me in a tomb." She shook her head, tried not to think about Harry. She'd liked him. She'd mourn him as soon as she regrouped. Right now, it took all she had to hold it together. "It took me a while to make it out."

"You had rations in a tomb?"

She looked at Jim as if he'd lost his mind. "I had the tip of a broken arrow."

He thought a long moment, his sober expression eerie in the green light cast from the chopper's control panel. "So you're saying," he spoke slowly, "that you haven't been on an insertion mission. You've been in a tomb. And you've lived in that tomb without food or water for three months?"

"Damn right—no, that's not what I'm—" Cold chills swam up and down her backbone, set the roof of her mouth to tingling. "Did you say, *three months?*"

"Yes, ma'am." He nodded. "That's how long you've been missing."

"But—but that's outrageous." She'd been tortured, injected with something, and then awakened in the tomb and dug her way out. Okay, she didn't remember the IV, but she damn sure would have remembered *something* in three months. "Three days, maybe. But not three months."

"I'm telling you, it's been three months since we received any transmission from you, ma'am. I should know when you went missing. I flew the search team who went in looking for you."

*Three months?* She couldn't wrap her mind around it. How could that be possible? Why would Kunz want to knock her out of commission for three months? And again, what *exactly* had he done?

# Chapter 2

"Kate?" Amanda waited for her fellow S.A.S.S. operative, Captain Katherine Kane, to look up from her desk.

Relief flooded her solemn eyes. She stood up and hugged Amanda. "You're back." She clapped Amanda's shoulder, her turbulent expression at odds with her quiet features. "Damn, Amanda. We thought you were dead."

Kate, the unit's bomb-squad specialist with expertise in biological and chemical weapons, was the taller of the two at five-eight, with green eyes and short, curly blond hair. Amanda's eyes were blue and her hair was long and deep brown. Both women were in good physical condition—they had to be. "I thought I was dead, too, for a while." She nodded toward Colonel Sally Drake's office door. "Is she waiting for me?"

Kate nodded. "Jim radioed the tower from the chopper. They let her know you were on the way in."

Well, here it came. No moment of truth waits forever. She

had to choose: lie and stay safe, or tell the truth and be sacrificed.

"You don't look happy to be back."

Amanda shrugged. "Overload."

"Rough?" Empathy shone in Kate's eyes. She knew what could happen to an exposed operative stuck in the field.

"Yeah." Amanda didn't hesitate or bother trying to lie. It'd be futile. "Let's talk later, after I see Colonel Drake."

"We'll have dinner." They were both loners, like so many of the S.A.S.S. operatives, but Kate seemed to know that Amanda's first night home would be especially difficult. Flashbacks to captivity were most potent and disorienting in the early days after release.

"Amanda." Colonel Drake appeared at her office door. In her late forties, the S.A.S.S. commander looked lean and mean. She was a redhead; her hair cropped short and spiked, bold and brassy. It suited her style. "How was your vacation?"

Drake was already trying to cover Amanda's ass. She was a good woman and a great commander. "Fabulous." Amanda smiled. "Check out the tan." She walked into Colonel Drake's inner sanctum and sat down.

The colonel took her chair behind her wide desk, dropped the light tone and got serious. "You okay?"

The moment of truth. "Yes, I am. But we have a problem."

"Scale?"

Colonel Drake assigned everything a value from one to ten. "Twenty."

Her serious expression turned grim. "Enough said. What do you need?"

Amanda nearly sighed her relief. She didn't know what had happened, and if Colonel Drake let her report that, then the colonel would have no choice but to act on it. This was a whacked-out version of "don't ask, don't tell"—dangerous as hell, considering—but Amanda grabbed it with both hands.

In a display of ultimate trust, the colonel was giving Amanda a chance to do what she had to do to protect the interests of the U.S. and S.A.S.S. without sacrificing herself or her job. But was that possible?

Amanda wasn't sure. She licked at her lips. "I need to see the medical officer right away."

"Can it wait until after the mission outbriefing?" Colonel Drake frowned.

"No, ma'am. Time is of the essence. I need some blood work done."

Drake leaned forward, laced her hands atop her desk. "Were you raped, Amanda?"

She couldn't do it. She couldn't lie to protect her own interests and leave S.A.S.S. wide open. Kunz must have believed she would—her career was all she had to lose—or he never would have allowed her to escape from the tomb. He needed blackmail fodder. Something important enough to her that she'd agree to spy for him in exchange for keeping the truth about her blackouts buried.

Same damn manipulation tactics as her father. An icy shiver swept up her spine, and anger flooded down it. *Use and abuse and to hell with the consequences.*

Anger boiled over into outrage and stretched deep down inside her, into memories she kept tightly locked away because they filled her with bitterness and hatred and smothered all that was good. She fought them. Long ago, she had chosen not to live her life hating, and she hadn't, but the memories were so dark and ugly, and so strong. God, but they were strong.

Her father had controlled her until she had stopped letting him. She was nine years old and recalled in intimate detail that entire day. He'd heaped abuse on her head, on her body, and she'd been totally removed from it, resolved not to let it touch her. And it was as if all those things were happening to someone else. Someone made of steel, who could take anything and not be destroyed by it. After that day, he had bruised her body, but never again did he poison her mind or heart.

And she'd be damned if Kunz would, either.

Visualizing a safe, Amanda shoved the dark memories, the anger and bitterness and hatred back inside it, and then slammed the door and jerked the key from its lock. *You control you, Princess. You choose. Kunz will not blackmail you into spying for him. No man will use you again. Ever!*

Kunz underestimating her was her only satisfaction in all of this. Amanda blinked hard. The next words out of her mouth would irrevocably change her life. She would forfeit all she had, her job, and leave herself with nothing.

"I don't know."

Amanda dressed behind a screen into her uniform, and then stepped out into the examining room, fastening the last of the buttons on her pale blue uniform top. Colonel Drake stood with arms folded over her chest by the door. She had to be here to protect Amanda's security clearance, but because it already had been violated, she avoided looking at her.

The medical officer, Dr. Vargus, sat at a small desk in the corner, writing in Amanda's records. Graying at the temples, he sported a permanent frown from too much squinting to read small print. Finally, he swiveled on his stool and looked at her, his glasses resting on the tip of his nose. "Well, there's no physical damage indicating rape. But you have had sex."

*With whom?* The question seared her mind, but she didn't dare ask it. He wouldn't be able to answer her anyway. The violation of her body infuriated her and she stomped down those feelings. She couldn't admit to Dr. Vargus that if she'd had sex, she *had* most certainly been raped. "What about the blood work?"

"The AIDS test results will take time. But there are traces

of flunitrazepam, a benzodiezpine—sometimes known as 'roofies'—in your bloodstream." He removed his glasses, looked up at her. "Are you having any symptoms of amnesia, forgetfulness? Time lapses?"

"Don't answer that, Captain." Colonel Drake stepped forward. "Next question, Dr. Vargus."

He frowned. "How can I help her if I don't know her symptoms?"

"National interests," Drake said. "Work around it."

Obviously he'd heard this before and disagreed with the policy. But a new respect for Amanda lighted in his eyes. He glanced at her then back at Drake, and bitterness etched his tone. "Fine. Sacrifice the patient for the nation. I've got it."

Amanda appreciated his concern, but couldn't show it. She stared at him, her expression blank, her eyes giving away nothing, and waited.

Finally, he went on. "Captain West. The traces of the drugs found in your blood would be consistent with memory challenges—if you were experiencing any. They induce amnesia and are most often used during surgical procedures, though lighter doses with short-term effects are popular in social drug-use circles."

Amanda chose her words carefully. "Are these drugs capable of inducing actual blackouts?"

"Absolutely."

Again, she approached with caution. "For extended periods of time?"

"How extended?" he asked.

"Several months?"

His face paled. Dr Vargus paused for a long moment, looking deeply into her eyes, clearly getting a grip on what had happened to her. "If a patient received repeated doses of these drugs at regular intervals, then yes, it's possible."

"Would there be long-term effects?"

"Not that we're aware of," he said, then paused to rub his chin. "But that type of use is atypical, so there's no scientific data to back up my opinion. The truth is, I don't know, Captain. There could be some residual effects."

"Residual effects?"

He scrunched a shoulder. "Slurred speech, slowed psychomotor responses, maybe symptoms of being intoxicated. These might be precursors to a more severe period of amnesia."

Amanda's stomach flipped. "And how long might this period last, do you think?" She lifted a hand. "Speculating, of course."

"A few hours," he said. "Maybe a little longer."

She could live with that. But Amanda didn't dare to look at Colonel Drake to see how she'd reacted to this possibility. "Thank you, Doctor." Amanda tucked her cap between her belt and slacks, and walked to the door. Colonel Drake opened it and stepped aside.

"Captain West," Dr. Vargus called out.

"Yes, sir?"

"If your security clearance requires you to have an escort during medical treatments to verify security breaches have not occurred, then mine requires me to remind you that if you have had any instances of memory loss, regardless of how minor or incidental they might seem, it's your duty to report them."

"Dr. Vargus." Colonel Drake stepped forward. The steel in her voice matched that in her eyes. "Thank you for fulfilling your notification requirements. Rest assured that we will utilize all means necessary to meet our obligations." Colonel Drake lifted a hand, motioning to the door. "Let's go, Captain."

Amanda cast a parting glance at Vargus. He knew. The question was would he report them. "Thank you, Dr. Vargus."

He held her gaze a second longer than necessary, then nodded, sat back down and buried his head in the file, signaling her he would play ostrich and forget the questions he'd been asked. There would be no report.

Shaking, Amanda followed Colonel Drake out of the office.

When they stepped out into the bright summer sun, they both put on their caps and walked toward Building 7, which housed the S.A.S.S. offices. "Thanks for the backup in there," Amanda said.

"It's my job." Drake looked down to the corner. "Must be trouble at the office. Kate's coming after us."

Amanda wasn't ready for more trouble. She needed time to get a grip on her current situation. But Kate kept on coming, dragging a black suitcase on wheels down the sidewalk.

When they met halfway, Colonel Drake said, "What's up?"

"I know we're not talking about this, but there's a lead investigator for the Office of Special Investigations in Florida at Providence Air Force Base who went missing for a while back for three months." Kate blushed. "I didn't mean to listen, okay? The walls in the office are paper thin and unless you're whispering, or in the vault, your voices carry." She passed Amanda the suitcase. "Everything you'll need for a few days is in there. Chopper's waiting on the pad to fly you down there."

Amanda wasn't sure what to do, and Colonel Drake looked torn. Kate lifted her eyebrows and Amanda stilled, waiting for the colonel's decision. If Amanda took that case and got on the chopper, then all three of them—she, Kate and Colonel Drake—would be deliberately violating regulations that could land them in Leavenworth for ten to twenty years. But if Amanda didn't go, her career was finished and the truth would never be exposed. She'd never know if Kunz really had done this to other military members, and if he had, how many times. She'd never know for what purpose. And she'd have to live forever with knowing she had deliberately left the U.S. vulnerable.

"Colonel," Kate said. "Captain Mark Cross isn't the only one. Two men in his unit also have three-month unexplained absences and both of them are being tried for murder."

"Murder?" Amanda shuddered.

Kate nodded. "One supposedly killed his wife, the other his significant other. The evidence is overwhelming, but Mark swears neither of them are guilty."

"The absences are pervasive," Colonel Drake said, then looked at Amanda, resolved. "With millions of military and civilian employees in the potential victim pool, we have to find out how pervasive." She parked a hand on her hip, mulled over her thoughts for a moment, and then continued. "I'm declaring this a Special Project."

That designation gave the case the highest priority. It also knocked out the need to abide by a million little regulations and courtesies that ordinarily they would endure. Amanda nodded at the colonel.

"You're primary," Drake told Amanda. "Kate, you assist her." After a brief glance in Kate's direction, Colonel Drake focused again on Amanda. "Get to the bottom of this fast, and keep me posted. S.A.S.S. doesn't leave the U.S. vulnerable, and neither its operatives nor its commander does jail. Remember that."

"Yes, ma'am." Amanda took the case from Kate. Since the truth was out in the open now, there was no sense in hiding it. "What about my clearance?" she asked. It should be revoked, but without it, she'd never find the truth.

The colonel hiked her strong chin. "Your clearance is in perfect order, Captain. Go—and make damn sure you pay attention to residuals."

The potential effects Dr. Vargus had warned her could happen. Big order. Huge, considering she didn't know what she didn't know, and what she didn't know appeared to involve a lot more military personnel than just her. "I'll do my best."

She would. And she'd pray like hell it was good enough.

When Amanda stepped off the helicopter at Providence Air Force Base in Florida, the humidity slapped her in the face like a steamy wet washcloth. A tall man in uniform, wearing captain's bars on his shoulders, stood waiting beside a standard-issue blue sedan. Seeing that he had her attention, he waved.

Assuming he was Captain Mark Cross, she walked toward him. As she stepped closer, his features cleared. Long and lean, broad-shouldered, with a hard, angular face framed by black hair and gray eyes that, at the moment, held distrust, surprise and just enough subdued appreciation to stroke her ego without caressing it. Looking at him had words like *interesting, intriguing* and *sexy as hell* flowing through her mind. "Captain Cross?"

He nodded, extended a hand. "Mark, please."

"Amanda." She shook his hand and liked the feel of his grip. Not too hard, but solid and firm enough to assure her she could depend on him. She'd always judged a man by his handshake and Captain Mark Cross passed.

"We're being watched. Get in the car."

She resisted the urge to look around, stowed her case in the back seat and then slid into the front beside him. "Safe?"

"Yes. I swept the car for listening devices. It's clean." He slid the gearshift into Drive, hit the gas and drove away from the chopper's landing pad.

"Who's following you?"

"I don't know—yet. Two cars. Two men. Civilian clothes. They locked on to me right after Kate called and they've been running a rolling-parallel maneuver, tracking me ever since."

So his office phone was bugged and the men tailing them were professionals. "You know Kate personally?"

"We worked together for a time before she got assigned to S.A.S.S. and we became close friends." He grunted. "Actually, we're more like each other's surrogate family. Neither of us has any."

"So you adopted each other. Nice." She turned the topic. "You think your shadows are connected to me, then?"

He spared her a glance. "That would be a logical deduction, Amanda."

"You've already got a theory. I see it in your face."

"It's pretty clear someone doesn't want us sharing information on our absences." Turning into a half-full lot, he parked the car near a tall building with no windows—the vault: a site for top-secret work. "We need a place to talk freely."

"Suggestions?" She assumed he'd recommend the vault. Vaults always had extensive security, including white-noise devices to prohibit communications being intercepted by unfriendly forces.

He didn't. "At this point, I'd prefer total isolation. Unfortunately, that can't be assured here."

Surprise had her skeptical. "Not even in the vault?"

"Not even there." His steady gaze didn't waver. "My boat is safe, if you have no objections to being isolated on it with me."

She wasn't sure if she should be insulted or honored that he'd asked. If he assumed she had been raped during her captivity, then his consideration was noble. If he assumed she feared him, then it was insulting to her operative skills. Unable to decipher his intentions, she elected to give him the benefit of the doubt and let the matter slide. "I have no objections."

Her lack of hesitation surprised him. "You're pretty trusting for a seasoned S.A.S.S. operative. Anyone can put on a uniform, Amanda. I haven't proven who I am to you."

Questioning her abilities. How typical. "You look exactly as you do in your dossier photo, Captain Cross. And you don't have to prove who you are, I know." Her temper rose just enough for her to want to knock him down a notch. "You were with Delta Force, pulling Black World operations, transferred out when you went missing for three months and your security clearance was lowered. You've won two Purple Hearts—one in Afghanistan and one in the second war with Iraq—and you've got a total of sixteen bronze stars. You've been at Providence Air Force Base for over a year, trying to find out what happened to you during your three-month absence and finally using that law degree you picked up somewhere along the way to prove two men in your unit are innocent of murder. You believe them. No one else does—the evidence is overwhelming, which in my mind brings the reliability of your judgment into question. You like to boat, to saltwater fish, and you listen to country music—station 105.5 mostly. You've never been married, you're thirty-two, heterosexual, you don't smoke, drink only socially, and you date heavily, though you never see the same woman more than six times—which in my mind also brings the reliability of your judgment into question."

She popped on her sunglasses and turned to look at him. "I don't trust at all, Captain Cross."

"Apparently, I misjudged you."

Damn right. "Allowing underestimation is an extremely effective weapon."

"We're on the same team."

"That's yet to be decided, and frankly I'm not eager to take you on."

"Why not?"

"You're high liability." Glancing over, she frowned into the side-view mirror. "You've misjudged your shadows, too. That's three judgment errors, Captain, and the third is about to cost us both a great deal." She nodded behind them, where two cars were parked side-by-side. "They're edgy, and if you don't get out of this parking slot in the next few seconds, they're going to shoot us."

He darted his gaze to the rearview mirror, saw the men she'd been watching raise their guns. "Damn."

She expected him to reach for his gun. He didn't. "You know you're being followed, and you're not even armed? What moron trained you, Cross?" She sighed. "Keep your head down and I'll take care of it. When I signal, cut around and pick me up on the street."

Amanda checked her weapon, got out of the car and walked straight toward the sedan. The driver tossed a look of surprise at the Lexus's driver, clearly unsure of what to do in a direct confrontation. She didn't recognize either of them. Just before reaching the black sedan, she veered out of reach, passed the passenger window, and then kept walking, pretending not to notice them. When she cleared the car and gained the protection of the Jeep parked one row over, she turned and fired, shooting out the sedan's back tires. The driver dived for the floorboard, and the black Lexus returned fire then screamed out of the parking lot, leaving half his tires on the asphalt.

Hearing another set of tires squeal, Amanda turned and ran for the street, hugging the parked cars for protection. Moments later, Mark skidded to a stop, flung open the passenger door.

Three shots fired. A bullet grazed Amanda's upper arm, hot and hard. It stung and burned. Grabbing her bicep, putting pressure on the wound, she dived into the car, grabbed for the door and slammed it shut. "Go, go, go!"

"You're hit." Mark stomped the gas, heading for the base gate.

Blood soaked her sleeve and ran down her arm. Amanda rolled her eyes at him. "Very observant, Cross." Maybe she'd been wrong about that handshake after all. "Just get to the boat, okay? They'll be right behind us." The Lexus had already doubled back.

"You need a doctor."

"I need a first-aid kit," she corrected him, feeling the first serious wave of pain wash through her. "It's a flesh wound."

"There's a kit on the boat."

Her arm started throbbing; she felt it in her temples and fingertips. The adrenaline rush weakened and pain slammed through her. She broke into a cold sweat, seeing spots. "Then kindly move your ass and get me to it."

With a little luck, she'd still be conscious. Without it, she'd be at Cross's mercy. He could choose to report it.

*You will not give him that opportunity, Princess. You will stay conscious. You will endure the pain, and you will not pass out.*

"You're really pale, Amanda."

She glanced into the mirror. The two men were behind them, both in the black Lexus. "Damn it, they've caught us," she shouted. Totally irritated, she stretched over and slammed her foot down on the accelerator. "Will you drive?"

Amanda twisted on the seat, took aim and blinked hard, trying to clear the spots from her eyes. She put one bullet through the Lexus's windshield, then another one in its front right tire. The driver hit the brakes hard. The car screeched, skidded, its tires churning smoke. The driver lost control. The car careened off the road, over the shoulder, and onto the grass, where it fishtailed to a stop.

A cloud of dust enveloped the car and Amanda collapsed back on the seat, her head spinning, the spots blinding her. She fought against passing out, but there was no way she could avoid it. Her body was too worn down from captivity and the tomb, too vulnerable. The darkness was coming at her from all sides and sucking hard. "Cross. I think I'm going to…"

"Well, I'll be damned. You're human, after all."

# Chapter 3

Amanda awakened on a 26-footer with dual 150 Yamahas mounted on the stern. She lay sprawled on a bench seat and twisted her neck to check out her surroundings.

Mark Cross sat at the wheel. They were surrounded by water—the Gulf of Mexico—and a finger of land with tall bumps of buildings to the north looked small and distant. Her arm throbbed and she looked down at it. It was bandaged.

As if sensing she was up, Cross glanced back over his shoulder, then slowed the boat and let it idle and drift. "You okay now?"

She nodded, embarrassed. "Yeah."

He reached into a cooler under the seat, pulled out two bottles of water and then passed one to her. "We have privacy out here. When you're ready to talk about your experience, let me know."

She took the bottle. "You've got to be kidding."

"Excuse me?"

He was serious. "Why should I be willing to put my life and career in your hands by telling you anything?" Unscrewing the cap, she took a long drink. The cold water felt good sliding down her parched throat. "I'm here to *get* information not to give it."

He sat down opposite her, stared for a long moment. With a breathy sigh, he reached under his left slacks leg, removed a gun strapped to his ankle, then set it on the seat beside her. He paused, measured her nonplussed response, then removed a second gun from his right ankle and set it beside the first one.

She showed no reaction.

His challenging gaze locked on to hers, he stood up, shoved a hand down the front of his slacks, withdrew a third gun and then set it on the seat beside her. It brushed her thigh and the metal was warm from his body.

Finally, he spoke. "Allowing underestimation *is* an effective weapon. There's value in knowing the strengths and weaknesses of your allies, as well as your enemies."

So he'd been testing her abilities. Respect for him welled in her, as did amusement. Her handshake test had been on target after all. "Sound policy."

He chewed at his inner lip. "Look, we share the same unique problem, Amanda, whether or not you want to admit it. I know you were missing for three months."

"Kate wouldn't dare reveal that."

"She would and she did. To me, where revealing it was safe," he said. "Kate was terrified for you, and I supported her like any decent brother—surrogate or otherwise—would."

"Just like she supported you?" Amanda asked, gaining insight. He and Kate were really close. Family. Inside, she felt a little ache. She didn't have that.

"Yes," he admitted, then stared down for a moment before looking back into her eyes. "We were both missing for three months and we don't know why, Amanda. We both need the truth. The only reason I haven't been dumped on my backside is because I have an advantage."

She looked at him, questioning.

"Secretary Reynolds," Cross continued. "He knew me well and he trusted me. That's the only reason my career isn't in the jeopardy yours is in. But that doesn't mean I don't think about those three months, or worry about what happened during them. Will what I said or did be the reason people are killed?" He lifted his shoulders. "I don't know. I need to know, Amanda. Just as much as you do."

Empathy streamed through her. She knew this hell, this doubt and fear, and saw all her deepest feelings reflected in his eyes.

"So, do we work together to find the truth, or not?"

Their gazes locked and the truth settled over Amanda like a shroud. Whether or not either of them wanted it, they shared a bond birthed in fear and doubt, and it created an intimacy between them she'd never felt before in her life. An intimate bond that she never would have allowed herself to feel, much less admit existed. But this refused to be denied. This…connection.

"We do." Amanda nodded, totally intrigued by Mark Cross. "Absolutely."

"Good." He swallowed a drink of water. "You look hungry. Are you?"

"Yes." She'd been eating practically nonstop since her return, but still couldn't seem to stay full for more than an hour.

"Let's go to the galley and fix some lunch." He moved toward the metal stairs, his long body casting a shadow on the white deck.

Amanda followed him, glad to be out of the relentless sun. The glare was strong; inviting a wall-banger of a headache she wanted to avoid. When they sat down, she said, "So tell me about your experience."

He opened a picnic basket and pulled out fried chicken, potato salad and baked beans. Then a bowl of fresh fruit: strawberries, raspberries, blueberries and kiwi. "I'd just finished a high-risk rescue mission and was starting my leave. I had three months, including use-or-lose days, and things were relatively quiet at the office, so I decided to binge and use all the time off at once. I planned a whale of a vacation. I'd take the boat down to the Bahamas and cruise the Caribbean, being totally decadent."

Decadent she could believe. The man oozed testosterone. But a man who lived by a self-imposed, six-date limit didn't get decadent with the same woman for three months. "Alone?"

"Yeah." He seemed uneasy about the question. "I like my privacy."

"Me, too." She gave him the lie. They didn't get close to people outside of work because it took too much effort. It was easier to avoid relationships than to live lies and make excuses for unexplained, extended absences and some of the "dark side" mission requirements that came with the job. She popped a tangy raspberry into her mouth, and immediately wanted another. "So what happened?"

"Day three, I went to sleep on the boat in the Bahamas." He scooped potato salad from a carton onto his plate. "I woke up on my boat, thinking it was the next morning, only it wasn't. Three months had passed, and I wasn't in the Bahamas or anywhere in the Caribbean. I was docked at my home port in Destin." He shook his head, obviously reliving the disbelief he'd felt then. "I have no idea how I got there, or what happened during the three missing months. No memory of any of my vacation after the first three days whatsoever."

Unlike her own experience and yet similar, too. Kunz could be responsible. Mark's incident had GRID's pseudo-signature. He had chosen not to conceal the truth about his three-month absence, to tell Secretary Reynolds the truth, admitting he had no recall of that time and the security breach his blackout created. That put his life and career squarely in the secretary's hands.

Amanda rubbed her temple, considering all the angles. In the end, Kunz letting Mark go didn't make sense…unless he *wanted* Mark to be honest with the secretary. Or unless Kunz deliberately took the risk because those risks were unavoidable.

Mark remembering nothing of that three months, her remembering nothing of it… It was certainly possible he, too, was a Kunz victim. The odds of them experiencing the same thing for any other reason were astronomical.

"What about you?" Mark asked. "What do you remember?"

She dabbed at her mouth with a paper napkin. "I was inserted undercover on a mission and exposed—I don't know how—and then I was taken hostage and tortured."

Mark stopped eating, leaned forward, giving her his full attention. "You remember what happened to you?"

"No, not really. I remember bits and pieces of being tortured and drugged and someone told me I'd be sealed in a tomb. I'm not sure who. I heard one voice in my head, but I see two different men." She shrugged. "The next thing I remember is waking up in the tomb. The brick mortar was still wet but it took a while to get out—maybe a few days. When I did escape, I found out I was in a different country and three months had passed from my last call-in. I thought it had only been a few days. Now, I'm not real sure when the things I remember took place."

"No other memory of that time at all?"

"None. Blank slate." She stabbed a chunk of potato. "The only thing I'm certain of is that I wasn't in that tomb for three months. No rations. Beyond that, I don't have a clue."

He sighed. "Who held you hostage?"

She munched on a strawberry before answering. "What is your security clearance now?"

"Above yours."

She gave him a level gaze. "Unless you've been elected president, that's not possible." Her job required open Intel access.

He held her gaze, and then decided to trust her. "My clearance being lowered was for public consumption, Amanda. To protect my unit and me. Whoever did whatever was done to me had to be put on notice that I was out of commission, that all my access codes and the intelligence I had access to was obsolete."

She believed him. "Okay," she said. "So where are you now?"

"I answer directly to Secretary Reynolds."

The secretary of defense. *Major clout.* That worked for her. "GRID held me," she said. "Thomas Kunz." She imaged a photo of him in her mind: black hair, brown eyes, and a sharp face full of angry angles. Something niggled at her, as if Kunz's image wasn't quite right, but it persisted so she didn't fight it. "You?"

"I don't know," Mark said. "I haven't been able to find any connections."

"What about similarities between you and the other two men in your unit?" Sitting across the table from him, she bit into a piece of chicken that was tender and juicy.

"We're all attached to Intel and assigned to Providence Air Force Base. But that's it. Totally different backgrounds, missions, training. Hell, we don't even share common hobbies."

"Are you familiar with GRID's organization, Mark?"

"Not really, no. I've seen it named on the Watch list, but I don't know anything about it. The records are sealed. Access is on a need-to-know basis. Officially, I have no need to know."

"The designation is necessary," she assured him. GRID was kept out of the news, out of the typical information-sharing channels, because discussing it only increased its ability to market its services to unfriendly forces. "It's the largest group of intelligence brokers in the world. They're experts on U.S. personnel, resources and classified intelligence," she told Mark. "The organization has only one known criterion for selling intelligence to anyone—payment must be in U.S. dollars." Talk about adding insult to injury.

"So the obvious link—intelligence—is the link between our incidents?"

"That's my guess."

He quietly absorbed that information. "And you think GRID is also responsible for the absences of the two men in my unit?"

"Anything is possible, Mark." She wished to hell it wasn't, but facts were facts. "I think it's worth investigating and making a final determination."

His eyes glazed, unfocused on some distant memory far outside the boat's cabin. "I interviewed extensively on the two men—Sloan and Harding. No one knew much about Sloan. He'd just reported for duty here and hadn't had much time to interact, but people from his old unit and all his records claim he's an exemplary soldier. No incidents of him losing his temper enough to hack a woman to death. And no evidence of post-traumatic stress, which is what the prosecutor's medical officer is claiming as the reason for his memory blackout."

There it was again. That god-awful word, *blackout*. A shiver shot up her backbone and set the roof of her mouth to tingling.

Mark went on. "Reactions were different with M.C.—Major Harding."

"How so?" She took a long drink of water to wash down

a bite of potato salad. Sweet relish would have been better in it than dill.

"Several people I interviewed said they had noticed small inconsistencies in his behavior before and his behavior after his absence. Nothing they could finger exactly, just little things. Apparently, those differences carried over at home, because his wife, Sharon, made an appointment with the OSI office to discuss something *troubling* her about him."

An alert went off in Amanda's mind. Spouses didn't make appointments to discuss matters troubling them. Those kinds of discussions negatively impacted careers. They talked to friends, other spouses—ones who couldn't wreck their marriages, their spouses' careers, and their livelihoods. "Interesting."

"It certainly might have been, if she had kept the appointment. She died the night before in a car accident. Her brake line had been cut. Within twenty-four hours, her husband was arrested for her murder."

Even more interesting. "What was Major Harding's security clearance at the time of the murder?" A chilling thought simmered in Amanda's mind.

"Top secret."

Just as she feared. "We need to talk to him, Mark," she said, crushing her napkin and clearing the remnants of their picnic. "Sooner than later, if possible." Amanda was seeing a pattern. A very disturbing pattern that could rock the entire world of military intelligence. "Can you get me in to see him?"

"No problem." He reached over and dabbed at her chin with a napkin. She started and he stilled, suddenly uncomfortable. "A seed," he said. "From the strawberries."

"Oh." She swiped at her mouth. "Thank you."

"Sure." He rinsed their plates at the sink. "Do you want to stow your gear at the VOQ first, or go straight to the jail? I made you a reservation and arranged for a rental car."

"Thanks." Registering for her room at the Visiting Officers' Quarters could wait. "To the jail, please."

"Okay. I'll have the car delivered there." He dried the dishes and stowed them in a cabinet over the sink. "We'll bypass the harbor, in case your shadows are hanging around, waiting for us to get back."

The air force standard-issue sedan was parked at the harbor dock. "What do we use for transportation?"

"We leave the boat at my house, pick up my Hummer, and go from there."

He had a Hummer, a house on the water, a huge boat. "Your pay grade must be a lot higher than an S.A.S.S. operative's."

"It's the same." He didn't look at her, but the corners of his mouth drew down and he shifted, clearly uncomfortable.

"Really?" She hiked an eyebrow but restrained herself from asking the question.

"Don't get diabolical on me, Amanda. I'm not on the take and I didn't inherit a fortune."

"Fair enough." She shrugged. "What did you do?"

"I designed a few mystery games called Dirty Side Down."

"The computer game?" It was all the rage with the college set and she and Kate had played often. Neither had won, but they'd played. "Kate never mentioned you had created them."

"You didn't know me, and I don't advertise it. Notoriety gets in the way of the job, so I avoid it."

He'd be worthless in his job if he had to deal with fame. "So Dirty Side Down is subsidizing your income."

"All four versions of it." He nodded. "Games pay well."

Interesting. Not a word about any of this was mentioned in the dossier Kate had given her. "How well?" She pushed, not quite ready to completely trust him.

"Very." He smiled and there was just enough playfulness in it to set her mind at ease. "If you're through being suspicious, we can get going."

"I'm reserving judgment on suspicions—you go through a lot of women. Odd, a six-date limit—but I am ready to go."

He ignored her not-so-subtle inquiry and smiled. "We're off to jail, then."

Amanda nodded, hoping that beyond visiting other prisoners, Mark's words didn't prove prophetic.

Major M. C. Harding sat waiting in an interview room typically reserved for attorney/client visits. Unlike words spoken, his appearance couldn't be faked, and it was consistent with that of an innocent man falsely accused who was grieving the death of his wife. He looked gaunt, his eyes sunken, as if his being in jail had sucked all the life out of him and left only a brittle, bitter shell.

He stared at her across a scarred table, his voice deadpan flat and hopeless. "I don't have anything to tell you, Captain West, that I haven't already told Mark several times. I don't know what happened to Sharon. I only know I didn't kill her. No one wants to hear that. They want me to talk about evidence, but I don't know anything about evidence, and I don't give a damn what it supposedly says. If it proves I killed Sharon, it's wrong."

He certainly came across as earnest and sincere, if hostile. Understandable, if in fact he was innocent. Ordinarily, she'd strive for more compassion and tiptoe, but considering the potential consequences, she didn't have the luxury of spare time. She'd have to be blunt and to the point. "In the interval between your initial absence and your arrest, is there any segment of time for which you can't account? I'm not looking for alibis from others. I'm talking about intervals of time where you don't know where you were or what you did."

He glared at her. The red flush of anger swept up his neck and flooded his face, and he shot a daggered look at Mark. "What the hell are you doing, bringing her here to ask me questions like this?"

"Calm down, M.C.," Mark said. "You don't understand—"

"The hell I don't. I understand plenty." He shoved back from the table. "I'm already convicted, man. I didn't do a damn thing, but that means nothing to anyone but me. I trusted you, and you bring some hotshot in here to ask me questions like that. What? You expect me to spill my guts and help her shove the freaking needle into my arm?"

"She isn't here to push for the death penalty or a lethal injection, M.C."

Mark spoke loudly, but not loudly enough to be heard past M. C. Harding's temper. He glared at Amanda. "Here's the kicker, Captain West. I don't have any guts to spill."

She held her patience, kept her tone low and even. "Meaning, you don't remember what happened to you during that time? Or you're being coerced by a third party into not admitting what you remember about what happened to you during that time?"

"You want my life? You're going to have to take it without my help. I've lost all I'm going to lose in this deal, Captain." Harding stood up. His chair flew backward. "This interview is over." He walked to the door, pounded on it, summoning the guard. "Don't come back. I have nothing more to say to either of you."

"M.C.," Mark intervened. "This isn't what you think."

"Yeah, right. It never is, is it? I can trust them to find out the truth—of course I can. That's why my ass is parked in a four-by-six with bars. Because they're all so damn interested in the truth."

"She's one of—"

The guard arrived and Mark stopped abruptly. He took M.C. away and Mark dragged a frustrated hand through his hair. "Damn it, Amanda. Did you have to set him off like a rocket?"

"I had questions, and I asked them reasonably. Harding is hiding something." Residual effects of some sort that Dr. Vargus had mentioned; she'd bet the bank on it. "I got too close and he got nervous. That's what happened here."

"No, Amanda, it isn't." Mark let out a sigh that heaved his shoulders. "You pissed him off because you didn't give him the benefit of the doubt on believing he's innocent."

"Do you know how many guilty people in jail claim they're innocent?" She snagged her purse from the floor. "My faith can't be demanded, Mark. Not by anyone. If Harding wants it, he has to stop being hostile and earn it."

"Harding doesn't give a damn about your faith, he cares about his own."

"Well, that makes a lot of sense." It made no sense at all.

Mark rolled his eyes, then returned his gaze to hers. "He knows what he has and hasn't done and you're casting doubt on it. Knowing is all he's got left. Knowing he didn't kill his wife. Knowing he's innocent and rotting here. He's lost his wife, his family, his career—everything important to him in his life, including his freedom and reputation. Think about it, Amanda. He woke up just like you and I did—clueless—only he's accused of murder. All that, and you want him to stop being hostile and earn your faith? Situation reversed, would you be interested in earning his?"

She'd be beyond hostile, she'd be postal. "Probably not," she confessed. "Let's go run some data and see what turns up. I've got a bad feeling in the pit of my stomach that all four of us are in the same boat."

Mark looked into her eyes. "No, you don't. You have the feeling there are even more than the four of us."

He'd read her thoughts. She didn't know how he'd done it, but she didn't much like it, so she didn't confirm or deny his statement.

They walked out and Mark passed her a set of car keys.

"The green Honda is yours." He gave her directions to the VOQ, and then left for his own car.

He was a good-looking guy, and a considerate one, finding compassion for Harding when he had to be ticked off because M.C. wasn't cooperating. Intriguing man, Mark Cross. "You do know your office phone is bugged," she shouted back at him.

He stopped in his tracks, sighed so heavily it lifted his shoulders, then turned toward her. "We're backtracking calls on it, Amanda."

She tilted her head and looked over at him. "I did it again, didn't I?" Underestimated him. Insulted him.

He nodded. "Yeah."

Apparently, he was getting damn tired of it, too. "Sorry."

That apology earned her a killer smile that knotted a hitch in her chest. She swallowed hard and told herself it wasn't a hitch at all. It was too much potato salad. That was a lie, of course. It was him. But she needed this lie as much as he'd needed his lie about his love of privacy being the reason he'd set out alone on a three-month boat trip, so she hung on to it, slid into the Honda and keyed the ignition.

The baking sun had heat rolling up off the seats and the dash, nearly suffocating her. The engine roared to life. She cranked the air conditioner full blast, cracked open a window, then risked blistering her palms to hold on to the steering wheel to drive out of the parking lot and away from the jail. She left the facility and headed south toward Highway 98. According to Mark's instructions, she'd go through a five-mile barren stretch, then dead-end at 98, which ran east and west. She was supposed to hang a left and then drive until she saw the base. Providence was on high alert for terrorist attacks, like the rest of the country, which meant it could take a while to get through gate-guard security.

So far, base police hadn't turned up anything on the black

Lexus. Maybe by the time she hooked up with Mark, they'd know if anyone had registered one. Every vehicle on the base had to be registered or have a valid ID and visitor's pass.

Midway through the barren stretch of open road, a blue pickup got on her back bumper and, no matter how many times she tapped on the brakes to warn its driver to back off, she got ignored. The truck windows were tinted dark; she couldn't see who was inside. Getting more annoyed by the tailgater's persistence, Amanda slowed down. At a wide bend in the road, the jerk passed her and then swung deep into her lane. She swerved hard to the right to avoid hitting him. Her right tires hit the soft, sandy shoulder and grabbed, twisting the car. Off the road, she struggled to get back control, but failed. The car fishtailed, careened through a wooded area. It took total, constant focus to dodge clumps of pine and oak. Near a tall-grass clearing, she finally got the car slowed down. The truck paused on the road and waited. To avoid being seen by the driver, she grabbed her purse, cracked open the passenger door and rolled out onto the ground. Her upper arm hit an exposed root, throbbed, and she clenched her jaw to keep from screaming out. Hugging the dirt, she hid in the deep, stringy grass. She didn't recognize it, but it was pungent and she hoped, not poisonous. The car rammed into a sprawling oak and exploded.

*An impact bomb.* Breathless, Amanda watched the flames in horror.

The blue pickup slowly drove away.

Amanda watched it leave through tall, spiked blades of grass, then pulled her cell phone out of her purse and dialed Mark.

"Are you lost, Amanda?"

He'd known it was her. Caller ID? No way. Not on her cell phone. Had to be either powers of deduction or perception? Interesting. "Not exactly." She wiped the sweat from her forehead and watched the flames crawl through the car. "I had to make a pit stop."

"What? Where?"

"You know that isolated stretch of road? Well, I'm stuck without a car somewhere in the middle of it." And there wasn't another car in sight to confiscate to go after the pickup. She fought frustration on that, then warned herself to accept what she couldn't change to avoid wasting energy she didn't have to spare.

"Did the Honda break down?"

"Not exactly." The flames licked at the roof and the stench of burning tires made her queasy. "Someone in a blue pickup played road hog. There wasn't a decent shoulder."

"Are you okay?"

"I'm fine. The car's totaled."

"From a soft shoulder?"

"Not exactly." She didn't want to say too much. Cell calls were extremely easy to intercept.

"I'm on my way. Three minutes, max."

Relief washed through her. "Thanks." This wasn't an accident. Someone had taken serious exception to her conversation with Major M. C. Harding.

"Stay away from the road," Mark said. "Put a shoe out so I can find you."

"Finding me won't be a problem." She dragged a shaky hand over her sweat-dampened forehead, then brushed grit and dirt from her scraped knee. Her hose couldn't have been in worse shape if they'd been run through a shredder. "Just look for the burning car."

# Chapter 4

The police filed the reports and put out an APB on the blue pickup. Firemen from two different stations responded and extinguished the flames on the Honda.

When the tow truck pulled away with the charred remains, Mark seated Amanda in his black Hummer and then drove to the base. "You okay?"

"Actually, I'm pissed," she confessed. "But the only casualty is my hose."

He glanced down at the strings of nylon dangling on her legs. "Did you get a look at the driver?"

"Tinted windows." That set another wave of frustration rushing through her stomach and chest.

Mark frowned and a creased pit formed between his eyebrows. He parked in front of the VOQ, which looked like the temporary living quarters "hotel" that it was. Cool beige, square brick building, three stories high, unadorned by anything so softening as shutters, and tiny grounds meticulously landscaped.

Mark left the engine running and the air-conditioning blowing on high. She reached for the chrome door handle, but he stopped her. "Stay put and catch your breath. I'll check you in, then you can grab a shower and we'll go get something to eat."

Her growling stomach appreciated the courtesy as much as her weary body. The roll out of the Honda ordinarily shouldn't have been a problem. But she hadn't yet recouped from her hiatus in the tomb and the flesh wound, and her body ached, letting her know it.

A few minutes later, Mark came out, and got in behind the wheel. "Well, our luck's holding at lousy. They screwed up the reservations and they're booked up. No room at the inn."

"That's okay." Screwed-up reservations were a minor inconvenience that didn't rank worth being riled about when compared with everything else that had happened lately. "We passed half a dozen hotels on Highway 98, just take me to one of them."

"Not okay," Mark contradicted her. "It's tourist season here. No vacancies for forty miles in any direction."

"Figures." Amanda resisted the urge to scream. "If you have any suggestions, I'm wide open."

"If you want privacy, you could stay on my boat, but I think it'd be wiser to stay with me. There's plenty of room at my house and the security is better. Considering the two attempts there have been on your life since your arrival, I think the house would be the wiser choice, but it's up to you."

"That's gracious of you, Mark. Thank you." He was right about the extra security, too. "The house would be great."

He backed out of the parking slot, and then drove away. "While the desk clerk was searching for a hotel, I checked in with the base police. The black Lexus was stolen from a condo parking lot at the beach. The sheriff's office found it about thirty minutes ago, abandoned at the harbor docks."

The men had followed Amanda and Mark to the boat. "How did they get the Lexus on the base?" Armed guards were posted at the gates. Unauthorized people weren't permitted to enter. She rummaged through her purse for a stick of gum, offered a slice to Mark.

He refused. "Stolen access sticker on the car." Looping his hand over the steering wheel, he shrugged. "It belonged on a Blazer that had been parked at Wal-Mart—a woman shopping for school supplies with her three kids."

"Great." Disappointment mixed with disbelief. "Not very reassuring—as far as us keeping terrorists off the base, is it?"

"The guards are pulling a hundred percent cross-check on ID cards."

"Now." She tapped her sunglasses at the bridge of her nose and cracked her gum, totally annoyed.

"Now," he agreed, giving her that one.


Mark's home was in an upscale, gated community on the bay. He paused at the guard shack, a pretty, white clapboard surrounded by a riot of zinnias, marigolds, petunias and lavender—the blend of which drifted in through the window he opened to address the guard.

"Sam, this is my guest. Give her unfettered ingress and egress, okay?"

Surprise lighted in Sam's eyes, but he quickly masked it. "Yes, sir, Captain."

"Thanks." Mark started to pull away. "Oh, and expect a rental-car delivery in an hour or so, too. It won't be a Honda."

"Yes, sir." Clearly not getting the significance of that comment, he nodded. "I'll need a name, sir—to post so there's no problem with the other guards in giving your guest access."

"No, you won't. I don't want anyone to know she's here."

Sam frowned, clearly not sure what to do with that.

Amanda interceded. "My husband is trying to kill me, Sam. Mark is hiding me from him."

His entire expression changed. The hesitation and uncertainty faded to a fierce protection that Amanda found endearing. He glanced at Mark and then back to Amanda. "Don't you worry. No one will know you're here and we'll be watching for possible intruders, ma'am."

"Thank you." Amanda tried not to bristle from the lie, and from needing a man to protect her. It was a little tough on the ego for someone with her skills and training, but Sam's intentions were honorable, and it would be good to have extra eyes monitoring for intruders.

Mark drove on, and when they'd cleared the gate, he gave her a sidelong look. "Your husband?"

She shrugged. "Sam was thinking our relationship was personal. You were letting him."

"Yeah, I was," Mark said, apparently not too happy that she'd screwed up his plan. "Anonymity and a personal connection rather than a professional one gives you a little protection."

She'd like to argue with that, but she couldn't, so she silently seethed about it and expanded on her rationale for upsetting his applecart. "You give people a reason to cover your ass, Cross. That satisfies their curiosity and bonds them to you. Curious people gossip, speculating on their curiosity."

"Okay. Different approach, same results." Mark drove down to Bayshore Drive, took the last right turn before the street dead-ended onto Bayside Circle.

"Different approach, different results," she countered, noting his was the only house on the street: a sprawling, two-story Mediterranean with a terra-cotta tile roof.

"Do you always have to be right?" He drove down the softly sloped driveway into the four-car garage. "Or is it just a personal goal to always be right when dealing with me?"

"I do my best across the board," she said. "My survival often depends on it."

The look in his eyes softened. "I'll try not to take it personally then."

She smiled. "Take it personally, Cross. You're keeping dangerous company these days. Mine. And it could get you killed."

He smiled back. "I'll take my chances."

Defusing the sparks between them, Amanda turned the topic. "This house isn't large, it's obscenely huge." She glanced back at him. "Don't you get lost in it?"

"It's a house." He hiked a shoulder. "Would you be more comfortable at the boat?"

"No." She had the grace to blush. "I'm sorry. I didn't mean that as an insult. I just meant that if I lived alone, I'd feel lost in a house this big."

"Not if you lived in just part of it and ignored the rest." He cut the engine and removed the key.

Cross's white elephant. "If that's what you do, then why did you buy it?"

"Because I love the view of the bay from the back deck."

"So you bought the deck. The house just came with it."

"Of course not. That would be foolish."

She didn't believe him for a second. "Would it?"

"No. Not if that's what you wanted," he admitted. "The truth is, I bought the view. The house and the deck came with it." He smiled. "Come on inside and let's get you settled. Then you can see what I mean."

Amanda had no problem believing Mark, but he was different than most men she had known. He wasn't into image or money. He was into simple joys, compassion and breathtaking views. She liked that. And his killer smile.

Mark snagged her case and paused to punch in the five-digit code to disarm the security system. "Did you get that?"

"Got it," Amanda admitted, hoping she was supposed to have gotten it.

They stepped inside through the garage. Cool, crisp air washed over her. Beyond a tall tile entry, a den ran the length of the house decorated "beachy" in soothing sea colors, overstuffed leather sofas that looked like sun-warmed butter, and cushy pillows and plush rugs scattered everywhere. It was clear that this was Mark's favorite part of the house. She understood why. It was calming and it had a good feel to it. The back wall was glass, and beyond it, his deck, a patio, a stretch of lawn, and then the bay, which had whitecaps and was just rough enough to sparkle like diamonds winking under a puffy pink-tinged sky. "You're right." His beloved view was breathtaking. "It's gorgeous."

"Wait until sunset." He smiled, pure pleasure in his tone. "Your room is this way." Carrying her case, he led her down a hallway to a large room that faced the bay.

Sheer white drapes hung from the ceiling, fell in soft folds down the long windows and puddled on the floor. The furniture was hand-carved teak, and she couldn't help but wonder how many women had slept in the bed, and how many of them had slept there with Mark beside them.

Not that it was any of her business.

Still, she was curious.

"There's a bath and sitting room around the corner there." He motioned left. "If you need anything that isn't here, yell."

She looked at him, saw the gleam in his eye, and couldn't resist a little good-natured teasing. "This is your date-six room, right?"

He didn't return her smile or her teasing tone. "Actually, you're the first woman to ever stay in this room."

She'd gone too far. "Don't get defensive. I was just teasing. You certainly don't owe me any explanations."

He nodded but didn't take the bait to tell her where his women did stay. "I'm sure you itch from rolling around in the grass out there," he said. "Why don't you grab a shower and then meet me on the deck for a snack."

He seemed to always know when her low-fuel light came on. "Are you hot-wired to my stomach, or what?"

"No." The look in his eyes turned serious. "I remember."

"Remember?" She deposited her case near a walk-in closet the size of her apartment in D.C.

"For a few weeks after I returned, I was constantly starving. I couldn't get enough food, or enough to drink."

"Same here."

"See you in a few." He walked to the door.

"Okay. I'll be a few minutes longer, though. I need to report in to Colonel Drake."

"Use the house phone. It's satellite secured at all times."

"Thank you." She waited to really look around until Mark walked out and closed the door behind him. The room seemed cavernous without him in it, and not sure she liked that, she rounded the corner to the bath, which was sinfully gorgeous, with a garden tub large enough to swim in. "Well, Princess—" she toed off her shoes and sank deep into the plush carpet "—you're definitely in a room fit for royalty." The amazing thing was, it felt comfortable, too. Homey touches of peach-scented potpourri and candles and shells and stones sprinkled atop counters and ledges and in alcoves carved into the walls softened the formality and made the space welcoming.

Back in the bedroom, she lifted the receiver of an ornate ivory phone and dialed the office. When Kate answered, Amanda plopped down on the edge of the bed. "Hi, it's me. Is she available?"

"Well, thank God. She's been waiting all day for you to check in. What the hell is going on down there, Amanda? There's been a steady stream of honchos going through here all day. She's been on the phone with Secretary Reynolds at least three times, and General Shaw is calling hourly for updates."

General Shaw was Colonel Drake's boss at the Pentagon.

Secretary Reynolds was General Shaw's boss. This was not good. Baffled at the cause for the heavy honcho traffic, Amanda swept straggling strands of hair back from her face. "What's broken loose?"

Kate hesitated. "I think that's what she's hoping you can tell her."

Surprise shot through Amanda. "Me?" She jerked down her panty hose, then sat down in a stuffed chair beside the bed and pulled them off her feet. Her knees were scraped and covered with grit, and a new bruise already purple covered half her right thigh. She frowned in disgust. There shouldn't be a mark on her. The car was going less than ten miles an hour. Definitely a rookie rollout.

"Yeah. You've been the topic of conversation all day."

Oh, hell. She swiped at the sand and dirt clinging to her shins. This sounded worse than bad. Colonel Drake had to be taking major heat for not yanking Amanda's security clearance. What else could it be? "You'd better put me through." Get the bad news over with sooner rather than later.

"West?" Colonel Drake answered, sounding loaded for bear.

Amanda cringed. "Yes, ma'am."

"What the hell is wrong with you? I said, be discreet. Didn't I say to be discreet?" She didn't pause for an answer. "Do you have any idea what's gone on here today?"

"No, ma'am. I've had my hands a little full."

"Yeah, I'd say so. So far, I've heard from the warden, who says you're banned not only from Harding but from his entire facility, and General Shaw has been listening to complaints from base security about your discharging a firearm in a parking lot outside the vault— I don't know if I've convinced him not to arrest your ass, but I've eaten enough dirt to get you a presidential pardon—"

"That was self-defense, Colonel. Two men had drawn down on Captain Cross and me."

"So I hear. I also hear there is no sign—aside from your report, of course—any two men accessed the base."

"Then they need to review the security tapes at the gates. They'll prove—"

"They don't. There was some kind of malfunction."

"Well, doesn't that strike anyone as just a little odd, ma'am?"

"Don't get flip with me, Amanda. Right now, I'm maxed on patience and I'm ready to rip someone a new one. You're a pretty good candidate for the privilege at the moment, so stop tempting me."

Amanda rolled her gaze ceilingward, softened her voice. "The civilian authorities found the car this afternoon at the docks."

"That doesn't prove it was on the base," Drake pointed out. "You've pissed off an entire detail of base security, blowing out of the gate and ignoring the guards' orders to stop. Base commanders are damn touchy about perimeter violations— especially since 9/11. You know that."

Blowing past security at the gate? Amanda nearly choked. "I wasn't even driving the car." Mark had ignored the guards' orders and blown past them, leaving the base to lose the Lexus would-be assassins.

Colonel Drake's sigh could have powered a sailboat across the bay. "Captain Cross is one of theirs. You're an outsider. You know how this works."

Amanda was too damn tired for this. "Look, I've been here less than a day, and I've already—"

"Damn it. Hold on a minute."

The line blanked out. Amanda waited, working to keep her temper down when she really just wanted to hang up, crawl into the tub filled with warm water and sink.

"You *blew* up a Honda?" Colonel Drake returned with a mortified vengeance that had Amanda's ears ringing.

"Actually, I didn't," Amanda said. "Someone in a blue pickup truck ran me off the road. It was deliberate. I jumped out, but the car hit an oak. An impact bomb detonated. I didn't plant it there."

"So you've got two guys in a stolen Lexus drawing down on you and someone in a blue pickup running you off the road and bombing your rental car?"

"Yes, ma'am. That's what I've got." That, and a hostile Harding holding out on her.

The fire left Drake's voice. "What are you into down there, Amanda?"

Well, it was about time. Relaxing, she slumped back against the headboard and drew up her knees. "It appears GRID may be responsible for all four absences. The common bond among us all is high-level security clearances and access to classified intelligence resources. No one is more interested in that information than GRID."

"If you're all in the same boat, then why is Harding screaming abuse and rights violations against you to everyone short of God?"

"Because he doesn't know we're in the same boat. I'm not a hundred percent sure myself—not yet. But the evidence is pointing in that direction. The worst of it is that both Mark Cross and I have the feeling there could be others."

"That's not good news." Drake's sigh sent static through the phone. "Kate ran a search on all Intel operatives, and there aren't any other reports of absences filed."

"What does that tell us?"

"That there aren't any others?"

Colonel Drake had obviously had a killer day. Otherwise, she'd be all over this. "Oh, so then you've filed a report on me and they've jerked my security clearance?"

"No," she grumbled. "People aren't reporting the absences to avoid losing their clearances and their jobs. Point made."

"Noble intentions for not doing so, I'm sure." Amanda rubbed her aching arch, then her instep. "But the lack of reports is causing us a lot of challenges at the moment."

"Can we resolve them without shoving open those doors?"

"I certainly intend to try, ma'am. I'm not eager to be unemployed. I like my job. I'm pretty sure that and not some nefarious plot is the reason the other cases have gone unreported. It's the only thing that makes sense, because it would require superiors go along with the deception."

"You love your job and you're damn good at it, which is why I'm going along with the deception." Sally Drake knew her people, often better than they knew themselves. "I'm taking that as a sign on the other cases. I'll back you on this, Amanda. But I'm under extreme pressure from General Shaw and Secretary Reynolds not to in any way undermine the credibility of our paramilitary and Intel forces. You know exactly what I mean here."

"Yes, ma'am." Amanda closed her eyes. Their missions were difficult enough without an S.A.S.S. creating doubts about their character. Trust in them was essential to their missions. "I don't want to make life harder for anyone. But if Thomas Kunz is behind these absences, he damn well has a reason for them. That reason is bad news for the U.S. and there's no way around that. We have to know what his reasons are."

"Officially, I have to order you to back off, so I am. Back off, Amanda."

"But ma'am—"

"Unofficially," Drake interrupted, "I know you too well to think for a second you're going to obey those orders. So be discreet, will you? If I can help you, I will, but keep in mind that the warden, General Shaw and Secretary Reynolds have already chewed my ass so much, I've lost two dress sizes. I don't have a lot of grace or ass left with any of them."

"I'll do my best."

"And for God's sake, don't get yourself killed. The paper-work king, Colonel David Gray, runs Providence and the bastard hates me."

Why would the base commander hate her? Amanda shouldn't ask. But of course, she would. It could, on a stretch, be considered essential to her success. Personal grudges could jeopardize resolutions. "Whatever for?"

"We were both up for the S.A.S.S. command and I got it. The man holds a good grudge."

"I'll keep that in mind."

"Oh, and if you have to kill the Lexus or pickup drivers, be sure to do it off base. I'd rather deal with civilians than with Gray."

"I'll do my best not to inconvenience you, ma'am."

"Report often, and be discreet."

"Yes, Colonel." Amanda hit the hook button, resentment churning in her stomach. Right now, the last thing she, Mark, Sloan or Harding needed were political games. They were the victims. They deserved justice. And she intended to get it for them.

Discreetly she dropped the receiver into its cradle—if possible.

"Obviously the report didn't go well."

Showered and dressed in white slacks and a lemon top, Amanda smiled across the wide expanse of deck at Mark, who had stood up at a glass-topped, ironwork table. "Very observant, Captain." She let her gaze slide past the table and thick-cushioned chairs and potted bursts of spring bouquets to the water. It had calmed down and was as smooth as a glass mirror, reflecting soft amber and warm pinks in the setting sun. "But you were right about this view. It's very…"

"Calming?"

She smiled at him. "Yes." He had showered and changed, too, into a pair of jeans and a sage shirt that clung to his body. The man was fit. Sexy and fit.

"Come eat and tell me what's going on."

She walked over, sat down at the table. On it, he'd placed several trays of food. Peeled shrimp and dip, crackers and cheese, fresh veggies and fruit. Her stomach growled.

"Beer? Juice? Soda?" he suggested, then looked at her again. "Or do you need something a little stiffer."

"I'd love a martini but I'm too worn down to risk alcohol. I need to think straight. Better make it one of those Snapples. I like them all."

He passed a bottle and a tall slim glass filled with ice. "Who complained?"

She ignored the glass, popped the top on the bottle, and then took a long drink. The chilled drink felt good sliding down her throat. "Who hasn't?"

Mark sat down, motioned for her to eat, and filled his glass with bottled water. "How high up the food chain?"

She crunched down on a carrot, chewed, and then swallowed. "All the way to your Secretary Reynolds."

Mark swiped a broccoli floret through the veggie dip. "He's worried about undermining the credibility of the covert operatives."

"Yup." His crunching broccoli sounded so good, she had to have a bite. "And it seems your base commander is in a pissing contest with my S.A.S.S. commander, so I can do no right here."

"Colonel Gray has his moments. He was pretty ticked off about me blowing past the gate guards to ditch the Lexus. Fortunately for me, the guards typically only stop people from entering the base, not exiting it. But you work for Colonel Drake. He happens to be more ticked off at your boss than he is with me."

"Because she got the S.A.S.S. command, and he didn't.'"

"You got it. Gray really wanted that command." Mark looked out toward the water and watched a pelican pause atop a post on his boat dock. His voice dropped a notch. "What you're telling me is that Gray and Drake have their noses out of joint and they're ordering you to back off."

The broccoli tasted too great not to have another bite of it. "Now you've got it." She guffawed.

"So what are you going to do?"

She let her gaze drift to the butterflies in the yard, on to the gulls cawing overhead, and took in a deep breath of tangy salt air. "Drink my drink, eat until I'm full, and then do exactly what I would have done anyway."

Mark went for a carrot. "You're going ahead with the investigation, then?"

"Of course." A breezy gust blew her hair over her eyes. She shoved it back, behind her shoulder. "Look, my job is to carry out orders, but my duty is to protect the interests of the United States. If the colonels want to get bogged down in a battle of wills, fine. No problem. If the general and the secretary want to worry about operatives rather than the country, fine. No problem. They do what they believe is right, and I do what I believe is right. I've listened to their worries and concerns and even their orders, Mark, but that doesn't mean I won't do my duty." She snatched one of the last two grapes off his plate. "We were victims. I think Sloan and Harding might have been victims, too. Until I know what happened and that there aren't more victims with access to high-level classified information, I'm going to press on."

His jaw ticked, but he offered her the last grape. "Against orders."

She took it—it was too plump to refuse—popped it into her mouth, and then challenged him. "Doing my duty and honoring my oath to this country."

"If you push this, at some point it's going to lead to you making accusations against someone for suppressing the truth."

"Undoubtedly, it will," she admitted.

"Yet you're still going to do it?"

"When and if the occasion arises."

"Okay." Mark's expression darkened and the look in his eyes went flat. "Then it's my duty as lead investigator to forewarn you. You're treading on dangerous ground, Amanda. You can't accuse fellow operatives or military members of covering up the truth without serious personal consequences."

"I'm aware of that. I'm hiding the truth, too, remember?"

"I was beginning to wonder if you remembered."

"I do. Go on," she said, motioning with a fingertip. "But first, pass the water—and do you by chance have some peanuts? I don't even like peanuts, but I'm craving them."

"You're craving salt from all the water," he corrected her.

"Okay, do you by chance have any salted peanuts?"

"Sorry, but no. I'm allergic. Can't be anywhere near peanuts."

She tilted her head. "What happens?"

"My tongue swells up and I can't breathe." He frowned at the topic interruption, but passed over his water glass. "It's also my duty to forewarn you that if you do make any accusations against anyone and you can't indisputably prove them, you can be tried for crimes against those individuals, against the military, and against the government. And while it's not my duty, I need to make sure you understand the consequences don't start at the court-martials door. You could find yourself ostracized by the other operatives, Amanda. If you get into a jam on a mission and need their support, that could be fatal."

She sipped his water, returned the chilled glass to him, then chomped down on a cheese cracker. When she'd swallowed it, she responded to his formality with her own. "I acknowledge your warnings, Captain Cross, and I appreciate your clarity on the potential fallout with the other operatives." That part was personal and sincere and she was grateful for it. "I can't speak for you and what you would do in this situation, but I owe it to all of Kunz's victims and to the U.S. to find the truth."

"I want the truth as much as you do."

"Of course. That's why you've been doing what you've been doing for the past year." She shoved the bowl toward him. "Have some crackers, before I empty the entire bowl by myself. My arteries will love you for sparing them."

He refused. "Sorry, you're on your own for restraint. I'm full."

"In that case, I'll do my best to exercise discipline." She looked at the bowl and her mouth watered. "Maybe I could just take them into the kitchen."

Mark laughed. "I'll help." He sprinkled the crackers on the lawn from the end of the deck and then rinsed off his hands in the water. "The squirrels will have a feast."

She liked him. She really liked him. He was gorgeous, thoughtful, and he hadn't grown so cynical by the job that he'd lost his sense of humor or the ability to care about others. She didn't like the intimacy or bond between them—it scared the hell out of her—but she did like the man.

When he sat back down, he grew serious. "I admire your steadfastness in this, Amanda. Frankly, I admire much more. I didn't mean to come across like an ass, but I had to make sure you knew what you were risking by continuing with the investigation when you've been ordered to back off."

"How can I not continue?"

"That was how I felt about it, too." He leaned toward her, looped his hands on his knees. "But it could cost you your career, and if what happened today is any gauge, your life. Those are pretty high costs."

"We're all going to die, Mark." She met his gaze easily, calmly. "It's what we do while we're here that matters."

"Yes."

The look in his eyes burned her, and the truth dawned. "You were ordered to back off, too."

"Again." He nodded. "Colonel Gray phoned while you were in the shower."

"Are you going to do it?"

"Now that I'm certain you won't back out on me, I'm going to work with you." Mark reached over and covered her hand with his on the table. "And together, we're going to find the truth."

Just as he had felt obligated to warn her, she felt obligated to warn him. "You could lose your career, or maybe even end up in jail."

He tilted his head and slid her a look that left her nearly breathless. "I can live with that." A furrow formed in the skin between his eyebrows. "I can't live without self-respect. I have duties, too."

Self-respect. That was the one. The single comment heaped on all of his other comments that captivated her. The intimate bond between them expanded and, damn, but it was strong. So was her physical reaction to him, but this…this connection seemed far deeper than mere attraction.

*Don't be crazy. You just met the man.*

He smiled and thoughts of resistance faded, her blood heated, and her logic turned to mush. Sometimes you don't need time. You just know. She knew, and she liked knowing just fine—at least, at the moment.

"You look ready to fall over."

"I am. I haven't had time to recoup." She heard what she said, but still couldn't believe she'd said it. Amanda West, admitting vulnerability to a man? Inside, she froze. Outside, she shuddered.

"Are you cold?" When she nodded she wasn't, he added, "It took me about four days to get back to normal."

Amanda watched his expression and body language closely, but he hadn't sneered or gloated. Her father would have done both—and then ridiculed and beaten her for being weak.

Totally oblivious to her scrutiny, Mark glanced at his watch. It caught the light and the metal twinkled. "We're out of time for today. What do you say that tomorrow we reinterview a couple people attached to M. C. Harding's case? Maybe you'll pick up on something I missed, or make a connection I haven't. We should talk with M.C. again, too, but we can't get in to see him until normal visiting hours."

A lawyer banned from the correctional facility? How bizarre! "Aren't you a member of his legal team?"

"Yes, but at Providence Air Force Base that doesn't mean you have total access to prisoners. I have total access, but only during normal visiting hours. We're stymied until tomorrow morning."

"Colonel Gray?" she asked.

"He doesn't like routine being interrupted. It undermines order." Mark rolled his gaze. "So does our plan of action sound solid to you?"

She nodded. "It works for me."

He glanced at the boat dock, and then at a long, thin cabinet built into the back wall of the house. "Do you like to fish?"

"Yeah." What woman in her right mind could resist putting the world on hold for a few minutes when Mark Cross looked at her with little-boy hope and eagerness? Even if he had made the suggestion only so she'd relax and let her mind shut down for a while. She appreciated the gesture, especially knowing he remembered everything about his experience and how challenging it was to reorient and transition.

The hardest part was cutting off the adrenaline flood. Fishing, being calming and soothing and slow-paced, would help.

"Come on." He pushed back his chair. "I've got a killer Ultra Lite rod you're going to love."

An hour later, they were barefoot, sprawled in low chairs at the end of the dock, rocked back with their lines in the water and their thoughts lost in the quiet of twilight. Neither of them seemed particularly inclined to talk. The quiet settled around them, soothed them, and the tension knotting the muscles in Amanda's neck and stomach slowly melted away. It was the first time in over a year she'd felt so relaxed.

After a while, Mark sighed. "Amanda?" He sounded tentative, and he kept his gaze fixed on the water.

What should she think of that? "Yeah?"

"I, um, have a confession to make."

Interesting. "Oh?"

"Yeah." He dragged his gaze to hers and, judging by his sour expression, he felt pretty rotten about whatever he had done and was about to confess. "The VOQ wasn't overbooked."

Her heart rate kicked up to warp speed. "It wasn't?"

"Not exactly."

"Not exactly?" She rolled her neck and rubbed at a knot of tension in it. Available guest accommodations were fixed, not flexible. "Either it was or wasn't booked up, Mark."

His face reddened. "It wasn't."

"Then why did you say it was?" Afraid to read too much into this, she treaded cautiously. They were attracted to each other on a lot of levels, but that didn't mean either of them would choose to act on that attraction, and assuming it did could cause consequences that ranged from bad to downright embarrassing.

He gave his shoulder a little shrug. "I wanted you here."

The pulse in her throat throbbed and her chest cinched tight. "Because…"

A cigar boat sped through the water, cutting an angry

white-foam trail, and heading straight for the dock. Mark grabbed her arm and pulled her into the water.

Cold, Amanda gasped and choked. When she broke the surface, she pegged the boat's position and swam under the dock, following Mark.

A bullet hit the post, three inches from her head. Splinters of wood flew.

She dived underwater, swam out from beneath the dock, and took cover behind Mark's boat.

The cigar boat veered away, spewing water ten feet up off the water's surface, and streaked toward the mouth of the bay. Two men in blue parkas, wearing dark glasses and baseball caps, stood on deck.

Amanda looked at Mark, bobbing in the water beside her. "Aren't we going after them?" She looked at his boat.

"We won't catch them. Those things are speed demons." He looked from the vessel disappearing into the distance back to Amanda. "We should report the incident. Shots were fired."

Mark was right, of course, but bottom line was it would cost them more than they would gain. "It won't serve any purpose except to get Colonel Gray crawling all over you, and Colonel Drake crawling all over me again. The Coast Guard isn't going to catch them in that thing, anyway."

"You've got a point," Mark conceded. "Colonel Gray wouldn't miss any opportunity to stomp on Drake."

Having to work around the Providence Air Force Base commander irked Amanda. "This man sounds like a real charmer."

"He isn't all bad, but he is a major work-in-progress. Little-big-man syndrome—a bad case of it. Mostly, he's a retired-on-active-duty pain in the ass. Since he didn't get the S.A.S.S. command promotion, he's just doing his time until next fall when he can retire. But he holds a good grudge, and he totally believes misery loves company."

So Colonel Drake had warned Amanda. Mark was right

about them catching the cigar boat in his fishing boat, too. That wasn't going to happen. Those things nearly had flight status. "You knew they'd come back tonight, didn't you?"

"Yes." He shook water off his face that was running into his eyes.

"That's why you wanted me here rather than at the Visiting Officers' Quarters?"

"Yes." He held her gaze. When she didn't say anything, he searched her face, seeking something only he could identify, and added, "Then."

She swam closer to him, stared up into his eyes, the water softly rippling around them. "And now?"

He wiped at a rivulet trickling down her temple with the pad of his thumb. "Frankly, I'm not sure yet, but I think I want to find out." He risked a glance into her eyes. "If you don't have any objections."

"I have no objections." She smiled, wrapped her arms around his neck and kissed him. Tentative and exploring, undemanding, she let herself open and get familiar with the feel and taste and scent of him.

His response was electric, liquid fire and pure heat, and he pulled her close to the hard wall of his chest. Amanda sank into the kiss, into a riot of sensations, certain that Mark Cross might have lied to her, but she damn well appreciated his reasoning. And silently she admitted that if he hadn't lied to her about the VOQ, she would have lied to him.

Not that she would mention it.

The rewards of him doing penance were just too intoxicating to willingly forfeit. But to soothe her guilty conscience, she'd pay her own form of penance and see to it he felt just as intoxicated.

It was an acceptable compromise....

# Chapter 5

Amanda asked herself at least a dozen times between 1:00 and 3:00 a.m. why she didn't just knock on Mark's bedroom door. But she knew the answer. For the same reason he didn't knock on hers. They were feeling too much too fast and didn't trust it. So they had stayed in their respective rooms and she spent a restless night wishing they were twisting the sheets, lost in sensation.

If she had half a brain, she would applaud their common sense. She'd be grateful for their wise judgment.

But she didn't, and she wasn't.

By morning she was grouchy as hell and just frustrated enough to confess she would rather have had a robust romp. Maybe two.

Dressed in her uniform, a pale blue shirt and dark blue skirt, she smoothed the epaulets bearing her rank at her shoulders and met Mark in the kitchen. He was dressed in his uniform, too. Seeing that he looked a little ragged around the edges gave her a warm glow in the pit of her belly.

"Rough night?" she asked.

"Long," he admitted.

"Sorry to hear that."

He gave her a glare that lacked heat. "Yeah, I can see you are. It shows in every watt of your mega-smile."

She wiggled her eyebrows at him. "Hey, no one's tried to kill me in twelve hours. I'm celebrating."

He walked to the coffeepot. "Right."

"Okay," she conceded. "It was a long night for me, too. Does that make you feel better?"

"Yeah." Cup in hand, he looked back over his shoulder at her. "If it's true."

"It's true." He looked damn happy about that. Too happy. "Lumpy mattress." It was brand-new and pillow-topped and soft and scrumptious.

"Of course." He filled the cup and passed it to her. "Hungry?"

"Starved." Truer words had never been spoken.

They ate scrambled eggs and English muffins and fresh cantaloupe, talking about the incidents and where they intended to go in their investigation.

Mark sipped his orange juice and took a one-eighty on her. "So, are we going to act on this thing between us or pretend not to notice it's there?"

Surprised by his bluntness, she paused, slowly chewed a bite of muffin then swallowed it. Just looking at him had her blood running hot. "Do you really think we've got a choice?"

"We've always got a choice, Amanda."

She tilted her head toward her shoulder. "I'm not in the mood to be that disciplined."

Relief washed over his face. "Thank God."

He leaned across the table, clearly intending to kiss her,

and her heart rate kicked up a notch. But he ignored her mouth and pressed a tender kiss to her forehead, which seemed far more intimate somehow. She thought back to her former relationships, which were admittedly superficial, but couldn't recall ever being kissed on the forehead. The kiss was tender and gentle; a caress that made her feel treasured.

She liked it. A lot. Too much. She frowned at him. "You're going to have to explain the six-date thing. I don't enter relationships seeing them end and I'm not into sleeping with half the state."

"You wouldn't be," he said softly. "I'm not irresponsible or stupid, Amanda, and not nearly so loose with my body as you're imagining me to be." He rimmed the juice glass with his thumb and asked her frankly, "So are you?"

The phone rang, sparing her from answering.

He answered it. "Hello."

He listened for a brief moment, his expression tightening, his body stiffening, on alert. He put his napkin on the table. "We'll be right there." Mark hung up the phone and spoke to Amanda. "M. C. Harding wants to see us at the jail as soon as possible."

"Us? But I'm banned from the facility."

"Not anymore. He's got the warden's approval."

Uneasy, she cleared the table, rinsed the dishes at the sink. "Did he say why he wants to see us?"

"No, he didn't." Mark put the pitcher of juice back into the fridge, snitched the faucet from her and rinsed his hands. "But he sounded a lot less hostile today than yesterday. Maybe he's figured out that you're not out to kill him."

"Maybe." Amanda got a strange feeling in the pit of her stomach, warning her that wasn't the case at all. Harding hadn't been in a forgiving mood when he'd raised hell with the warden. No, this wasn't a moment of grace on his part. Yet he could have picked up on what Mark had started to tell him when the guard had come in—that she was in the same situation on the three-month absences. He could have replayed the conversation in his mind later, after he'd reported the incident to the warden, and realized what Mark had been about to tell him. "You ready to go?" She looked at Mark.

Standing beside her, he rubbed his hands dry on the dishcloth. "Almost." He tossed the cloth onto the counter, bent down, and then kissed her solidly. "Good morning, Amanda."

She laughed out loud and then kissed him back. "Good morning, Mark."

"Don't forget to leave your gun in the car." Outside the prison in the visitor's parking lot, Mark reached for the Hummer's door handle.

She took the gun out of her purse and stashed it on the floorboard so they could clear security and meet Harding.

Inside, the halls were eerily quiet and all but empty, which was vastly unusual for a federal installation and contrasted starkly with her previous visit. Wondering why, Amanda walked beside Mark, spotted three surveillance cameras and held her question. Despite the absence of human bodies, there were eyes and ears everywhere.

In the interview room, Harding sat waiting for them. Amanda stopped. He'd already been brought in? Typically, a prisoner wasn't retrieved until the visitors were in the interview room. Her instincts alerted, and the skin on her neck crawled. She reached for Mark's arm and heard him mutter, "Damn it." Simultaneously, they turned back for the door.

It slammed shut right in front of them.

Amanda darted her gaze to Mark. Every sense she had elevated to high alert and the truth smacked her hard, right between the eyes.

They had walked into a trap.

"Sit down," Harding said from behind them. "I've never

shot anyone off of a battlefield, and I'd rather not start now. But if you don't move, I will."

Amanda and Mark turned, sat down across the table from him, focusing on the barrel of a .38 he held aimed somewhere between them. With his elbows perched on the scarred tabletop, he stood ready to pivot and shoot either of them.

"What the hell are you doing, M.C.?" Mark asked.

"Surviving." Anger and pain flashed through his eyes. "That's all. Just surviving."

The door opened behind them and two men walked into the interview room. Two men Amanda immediately recognized. She warned Mark. "And who said GRID doesn't provide great service?" Amanda spoke to the beefy guard whose nose she had broken at the Middle Eastern compound. "Blown up any Hondas lately? How about potshots? Taken any of those at people fishing?" These were the men in the blue pickup and boat—she felt sure of it—but not the men in the black Lexus. They remained a mystery.

"Don't start with me, West," Beefy told her. "I underestimated you once. It won't happen again."

She bet it wouldn't. Still, her flesh wound was little more than a nick, and he again had two black eyes and a swollen and bruised nose. "Annoyed someone else, I see."

"Don't start with me, West," he repeated.

"That'll do." The other guard raised a hand, warning Beefy to hush. Carrying a black briefcase, he slid it onto the table and opened it.

Amanda couldn't see what was inside, but she knew enough to fear it.

"What is this about?" Mark asked.

"You'll see soon enough." The second guard filled a syringe, tapped the syringe and stepped to Mark. "I'm being paid to deliver you, Captain Cross. I don't care if you're alive

or dead when I do it. If you move, he'll shoot you." He nodded to the beefy guard. "Any questions?"

"He's not bluffing," Amanda warned Mark, giving him a
let's-go-with-it-and-see-where-it-leads glance that she hoped
he wouldn't miss. There were three of them, but only two
were armed. She and Mark could take them. But if they did,
they'd just be buying themselves more sniper attacks. It
wouldn't further them in finding the truth.

Mark evidently came to the same conclusion. He didn't op-
pose, just let the man with the needle inject him.

Afterward, Needle prepared a second shot and injected
Amanda. She ignored him, but laid a glare on M. C. Harding. "What the hell is wrong with you? They killed your wife,
and you're helping them?"

His face mottled red. "I have no choice. I have a daughter
living with her grandparents. I can't lose her, too."

"Shut him up," Needle said, dropping the used syringes
into his briefcase and snapping its locks. They clicked into
place.

The beefy guard put a bullet right between Harding's eyes.
The silencer on his gun glowed in the light. He slumped over,
dead before he hit the table.

Adrenaline rocketed through Amanda's veins. She darted
a glance at Mark. He gave her the slightest nod to be still and
mouthed the words "In plain sight," adopting a code phrase
to communicate signals between them.

He was following standard operating procedure for situations where two operatives were being taken captive by hos-
tiles. She nodded that she'd gotten it.

"Give these two five minutes and then haul them to the
van." Needle turned and calmly left the interview room. "I'll
meet you at the helicopter."

Vans, helicopters, guns inside the walls of the

prison...GRID clearly had infiltrated the prison to get this kind of access and cooperation. The question was, through whom?

Regardless, it didn't take a genius to figure out she and Mark had the deck stacked against them. Harding was dead. Murdered. And they were witnesses. And that was an aside to their own problems.

Without a doubt, they were marked for death.

## Chapter 6

Amanda's head throbbed, pulsing in her temples, and her throat felt parched. Definitely, one of the worst hangovers she'd had in her life. Her stomach pitched and rolled and she cracked open one eye.

Pale wooden floors. Her uniform hanging on the bedside chair. The sun streaking in through her tab-top bedroom drapes. She bobbed her head, sniffed, tapped the mattress with her fingertips. Her pillow. Her sheets. Her mattress. She looked across the room to the far wall and then the floor. Her sleek lacquered furniture and geometric red and black rugs.

She was at home? In her apartment in D.C.?

Disoriented, she frowned. Rubbed her head to shove down the pain coursing through her and threatening revolt by her stomach. Opening both eyes, she inspected further. Her silk robe lay draped over the foot of the bed and she looked to see what she was wearing. Her hot-pink T-shirt and panties. Her skin crawled. They were hers, but they were not the under-wear she had put on that morning.

What the hell was going on here? Fighting panic, she sat straight up—and remembered M. C. Harding. The glazed look in his eyes, the bullet wound in the center of his fore-head. The abduction at the prison. Mark!

Yet here she lay at home. In her own bed, in her own apart-ment, wearing her own clothes.

She definitely had not dreamed all that—or the trip to Providence, multiple attempts on her life, and certainly not Mark. She rubbed her eyes hard, fearing they were tricking her. But her surroundings didn't change. This *was* her apart-ment. She *was* at home. The memories of Florida seemed ex-tremely vivid, but hell, she'd been overworked and through a lot lately thanks to Paul Reese and Thomas Kunz. Maybe she had dreamed it all. Could that be possible?

It didn't feel possible. It felt too real and raw. Needing val-idation, she sniffed her wrist and inner forearm. Mark's scent on her skin. No, that was real. He was real. Dr. Vargus had predicted milder symptoms would precede any blackouts, and she didn't remember having any symptoms whatsoever. Could she have had them and not remember them?

Possibly. She'd lost three months, after all.

*With injections.*

She looked at her inner arm, saw the fresh needle track, and remembered the injection at the prison. Saw the wound on her upper arm where the bullet had grazed her. Her stom-ach clutched. Mark was real. But this—she looked around her apartment—was not. She was certain Kunz would never di-rect his minions to bring her back to her apartment. Would he? So what was this?

She shook her head to clear it. Saw the photograph of her, Kate and Colonel Drake at her promotion party parked on the corner of her dresser. Same photo. She'd framed it herself.

Her pearls were dangling from the corner of the mirror. Her driving gloves lay on the gleaming dresser top beneath them. She walked to the bathroom. Her toothbrush, her teeth-whitening kit, her shower gel and razor. Apparently, Kunz's minions *had* brought her home. And Mark was real.

Solid and real and connected to her in a way she'd be hard-pressed to explain because she had no frame of reference for it. God, but she resented being on unfamiliar emotional ground. It scared the spit out of her. Bonds were dangerous, irritating, overrated. Bonds were terrifying.

Feeling fear annoyed her. She cleaned her face and nearly scrubbed the enamel off her teeth, then met her reflection in the mirror. "You need coffee, woman." She dabbed at her mouth with a fluffy towel then slung it back onto the towel bar, her head still woozy. "Lots and lots of coffee."

She shuffled down the hallway, shoved her hair back from her face, rounded the corner to the kitchen and came to a dead halt. A woman stood at her kitchen sink. "Who the hell are you, and what are you doing in my kitchen?"

The woman turned toward Amanda and sheer horror flooded her eyes. Her jaw dropped open and her mouth rounded into a perfectly stunned, "Oh, no!"

Amanda's knees went weak. Down to her pink underwear, the woman was her mirror image!

Before she could recover, the woman bolted out the back door.

Amanda chased her through the yard, cutting through an island of blossoming jasmine and gardenias. Branches slapped at her legs. When she rounded an aged oak, two men dressed in black suits intercepted her and blocked her path. "That's far enough, Amanda," one of them said.

The woman disappeared from sight. *Amanda.* She didn't know these men. How had they known her name? How had they known she and not the other woman was the real

Amanda? She glared up at them, recognized Beefy from the prison. GRID.

Her chest went tight, her knees threatened to fold, and she locked them. None of it was a dream. But all of it was a nightmare.

"What's going on here?" Amanda backed up a step to better see Beefy eye to eye.

"This is your neighborhood, your apartment, and you're free to do what you do in your yard, but you can't leave it without an escort."

This wasn't her apartment or her neighborhood. It was a GRID replica of her apartment and neighborhood. And the woman…a staggering chill charged through her. "Where is Captain Cross?"

Beefy cleared his throat, careful to stay out of striking distance. The bruises on his face had faded from purple and green, but not so much that he didn't recall the pain of having her break his nose. "He's being processed."

"Processed?" What did that mean? Amanda had no idea, but she was certain it wasn't good. "Would you care to explain?"

"No. You need to go inside and get dressed," Beefy told her, nodding to the left where a little boy was kicking a ball. "Someone will be over within the hour to talk to you about your new life."

"My new life?" Temper fueled the confusion in her with heat. Why keep her alive? Why not just kill her? Kunz had to have a compelling reason, and the sooner she discovered what it was, the better. "I'm not through with my old life yet."

"Don't come unglued on me." He backed up a step. "I'd hate to shoot you in front of a kid, but I will. You're not breaking my nose or anything else of mine again."

She needed a grip on this place, and she wasn't going to get it from Beefy or his stalwart companion. That made get-

ting them out of her way her first goal. She could take Beefy
down. He was clumsy and slow. The other one she hadn't
fought before. She took his measure and figured her odds at
sixty percent. But she'd bide her time and if possible avoid
violence in front of the boy.

With a parting glare at Beefy, she turned around and
walked back toward her first-floor apartment. She didn't see
his relief at not having to tangle with her again, but she felt
it.

"That's the hellcat who put you down?" the second guard
asked, disbelief in his tone. "She's tiny."

"She's lethal," Beefy answered, irritated and not trying to
hide it. "You get off guard for a second with her and she'll
kick your ass all over this compound."

Compound. So they were back in the Middle East. At the
GRID compound. She needed time to absorb, to get the lay
of the land and devise an escape plan. A woman—the mirror
image of her—in her kitchen. A replica of her entire home
and neighborhood.

*Replicas.*

Cold terror sank into her bones, and Amanda feared she
knew how GRID had become so effective at accessing classified information and intelligence.

And, man, did she hope she was wrong.


Her clothes hung in the closet, filled the dresser drawers.
She pulled on a pair of jeans, a T-shirt and sneakers, and
fixed herself a cup of coffee.

There were cameras everywhere, recording every move
she made in the apartment, and she'd spotted at least three
separate audio devices. The whole place was wired to the
rafters.

Every move, every word, every breath was monitored.

Sipping from her cup, she looked out a window and saw

the little boy still playing kickball. Now, there she could get answers. Kids were unguarded and blissfully innocent and honest.

She walked outside, the steaming coffee cup in her hand. He looked about five or six, pale blond hair and full cheeks ruddy from the heat and from running to kick the ball on the stretch of lawn between two islands of shrubs. There were cameras mounted in the trees. Red dots lighted on them. She counted six, and determined there wasn't a spot of grass in the yard where anyone in it wouldn't be watched and heard.

The ball came toward her. She set down her cup and kicked it back.

The little boy grinned, returned the ball to her. On the edge of the sidewalk, Beefy and his companion watched, clearly wary, but they didn't interfere.

"I'm Amanda," she told the boy. "I live here now."

"My name's Jeremy." He whacked the ball. "I live over there." He pointed to the apartment next door.

"That makes us neighbors." She kicked the blue ball back to him. Neighbors were trusted. Strangers were not.

"Do you have a mom and a dad or just a mom?"

Apparently, he lived with just his mother. "Both," she lied, seeing no sense in telling him she was for all intents and purposes an orphan and had been most of her life. "But they live in their own house."

"My dad doesn't live with us anymore, but I got a mom." He belted the ball a strong one. It bounced off a spike-leafed bush and back into the expanse of thick, lush grass. "She's a doctor."

Divorced? "That's an important job." Amanda kicked the ball to him, saw Beefy dial a number on his cell phone and speak briefly into it. While she couldn't hear what he said, that he wasn't happy about her game of kickball was obvious.

Seconds later, a lean woman in her early thirties rushed out of Jeremy's apartment in a green bathrobe. "Jeremy!" she shouted. "I told you not to speak to strangers."

"She's not a stranger." He picked up the ball and held it to his chest. "She's Amanda. She lives here."

"Go inside, honey. Right now."

Jeremy frowned, clearly considering rebellion, but in the end, he turned and silently walked into the apartment. The door closed behind him.

"I'm sorry." Looking embarrassed and exasperated, Jeremy's mother glanced at Beefy and then back at Amanda. "I hope he didn't bother you."

"Not at all. I was enjoying his company." Amanda smiled and extended her hand to the woman. "Amanda West." Beefy's companion started to walk over. Beefy grabbed his arm, held him in place.

Jeremy's mom shook Amanda's hand. "Joan Foster," she said, one eye on Beefy. "Again, I'm sorry. I'll talk to him so he doesn't bother you anymore."

Amanda's initial instincts were that Joan Foster was a decent woman, and that she was terrified. Her body language proved it—she fell just short of wringing her hands—but it was her scent that was a dead giveaway. Nothing in the world—nothing—smelled quite so distinct as fear. "Please don't, Joan. Jeremy wasn't bothering me. I approached him to play ball."

"Oh, okay." Joan cast a confused look at Beefy, who obviously had called her to end the powwow between Amanda and Jeremy. "I'd say welcome to the neighborhood, but under the circumstances..." She turned and walked back into her apartment.

*What circumstances?* Amanda would have loved to ask, but Joan didn't linger long enough to get the question out— and maybe that was for the best. One of the first rules in Intel was not to ask questions you couldn't answer. For now, Amanda had no answers, only questions.

The hour came and went and no one appeared to talk with Amanda about her new life or anything else. Patience never had been one of her strong suits, but fortunately neither had stupidity been one of her shortcomings. Until she knew what this place and these people were about, she had to move softly and slowly. Especially considering Mark was also here. *And being processed.* Her actions definitely could impact him, and she couldn't afford to forget that.

Amanda stayed put in the apartment, observing Beefy. His companion was gone. Beefy stayed put on the sidewalk, observing her. Three hours passed, and then four. Another man drove up in a blue Camry. He and Beefy exchanged a few words and then Beefy left in the car. The replacement guard turned toward her, and she recognized him. Her blood boiled.

The driver of the black Lexus who'd winged her.

Clenching her jaw and gritting her teeth, she debated killing him and decided against it, for now. She had more to lose by giving in to her temper than to gain by restraining it.

Jeremy went back outside with his ball.

Amanda didn't hesitate. She hit the door and joined him. "Ready for a game?" she called out.

Jeremy smiled, showing her every tooth in his head, which did not include either of his front teeth. Both were missing.

The Lexus maggot straightened from his slump against the street lamp. Alert and obviously uneasy.

Jeremy and Amanda kicked the ball back and forth a few times. Then Jeremy dived for a shot and kicked crosswise. The ball popped the guard right in the chin.

"Damn it!" He cupped his face and stomped across the yard, heading for Jeremy.

When he raised his hand to hit the boy, Amanda saw a cold gleam in his eye that she recognized too easily, and her stomach clutched with the same horror and dread she'd felt as a child. She grabbed Maggot's arm, twisted, and spun him around to face her. "Don't even think about hitting the kid."

He took a swing at her.

She blocked it, followed with a right uppercut to his jaw. He stumbled backward and fell to the grass with a healthy *"Oomph!"*

Jeremy stood statue still, his eyes wide with fear. His little chin began trembling.

Amanda reached over and pulled Jeremy behind her, blocking his vision of the guard and planting herself between them, sending the guard a clear message. To get to the boy, he'd have to go through her. "Get the hell off our grass."

Jeremy gasped, burrowed his head against the backs of her legs.

"Watch it, West. I know about you and I'm not running."

"You probably don't run any better than you shoot or fight. Unless you want to go toe-to-toe, I recommend you get off our grass. You're interrupting the game." He didn't move and her voice shook with outrage. "You can do that, right? Or are you only good at hitting kids? I'm sure Thomas Kunz is going to love hearing about this."

"Don't try pushing me around." Maggot straightened his jacket with a shoulder shrug. "Mr. Kunz doesn't give a damn what you say."

"Are you misinformed or just stupid?" Amanda asked. "Kunz has his faults, but there's no way he'd put up with a GRID member beating on a kid, especially without his say-so."

"How could you know that?" The guard pulled himself to his feet. Slapped at the blades of grass clinging to his slacks. "You can't know that."

"He was abused, genius. He knows what it's like to be on the receiving end of ham-fisted cowards, and there's no way he'd tolerate a lack of discipline in his people." She swiped her hair back from her face. She was certain Kunz had no such hesitations, but this guy didn't have to know that. "Don't these jerks give you any background on your own organization?"

Insulted, but clearly unsure whether or not he should believe her, he ignored her and warned Jeremy. "Next time, you watch where you're kicking that ball."

"It was an accident," Amanda said from between her teeth, then issued him fair warning. "If this kid has an accident— any accident—I'm coming for you. So you'd better go out of your way to keep him safe."

Maggot grunted. "You're not even armed."

She pulled her lips back from her teeth in a smile meant to freeze him in place. "You are stupid." She grunted her disgust. "I'm always armed."

He swallowed hard, obviously uncertain what to make of that remark. He debated, but apparently decided he didn't want to know badly enough to find out, because he backed off and returned to the street lamp.

Joan Foster came running out of her apartment, looking frazzled and weary. "Jeremy, are you all right?"

"Yeah. I'm fine, Mom." He smiled up at Amanda. "Can you really beat him up?"

She couldn't resist a chuckle. "Yes, I can."

His expression went serious. "Will you teach me?"

Joan caught a gasp in her throat. "Jeremy, no."

Amanda looked from mother to son. "Why, Jeremy?"

"So they don't hit my mom anymore." He gazed up at her, the look in his eyes far too old for his years. "I don't like it when they hit my mom."

Amanda and Joan locked gazes and the woman's fear grew thick and dense between them. "Yes, Jeremy, I'll teach you," Amanda said. "I'll teach you both."

Jeremy smiled and hugged her leg.

Startled, Amanda wasn't sure what to do. Stiff and unfamiliar, she patted him on the shoulder.

"Thank you for protecting my son, Amanda." Joan extended her hand and clasped Amanda's.

Inside her fist was a note. "Of course," Amanda said, taking it.

Joan looped an arm around Jeremy's shoulders and they walked back into the apartment.

Amanda palmed the scrap of paper and went inside, wondering where the hell she could go to read Joan's note in privacy. If she ran to the bath, which appeared to be unmonitored, after every encounter or interaction with Joan, the men minding the monitors would pick up on it. She needed a second safe place. When she toed off her sneakers near the bed, she found one. She kicked them under the edge of the bed.

Hoping whoever was supposed to be coming to talk with her would be a little more late than he already was, she waited twenty minutes, then pulled a fake search of the apartment for her shoes. She checked inside and out, the closet, the bath, and then "remembered" taking them off at the bed.

She looked under the bed, saw no cameras or devices. "Great."

Crawling on her belly, she slid under, grunted, pretending to stretch for her sneakers, and unfolded the note. The lighting was awful, but just enough that she could make out the words.

Thank you for protecting Jeremy.
Mark is alive. The entire compound is under constant surveillance. There are a few safe zones the camera doesn't reach. At 5:00 p.m., come and ask me to take a walk. I'll show you.
They go through the trash. Eat this note.

# Chapter 7

Amanda discreetly watched the clock. Promptly at 5:00 p.m., she walked out the front door, cut across the lawn to Joan Foster's door and knocked.

Joan answered, wearing jeans, a yellow sleeveless top and sneakers. Her brown hair was pulled back into a ponytail and clipped at her nape. "Yes?"

"Hi," Amanda said. "I want to go for a walk. Being inside has me edgy. But I don't know where I can and can't go. I was hoping maybe you could spare a few minutes to show me."

"I suppose I could." Joan's knuckles were white from the tight grip she held on the edge of the door. "Wait here while I tell Rosalita. She helps me with Jeremy."

The older woman had come to Joan's about one o'clock that afternoon, dressed in a gray maid's uniform. Amanda's nerves had been like live wires all day. Hour after hour she'd been armchair investigating from the apartment, waiting and waiting and waiting, but the guards had been wrong. No one had shown up to tell her anything, though the guards posted on the front sidewalk had switched every two hours. They hadn't budged long enough to give her a chance to slip away and do any serious reconnaissance.

Joan came out and closed the door. They stepped off the stoop and walked to the sidewalk. The sun beat down on them relentlessly, and the pavement felt hot through Amanda's shoes.

When they got close to the guard, a burly guy with a severe overbite, Joan paused to speak with him. "I'm going to show Captain West where she is and isn't permitted to walk."

Sweating profusely, he dabbed at his forehead with a white handkerchief and nodded but held his silence. Why these guards had to stand out in the sun in the middle of the day in suits, Amanda had no idea. It wasn't only impractical, it was vicious, and it surprised her that none of them had collapsed from heat exhaustion.

No doubt Thomas Kunz insisted on the suits to prove he was the ultimate authority and in total control. He seemed to have a penchant for little reminders to his staff, as well as his captives. Though, on second thought, the formal attire seemed more like something Paul Reese would insist on rather than Thomas Kunz. The fallen white knight with now-scarred face was very much into image.

Joan motioned, and Amanda moved down the sidewalk. She didn't dare to hope that the guard wouldn't follow them, and she'd been right. He paced himself to stay about twenty steps behind them. "Jeremy is a cute boy," Amanda told Joan.

"He's a good child." She spoke softly, gazed off down the street then whispered, "I hate him being raised in this place." At the corner, she left the sidewalk and walked through a patch of grass that led to what appeared to be a golf course. How bizarre. Kunz must be into golf. A clump of trees stood on the right.

Joan didn't walk up to them, but paused about fifty feet out, where the trees were at a perfect right angle to them and to a sign that they were at the seventh hole. She deliberately stared down at her feet.

Amanda saw a red tee stuck in the dirt, and nodded to Joan.

"This is a safe zone. Move one foot in either direction and you're back on camera, with audio. There's video everywhere out here. That's why the guards never get too close." The wind blew her hair loose from its clip at her nape and across her face. She smoothed it back. "Because of what you did for Jeremy today, I'm going to trust you, Amanda. For God's sake, don't make me sorry I have."

Amanda gave her a solemn look. "Because of what you did for me today," she said, referencing the note, "I'm going to trust you. Please don't make me sorry, either."

Joan looked deeply into Amanda's eyes. "Mutually assured destruction."

"Yes." Amanda acknowledged what she believed to be true.

For the guard's benefit, Joan smiled and pointed across the course, as if she was telling Amanda about the place. "Mark is alive. I'm doing what I can for him. Don't expect anyone to come for you until tomorrow. They always tell you someone is coming and then make you wait so you have a lot of time to dread it, and to show you that things here happen at *their* convenience, not at yours. The whole place is one long succession of mind games."

"I've more or less gathered that." Amanda faked a smile, glanced at the guard, who had stopped out of earshot, as Joan had said he would, and stood watching them. After her foray into the tomb and seeing her double in her kitchen, nothing about the level of psychological warfare GRID practiced here could stun her. Mark was alive. That was good news. Provided he wasn't being tortured. "Is Mark safe?"

"He'll survive it, Amanda." Joan's eyes held pity. "I'm sorry. I'm doing what I can."

Not the reassurance she had hoped for, but at least Joan was honest and helping Mark as much as possible. "I'm not surprised, but it's unfortunate that it can't be stopped."

"You have no idea how unfortunate matters can get for people around here." Joan shuddered.

"Tell me."

Again she pasted on a smile, but this one barely curled her lips and never came close to touching her eyes. "My husband, Simon, is being held hostage in the cabins farther down the course. His living conditions are not nearly so nice as ours." Her expression changed, puzzled. "You do know that this is a GRID compound, and what GRID is, don't you?"

"Yes," Amanda admitted without hesitating. True, the information was classified, but with her son living in this hellhole and her husband held captive in it, no one had more to lose than Joan Foster. "Why does GRID want Simon?"

"It doesn't." That truth caused her pain. "It wants me."

And the guilt she felt about that threatened to bury her. It pounded off her in roiling waves. "Why?" Amanda asked.

"Because I'm an expert in my field." Joan tilted her head, blocking the sun from her eyes with a hand cupped at her forehead. Still, she squinted. "Though I never thought I'd hate to say that, I do." Her eyes filled with tears and she blinked hard to keep them from falling down her face. "You have no idea how many times I've cursed myself for becoming a doctor. I wake up at night praying in my dreams that I'm a clerk in a grocery store or a gas station attendant. Anything other than this."

Amanda picked up on the problem. "What are they making you do that you don't want to do, Joan?"

Pain flooded her face. Her chin quivered and she clamped her jaw, looked Amanda right in the eye. "Every kind of work they tell me to do. I won't insult you or myself by saying I have no choice. I do, Amanda. I can do what I'm told when I'm told, or Thomas Kunz will torture Simon and Jeremy in front of me until they die, and then do the same to me."

An effective motivator for a loving wife and mother. Heartless, but effective. "What kind of work are they ordering you to do?"

"Illegal and immoral work," she said, bitter and blunt. "The kind of work that will have me burning in hell for eternity."

Amanda frowned. Obviously the spiritual ramifications of Joan's work here troubled her enormously. "Be specific, Joan. It's important."

"I drug intelligence operatives and plunder the depths of their minds. I expose every dark secret buried in every nook and cranny inside them and I plant specific 'memories' that are manufactured and not memories at all."

Horror swept up Amanda's back, tingled the roof of her mouth. "Just how successful are you at this?"

"Very."

Amanda's heart stopped, flipped and folded. Thomas Kunz was identifying operatives with high security clearances and then generating duplicates to gain access to intelligence and classified information. God help them all. "I've got to see Mark, Joan. The sooner the better."

"I'll work something out." She cast yet another sidelong glance at the guard. He was definitely getting antsy. "We'd better go."

## Chapter 8

Someone pounded on Amanda's front door so hard her apartment walls shook.

She awakened from a doze on the sofa and glanced at her watch: 2:00 a.m. Who the hell— Wait. Kunz. Proving he's in control.

Amanda regrouped, then answered the door with a resigned, "What?"

Standing on the stoop, Beefy took two steps back, staying out of striking distance. He didn't say a word.

Amanda glared at him. "Are you just beating on the door because you're bored and have no life, or do you actually want something?"

"Mr. Kunz wants to talk with you." Beefy backed down the steps, waited on the walkway. "Let's go."

A white sedan was parked at the curb with its lights on and its engine running. Beefy had come for her alone? How interesting was that?

Liking her odds, she walked to the car, then reached for the handle to open the front door.

"Get in the back seat." Beefy motioned with his head. "I don't want you up front with me."

Smiling to herself, she paused and let Beefy get within range. When he did, she whipped open the door and broadsided him with it.

Heaving a hefty grunt, he doubled forward and expelled a swooshed breath. Before he could recover, she twisted, hiked her knee into his stomach and drove the heel of her hand into his throat.

He crumpled to the ground, out cold.

She scrambled into the car behind the wheel and then took off, her tires screeching on the pavement.

*Okay, Princess, what now? Where do you go? Out of here, or after Mark?*

"Out. Definitely out." There were guards every six inches on this damn compound. She needed backup—a lot of it to get Mark, Joan, Jeremy and Simon out of Kunz's clutches. And she still had to kill Paul Reese for hitting her. That job headed her personal list.

Taking the corner at forty, she slammed on the gas pedal, and ate up the road. There were no lights in the distance, only darkness. She shot a glance into the rearview mirror. All the lights were behind her.

There was nothing out there.

The car lurched, hit the dust-dry dirt. She'd run out of road. Silently swearing, she kept going, but the dirt was beyond dry and loose and she couldn't gain traction to get up her speed. Swearing she'd kill for Mark's Hummer at the moment, she tried every maneuver she'd been taught on driving and even a few she hadn't tried before, but nothing worked. The car slowed, then stopped, bogged down in a thick cloud of choking dust.

She turned off the headlights, got out of the car and looked around. Desertlike. Nothing. No place to seek protection or coverage. Nothing at all, actually. No lights, no buildings, no signs, not even a self-respecting weed.

Something didn't feel right.

*Humidity.*

The air was humid. And it was the middle of the night and hot. Baffled, she made sure her perception was right; that it was humidity and not anxiety. It wasn't. The air was thick and heavy and almost wet, which didn't fit at all. The desert cooled down at night and the air was dry, arid. Right now, Amanda didn't know a lot, but she knew one thing without question.

She was not in the Middle East.

A broad stream of light streaked through the sky and shone down on the ground. Amanda tracked its sweep long before she heard the whine of the helicopter's props. Running would be a futile waste of energy. Her best shot was to take the chopper.

It spotted her and she stood still in the blinding light, until the aircraft set down on the dirt nearby, kicking up a dust cloud that would have her coughing for a week. She didn't move.

A disembodied male voice barked out an order. "Come to the chopper."

She still didn't move.

"Now, Captain West." To punctuate that order, he fired a shot six inches to the right of her feet.

She stirred, slowly heading toward the chopper, veering toward the pilot's side. When she stepped under the beam of the light, she could make out two shadows inside. Both men. Both large, and no doubt armed.

The pilot stayed seated, but the other man opened the passenger door and left the chopper. She recognized him as one she'd seen before, the guard with the extreme overbite. He took aim on her with a submachine gun and motioned with its barrel for her to get inside.

A submachine gun? Talk about overkill. It was another of Kunz's "I'm in control and don't you doubt it" dominance reminders. Arms raised, she walked around the chopper, "accidentally" bumped into the flat of the gun barrel to knock out Overbite's aim, and then backed off. "Sorry. Loose dirt. Not quite stable."

"Save it, West." He hiked the barrel. "Just get your ass in the chopper."

She snagged the cool metal, shoved the gun back into his shoulder, throwing out his rotator cuff, and he went down. Flipping the gun from her right to left hand, she shot him without taking aim, then spun on the pilot—and stopped in her tracks. "Harry?" She couldn't believe her eyes.

"Hi, Amanda." He smiled. "Get in, will you?"

She scrambled into the chopper. "I thought you were dead."

"So they've been telling me." He sighed. "Guess it's true then."

*Replica.*

How could she tell if the man flying the chopper was Harry or his double? "Frank told me you died in Iraq." It had been Jim.

"GRID faked it," Harry said. "Is Frank still flying relief for me?"

No pilot named Frank had ever flown on Harry's CIA drop-zone route. "Last I heard," she lied. This was *not* Harry. But Kunz wanted her to believe it was.

Or it was Harry and he was trying to let her know that things weren't right.

Which one, she had no idea. But she couldn't shoot Harry, if he was Harry.

In a fluid motion, she shoved open his door and kicked him

out of the chopper. He hit the ground with a thud and a swooshed breath. "Sorry." Maybe she was, maybe she wasn't, but now wasn't a good time to debate. She slid into his seat, slammed the door shut and lifted the bird off the ground.

Amanda wasn't on steady feet here. She could fly nearly any fixed-wing aircraft, but a helicopter was a different breed, and she hadn't been checked out in any of them. The craft, all too aware a rookie had the stick, lurched wildly, erratically, and she scanned the gauges looking for assistance. Her gaze locked on the fuel gauge. A red light flickered and began blinking. Low fuel light.

The tank was empty.

"Damn it!" She cranked her head back and groaned. "Can I *please* catch just one break here? Just one? I don't think it's asking too much for just one single thing to go right."

She looked around for additional fuel, checked the panel for a spare tank and found nothing.

A warning beep pierced her ears, joining the flashing red light. The engine was fuel-starved and about to choke; she was running on fumes....

Noise outside the chopper grew loud and then deafening. Four helicopters came into view. They swooped down from above and surrounded her.

Her stomach sank and the hope that she would escape died.

Apparently, God was fresh out of breaks.

# Chapter 9

Beefy blindfolded her, shoved her into a second helicopter and took her on a short flight across the compound.

Upon landing, he jerked her out of the aircraft and led her across rough ground into a building with smooth, dirt floors that smelled of freshly mown grass.

Fresh air quickly disappeared and the stale stench of recycled air filled her nose. The sound of six men's footsteps—no doubt, armed—escorted her down what echoed like a long corridor. The floor was hard and slick here, like tile. She hadn't seen the building or the corridor, but from the moment she stopped sensing the wind, and the air smelled recycled, she began counting her steps.

In her mind, she saw the building Beefy had dragged her through on her first visit with them. Every six feet, there had been a framed photo of Thomas Kunz. Black hair and evil eyes that glared out at whomever walked past. On passing each photograph, Amanda had felt a little niggle of something not quite right that had put her instincts on alert.

Though she couldn't see a thing, and she somehow knew this wasn't the same building, she was having the same experience now. Oddly, she was also recalling the image and feelings of seeing that photograph.

"Wait." Beefy spun her by her shoulders. "Go right."

Disoriented, Amanda veered right at what must be a T-section in the corridor. When Beefy ordered her to stop, she had just taken step number one hundred twenty-seven.

He removed the blindfold and she stood in a white corridor with doors lining both sides. They were all closed. "In here?" She motioned to a door off her right shoulder.

"Yes."

She entered an office that was totally at odds with the utilitarian buildings she had seen up until now. It was plush; rich woods in the desk, gray leather wingback chairs; thick Persian rugs that cost more than her car. This had to be Kunz's private office. And she didn't kid herself. Her being in it did not bode well for her or her future. Men with secrets kept them, unless they felt certain revealing them created no threat.

Very bad news for Amanda.

"Sit down." Beefy tipped the end of his rifle toward a visitor's chair.

Impressive night scope. Seeing it on his rifle ticked her off. The bad guys had better, more advanced equipment than the good guys. Where was the justice in that? "Why am I here?"

"To wait."

"For what?"

"Sit down and shut up, West."

Amanda frowned at Beefy and sank down in the chair. Even under these conditions, she appreciated the creamy soft leather and couldn't resist the urge to stroke its arm with a lazy fingertip.

Total silence enveloped the office, had her wishing she knew more about Mark and his condition. That she didn't know drove home the reason she had chosen not to encumber herself with relationships. You care about someone else and you're vulnerable. Your focus slivers because you're worried about them and their condition. Sliver that focus at the wrong time or place and you wake up dead—or worse, causing someone else to wake up dead. Those kinds of complications were albatrosses, not assets, for a woman in her job.

Unfortunately, she was in the same boat as the rest of the human race. Sometimes you don't get to choose. What's logical falls to what is. And what is just is, and you're stuck accepting it.

That frustrated the spit out of her. Not because it was fact, but because she didn't know how Mark had slipped in under the radar. It was as if she'd been fine one second, and the next second she suddenly noticed their bond had changed, become more heartfelt. Never having had a connection with a man—sex was *so* much simpler—she'd had no idea one could be so strong, so persistent.

Afraid, she let her head loll back, and had a serious conversation with herself. She couldn't be open to this stuff. These were lethal vulnerabilities for anyone, much less an S.A.S.S. operative. She didn't do lethal vulnerabilities any more than Colonel Drake did jail.

"We meet again, Captain." A group of men stirred behind her.

She shifted her attention, but didn't turn to look.

In her peripheral vision, she saw three of the guards stationed against the back wall, near a painting that looked like an original Dali. Beefy and Maggot stood sentry at the door and another guard positioned himself just outside it in the corridor. It fed her ego that they weren't taking any chances on her overwhelming them again. It also warned her that they were learning from her past behavior and anticipating her future conduct on that basis. First chance—any chance—and she'd mow them down to get out of here.

A blond man soundlessly walked across the office. Casual and elegant, he sat down at the desk. It was obviously his; his body language oozed confidence and control. This was unquestionably his office and his domain.

He laid a stern look on her. "I would say it's good to see you again, Captain West, but the fact is you've injured yet another of my men, and I'm weary of your behavior."

The real Thomas Kunz. She knew it. The voice matched the one in her memory. But the photographs hanging on the walls and everywhere else around here were not of Thomas Kunz. She'd thought they were, but they were not. This man, this blond, elegant, nonthreatening, sunny kind of guy was the real Thomas Kunz. "I'm a bit weary of your behavior, too, Thomas. Two in the morning is hardly an appropriate time for a social call, and your hospitality leaves a lot to be desired."

Maggot gasped.

Apparently, she'd been a little more blunt than most with Kunz. He didn't look angry, though—quite the contrary, he seemed pleased. "I said you'd be amusing, my dear, but don't goad me. At the moment, I don't have the patience to play."

She lifted a hand. "Then why do you keep inviting me into the game?"

His affable nature died and his eyes lost their humor and warmth. "There are a few truths you need to accept." His voice turned to sleet. "The sooner you do, the better."

"What kind of truths?" The new life Beefy had mentioned? She didn't flinch, but she did fear Kunz. He was too confident. Men couldn't fake that confidence; it was second nature to them. And second-nature confidence signaled that they had all they needed to back up that cocky self-assurance with decisive force and effective action. Every bit of which was bad news for her.

"Your old life is gone. You're no longer in it." Bluntly put, and Kunz poured himself a drink at a bar off his left shoulder to celebrate his victory over her. It smelled like bourbon. He took a sip, his back to her—again confident and unafraid of being attacked—and then in his own good time, swiveled his seat to face her. "Your new life is here, Amanda. You will never leave this compound again. Not alive." He again sipped from his glass. "You'll teach others of my choosing to be S.A.S.S. operatives. If you do this well and without causing trouble, you will live."

The man was crazy. Serious, but crazy. "And if I refuse?"

He smiled. "Then, of course, you die."

Like Joan Foster. Only in Amanda's case, far less effective. "You're overestimating the value I put on my life, Thomas."

"Perhaps, but perhaps not." He sipped from his glass. "You see, Amanda, I do realize that you don't fear death. But I also realize that you do fear the box." He rocked back in his chair, tipped his chin to his chest then looked over at her. "So my power is in keeping you alive and in the box, not in killing you—which I will do, if I so choose. Imagine it. You'd be like a rat mired in a maze. How intriguing it would be for me to watch you living in a box, day after day. How would you keep track of the years? You're quite a long way from death due to old age. Year after year, just you in the box—you and your memories of life beyond it."

"That's not going to happen."

He laid a look on her that could melt steel. "It will happen, if I choose for it to happen."

"It won't."

"I'll put you on a feeding tube and IVs to keep you alive, Amanda. You'll die on my terms and at my pleasure, not your own. Believe it."

Inside she fought a battle between fury and fear, but outside she let neither show. "What about Captain Cross? Do you have similar intentions planned for him?"

"He doesn't fear the box." Kunz looked at her a long moment. "I realize you feel an affinity to him because you were together when joining us, but I also know that you've only just met the captain, so don't pretend your concern is greater than it truly is to slant my plans for you, Amanda. It won't work."

So much the better. "I simply asked a question about a professional associate. Is he alive?"

"Of course." Kunz looked at her as if she'd lost her mind. "What good would he be to me dead?"

"Well, I don't know, Thomas. How could I know?"

Kunz frowned. "You're testing my patience. A woman of your intelligence should not try to appear stupid. It's neither believable nor flattering. You now know what I'm doing here."

"I have no idea what you're doing here—or where *here* is, for that matter."

"Don't lie to me!" He cracked a hand down on his desk. The smack popped her ears, echoed. "You do know. You knew in the interview room with Harding. You knew or you wouldn't have fought my men. You're totally predictable. You always fight."

Not true. Never when she couldn't win. She was a woman who had a healthy respect for odds. "Okay, so I know you're kidnapping intelligence operatives, drugging them, discovering everything you can about them and then cutting them loose."

"Very good." Kunz refilled his glass, set the bottle on his desk and nodded to her. "Have you decided to be civil?"

"I don't seem to have much choice. Though the audience isn't necessary at this point, Thomas."

That she had the audacity to repeatedly address him by his first name clearly amused him. "Leave us," he told the guards. "Captain West has elected to be rational."

*Only until I find a way to bust your ass, Kunz. Only until then, and until after I kill Paul Reese for hitting me.*

He poured her a shot of bourbon, passed it over. She threw it back, downed it, setting her throat on fire.

"You haven't asked about Paul," Kunz said. "I would have thought you'd be interested in knowing how he is doing."

"He's scarred," she said, her voice flat and unemotional. "That tells me exactly how he's doing."

"There's my astute Amanda." Kunz laughed. "He wants you dead, you know."

"And this is news because…?"

"Touché." Kunz sipped from his glass. "Have you determined why I cut you loose in that tomb? Why the three-month absences?"

"I've speculated," she admitted. She had nothing to lose and everything to gain by cooperating with this line of discussion. She could learn valuable information. "You choose the operative you want to create a double for and then bring in the operative to study and probe. That takes about three months. Afterward, you turn them loose, to avoid anyone finding any differences in them, but also because you need time to substitute the double's identity for the real operative's. X rays at hospitals, medical and dental records, blood types, fingerprints, biometric scans—and of course plastic surgery on the doubles. That gives you time to substitute the double's identity in the system and to prepare the double for the infiltration. For all intents and purposes, the double becomes the operative."

"I'm impressed." Kunz lifted his glass to her, rocked back in his seat. "It normally takes much longer for selected operatives to put the pieces together."

"Most operatives probably don't run into their double face-to-face in their own kitchen."

"No, most don't." He smiled. "I admit it. I wanted to speed things up with you."

"Why?"

"Mainly because Paul wants you dead and I want to minimize the attrition rate on my guards before he kills you."

Possibly true, but Kunz's reasons were more self-serving than that, and she'd bet on it. Amanda twirled her glass. "This won't work, you know. There are too many little details about a person to duplicate."

"It works." His voice blunted like a dull knife. "You see, that's why you're here. All the operatives we've duplicated are at one of my compounds. So they're available for consultations when those little details crop up, so to speak."

*One* of his compounds. So he had more than this one and the one in the Middle East. If he actually had one in the Middle East, that is. Extremely bad news. She guffawed. "And as an operative, my incentive to do this for you is…what?"

"Life, Amanda." He spoke simply, softly. "You and the other operatives who are my permanent guests get to live."

Amanda understood what Kunz was doing and how, and it certainly answered the question of how he obtained such accurate intelligence to broker on the black market. "You're definitely overestimating the value some put on their lives, Thomas." She motioned to the bar. "I'm not crazy about bourbon. I'd like a whiskey, please. Neat." She turned back to his program. "That's a serious flaw in your process."

He poured her a double shot of whiskey then slid the glass across the desk to her. "Others don't share your eagerness to die. You never have feared it." He set down the bottle, adding, "That's one of your most appealing traits, by the way. It fuels your willingness to take enormous risks. That makes you a formidable asset to S.A.S.S. and, frankly, to me."

So he would be reluctant to kill her—to lose the asset. But life in the box on IVs and a feeding tube…?

There were fates worse than death. In that one, she'd have to kill herself.

"However, don't foolishly overrate your value to me." Kunz refilled his glass at the bar. "You've established that you've suffered memory lapses and you're in your job only because you're being protected. That protection can be withdrawn at any time I choose. Or used as I see fit. Never doubt it."

Was that a backhanded way of saying he could manipulate Colonel Drake? Impossible. Only God and the president of the United States could manipulate her—God alone, without protest. "I don't doubt your ability to kill, Thomas. It's well documented." Amanda stood up. "I'm ready to take a look at this new life you have planned for me. If I like it, I'll keep it. If not, you won't be able to keep me alive." She gave him a matter-of-fact look. "No man uses me. Not unless I issue him a personal invitation to do so."

"Ah, yes. Your father." Kunz's level tone sharply contrasted with his gentle expression and the respect in his eyes. "Being a victim is a bitch, isn't it, Amanda?"

"Truthfully, I've forgotten." He might as well get a grip right up front. She wasn't giving in or up or going to be content following his rules for his purposes. She was going to do her job and rescue Mark. If possible, she'd also like to survive. "I haven't been a victim in a long, long time."

Uncertainty flickered in his eyes, and Amanda was glad to see it. He didn't know all he needed to know about her or he'd be certain she meant exactly what she said. She wouldn't be a victim. Not his, not anyone's. Not without a fight.

And in the years since her father's first beating, she'd become damn good at fighting.

"Guards!" Thomas called out.

The door swung open and Beefy came through, into the office. "Yes, sir."

"Take Amanda back to her apartment," Kunz said, then looked at her. "Get used to your new environment. You're no

longer a captain in the U.S. Air Force. You're no longer an
S.A.S.S. operative. Actually, you're no longer anything I
don't specifically order or grant you to be. That's your inevitable reality now. You can make it pleasant, or your worst
nightmare. I'm up for either. I'll give you twenty-four hours
to decide which."

Her wisest response was no response, though a scathing
rebuttal had her throat burning like a five-alarm fire. It cost
her dearly, but she set her glass on the edge of his desk and
headed toward the door without a word. Beefy read her mood
accurately and backed up out of her way, giving her lots of
room. She stunned him by smiling. "Thank you."

Having no idea what to do with that, the man backed up
another step and shot a questioning look at Thomas Kunz,
who issued him a solid frown.

Amanda decided right then Beefy was weak and vulnerable. He would never be won over much less become an ally,
but he shouldn't be too difficult to neutralize—without her
threatening to do him bodily harm. True, that held less appeal
than cleaning his clock, but Kunz did seem to take particular
offense to her inflicting injury on his men, and having Beefy
guard her could be far more productive than someone she
hadn't physically beaten. She'd have to prove herself all over
again. Beefy already had a healthy fear of her.

As well he should.

As well they all should.

*Meet me at S.Z. at 12.*

Amanda read the note printed on a tiny scrap of paper,
twice. She'd found it in the ice bin in her kitchen. Joan had
been clever to put it there. As hot as it was, ice was an often-
used and appreciated commodity. Okay, so she wanted
Amanda to meet her at the safe zone at noon. Hopefully—
*please, God*—she had arranged for Amanda to see Mark.

She really needed to see Mark. Her insides twisted like a knotted mass of whipped hotwires. What Kunz was doing—the potential scope of it—was horrifying, even for a seasoned operative who had experienced a lot of horror during her career. This program of his left her staggering. She needed Mark's grounding.

Okay, maybe she didn't need it. She stared out the window at a blue jay perched on a tree limb. But she wanted it.

She would kill Paul Reese, who had been avoiding her like the plague—whether by his own choosing or under Kunz's orders, she didn't know, nor did it matter. She would get out of here, and she would bring Kunz down. But she wanted to bring Mark out with her.

And she would. She'd do whatever she had to do to make it happen.

*That, Princess, is a promise.*

At 11:45 a.m., Amanda put on a pair of sneakers, running shorts and a visor to block the glare of the relentless sun, then headed out the door.

Beefy wasn't in sight, but a different guard—one she hadn't seen before—stood on the sidewalk. She ignored him, did a few stretching exercises, then took off on a jog.

She wound around the neighborhood a bit and then checked her watch—11:54. Time to get to the golf course. She took the path, certain she had timed it right to arrive at the safe zone promptly at noon.

Joan wouldn't be late. Why Amanda felt confident of that, she wasn't sure. Maybe it was Joan's knowing that as well as her own life, the lives of her husband and child depended on her actions. Whatever her reason, Amanda sensed Joan would be on time.

And she was. Promptly at noon, Joan paused on her run in the safe zone and bent down to tie her shoe.

Amanda called out. "Hi, there."

Joan smiled and stood up, still breathing heavily from her run. "Hello."

By that time, Amanda had reached her. She hiked an eyebrow, verifying they were safe to speak openly.

"We're fine," Joan said.

"How's Mark?" Amanda kept the smile, but had to work at it. The guard paused far enough away to be out of reach and just out of earshot, provided they kept their voices low.

"He's still in isolation being interrogated. I can't get to him yet. But he'll be coming to me later today."

"They're not torturing him?" That they might be had her stomach in knots.

"No, they want to see **how he reacts** in hostile situations. It's part of his study. I **don't have** time to explain now," she said, stroking the sweat **from her** forehead. "But he's not being tortured."

"Joan, you realize we have to stop this GRID program."

Her look glazed. "I don't think we can."

Hope had been drained out of the woman. "You help me get the big picture," Amanda said, determined to restore it, "and I'll find a way."

"Don't you think I've tried? I did everything I knew to do, Amanda." Joan's eyes filled with tears. She blinked hard and fast. "There is no way to stop him. Everything I thought of, Kunz had already built in a contingency to cover. Everything. You have no idea how hard I worked at this."

"You were alone, then," Amanda quietly insisted. She shook her leg, shifted her weight as if walking out a cramp. "You're not now."

Joan bent down, rubbed Amanda's calf. "I'm supposed to be befriending you so you don't fight me on your debriefing," she confessed, obviously realizing the risks in doing so. "That's why Kunz is permitting us to meet and chat, and why I was moved into the apartment next door to you."

Amanda tensed, but kept her tone civil and her voice even. "So are you just doing your job, or are you sincere?"

Joan's hands stilled on her calf and her look went flat. "They have my husband."

"That tells me nothing. You could hate him."

"I love him."

"So you are sincere, then?"

"Yes." Joan let the truth show in her eyes.

Amanda believed her. "I need all the information you can give me. Is there a way for us to meet more than for just a few minutes at a time?"

"Not without monitors. Not yet. But I'm working on it." She kneaded Amanda's muscle one last time and then stood up. "Meet me here at eleven tonight. Don't let the guard see you leave. Convince him you've gone to bed for the night. By then, I'll have had a chance to talk with Mark and to see what Kunz plans for him."

"Whatever it is, nip it in the bud," Amanda said before thinking. "I have plans of my own for Mark."

Stark terror washed through Joan's eyes. "Tell me Kunz doesn't know that."

"What?"

"That you have a personal interest in Mark."

"*I* didn't even know it," Amanda admitted, shuffling her shoulders. "He couldn't."

"Well, for God's sake, don't tell him. He'll do horrible things to Mark to get you to do what he wants done," Joan warned her. "And you will do them, Amanda. You think you won't, but you will. Because love is stronger than fear or hate. It's stronger than anything." She looked off, past the green and sand trap to a distant cluster of trees. "I've learned that the hard way here."

She had. Amanda could see that in the sadness in her expression, in the defeated slump of her shoulders. "I'm sorry."

"Me, too." Joan looked up at her. A tear glistened on her cheek. "It should have been a beautiful lesson."

It should have been, but that was in a perfect world, and they didn't live in a perfect world. Amanda was sorry, but she couldn't control that. She had greater responsibilities she could control, so that's where she had to focus her energy. On the military, who were counting on her to protect and defend the country. And to the unsuspecting millions of people living in it. Her duty to those things had to have priority over her personal feelings for one man.

"Your guard is getting antsy," Joan said. "The monitors have radioed and told him they can't hear us. We'd better get going." She cast Amanda a parting smile that appeared frozen. "Eleven."

"Eleven." Amanda took off in the opposite direction and ran hard, pumping her legs and arms, releasing some anxiety and giving herself time to clear all of her thoughts.

"Captain West!" the guard shouted.

No one had called her "Captain West" since Kunz had stripped her of her identity, which begged the question, Why had this man used her title? She looked back. He waved, motioning her toward him.

She slowed and turned, jogged back to him, and ran in place to cool down a bit. "Yeah?"

"Mr. Kunz wants to see you right away."

"What for?"

"I didn't ask, ma'am," he said, his back rod-straight. "Does it really matter?"

He had a point. Her choices here were limited and she needed to not arouse tempers or suspicions, or everyone would shut down and she would learn nothing from them. And he'd treated her with respect. "May I grab a shower first?" she asked without a hint of the hostility she felt.

"I wouldn't recommend it, ma'am," he said softly, his Adam's apple rippling up his throat. "When Mr. Kunz says right away, he means right away."

"Okay, then." She looked down at her sweat-drenched shirt, then smiled at the guard. "When he gets a whiff, he'll remember next time to give me time to get cleaned up, eh?"

"I'd think so, ma'am." The guard's lips didn't move, but a humorous twinkle lit his eyes. "You pretty much reek."

"Yeah, I do." Amanda walked back toward the apartment. "What's your name?"

"Gaston, ma'am."

"Well, Gaston, you're looking a little peaked. You okay?"

"Frankly, your run damn near killed me."

She looked down at his shoes. His suit. His gun. Yet no way would a die-hard GRID member admit that. "You're not dressed for it," she said. "This heat doesn't help."

"Ma'am, I could be in running gear and in optimum weather conditions, and your pace would still kick my ass." Reluctant respect resonated in his voice. "What's your speed in the stretch?"

Definitely not die-hard GRID. So what was he doing here? "Four and a half."

He pursed his lips, blew softly. "Three's pretty average."

She graced him with a killer smile. "But I'm not average."

"No, ma'am. I guess you're not."

Another potential ally. If it took flirting and being a little crass to seal a deal, she wasn't above it. She'd done worse and the stakes warranted it.

Exactly what those stakes were, she didn't know yet. But everything in her screamed the same warning: The stakes were enormous.


A messenger rode up to Gaston and Amanda on the golf course and pulled to a stop a short distance away. Gaston walked over and the young guard whispered something to him that he obviously didn't want Amanda to overhear.

Whatever it was turned Gaston's skin a sickly shade of green. "I need the cart," he told the messenger.

The guy climbed out, grimacing. Sweat streamed down his thin, pasty face and Amanda supposed he wasn't enthused at the idea of walking back to wherever he'd come from in the midday heat.

Gaston ignored him, turned to Amanda. "Get in."

Her stomach did a little flip, but she climbed into the cart. When Gaston slid in behind the wheel, she kept her manner casual. "Kunz change his mind?"

"Only about where he wants you to go." Gaston frowned now, and didn't bother to hide it.

"What is it? A firing squad? More drug therapy? Or has he ordered you to bury me in another tomb?"

Gaston glanced over at her and unmistakable pity shone in his eyes. "For you, it's worse." He swiped at his damp forehead with the back of his arm and motioned for her to hike up the hemmed edge of her shorts. When she did, he pulled a pen from his pocket and wrote on her thigh: *No choice. Few want 2 B here.*

Thinking of Joan and her situation, she softened her gaze on Gaston and blinked, letting him know she understood. Then she dabbed her fingertip against her tongue and rubbed away what he'd written.

When she had, he wrote a second message: *Avoid Reese and broken nose. Both want 2 kill U.*

The guard whose nose she'd broken. Beefy. She gave Gaston the slightest of nods, and then scrubbed off that message, too, trying not to let fear eat at her. Worse than a firing squad or being drugged or buried. There was no telling what Kunz, the King of Torture, had in mind for her.

Whatever it was, she prayed it didn't include Mark.

Gaston cut across the course and onto a paved street lined

with low-slung gray buildings and two wooden shacks that seemed out of place. The pavement ended at a circular driveway before a sprawling white-stucco building that had no windows. He pulled to a stop. "This is it."

Amanda walked inside. The air chilled her, raising gooseflesh. Beyond the typical difference between midsummer humid heat and air-conditioning, this went to that hospital-like cold in surgical units that's essential for keeping germ counts low. Antiseptic in smell and in looks. They walked down concrete painted-white floors, surrounded by tall white walls and white ceilings. The only decoration or color in the long hallway was multiple photos of the black-haired man she once thought was Thomas Kunz.

But why had she thought that? Confused, her skin crawled, warning her of the reason. *Transference.* He, or his minions, had superimposed a visual image of the man in the photo over his actual image to avoid his being correctly identified by authorities.

Amazing, but if she hadn't seen him face-to-face again, she would have sworn the man in the photos was Thomas Kunz, just as Intel had purported. Yet on seeing him, she'd immediately known the truth.

Mind games. He loved the "miracles of modern medicine" and, while that memory surprised her, she'd be foolish to forget that he included corrupting those miracles.

"Turn right here," Gaston said.

Amanda turned and walked to where Gaston stopped, two doors down. He held open a door for her. "I'll wait here."

"Thank you," she said, then walked into the room.

It was semidark, shadowy, a screening room of sorts. Three rows of six red-cushioned theater seats were centered before a large blank screen.

Thomas Kunz sat front row center. He turned to look back at her. "Ah, finally. Come and join me, Amanda."

She sat down on the row's end seat. "I need a shower," she explained. "I was out for a run."

"Considerate."

Kunz's smile stunned her. He looked so charming and innocent. How could he look so at ease with himself and at peace with his conscience when he'd done so many horrible things?

She crossed her ankles. "You summoned, I presume, for a reason."

"Oh, yes." Kunz shifted to face her. "I have something I want you to see. I suggest you watch carefully, my dear, and with as much emotional detachment as possible. It might be a little discomfiting, but it will prove to be in your best interests."

"I'll do my best to muddle through it, Thomas."

"I'm in no mood for amusements, so kindly refrain from engaging in flippant remarks and sarcasm." He looked at her, his eyes cold and empty.

The sunny-to-frigid change startled her. Burying her reaction to him, she shrugged. "So what is it you want me to see?"

"Your fate."

Fingers of ice tapped at her spine, squeezed her heart. "Okay, then. Let's take a look." She tried to sound breezy, knew she'd failed, but he obviously took her comment as sass and not substantive because he again frowned.

Kunz lifted a hand and the lights dimmed to dark. The screen before them flickered, and the "movie" began. The first image had Amanda's heart slamming against her ribs and her throat swelling shut.

She was the star in this film. And she was in uniform, meeting with Colonel Drake and Kate in Colonel Drake's office at Providence. Only it wasn't Amanda. She wasn't there.

It was her double.

Living Amanda's life.

Thomas cued up the sound. The double was speaking, and she sounded like Amanda—right down to her slight southern drawl.

"After intense investigation and conferring with Captain Cross, ma'am," the double told Colonel Drake, "I'm convinced there are no links between the three-month-absence cases."

"But, Amanda," Kate interceded, flipping a hand through her soft blond curls. "The last time we talked, you were certain there was a connection. Mark believed there was one, too."

"We were wrong, Kate," the double said simply. "We scrutinized everything and then double-checked ourselves. We found nothing. No evidence whatsoever to suggest any link. It just wasn't there."

"Well," Colonel Drake chimed in. "In the absence of evidence, we have no choice. I'm downgrading the necessity for Special Project status on this. Lower the priority code on GRID right away, Amanda."

"Yes, ma'am."

Kate looked less than happy. Actually, she looked pissed. And she would be because she knew Mark and knew the quality of his work. He had felt something was there, and Kate would respect that. She also eyed Amanda's double warily, though Kunz didn't seem to notice. But then, he wouldn't. Kate was merely Amanda's peer. She lacked jurisdiction or authority over her. Colonel Drake was Amanda's superior officer, the commander of S.A.S.S., and Kunz would be hot-wired to her reaction to Amanda's double.

Inside, Amanda started to shake. Whether from fear or outrage, she couldn't tell. If honest, she had to admit it was probably a fair share of both.

Kunz turned to look at her. "I thought you should see this

yourself. You can be amazingly stubborn about accepting the truth."

"What truth is that, Thomas?"

"Colonel Drake believes your double is you. She's totally accepted her."

"For the moment," Amanda conceded. Verification of the reason for the three months of plundering the depths of her mind became terrifyingly clear: familiarity studies for her double.

Kunz smoothed a hand down the thigh of his slacks. "No one will ever doubt her. She's worked very hard and done an excellent job at becoming you."

Amanda slid him a cold look. "I don't care if you have half the medical community working around the clock, you're not going to learn everything about any person in three months, Thomas. Things come up. Judgments have to be made. Little details get screwed up. Something happens and the truth comes out. It always comes out."

"Of course," he said. "Little details do happen." He rocked back in his seat and lit a cigarette. As I told you at our last meeting, keeping you alive makes you available to your double at all times, doesn't it?"

It did. It also gave her endless opportunities to pass coded messages to Drake that would reveal the truth…maybe. "How many times have you inserted doubles? Have you just infiltrated the air force? It and the CIA?" He had known about the CIA drop zone in Carolina. Harry was supposedly dead, but he was here. "Or have you pulled these switches in all U.S. security forces?"

Kunz declined to answer.

"What?" She pushed. "I'm stuck here forever. I want to know."

"Ask me two years from now, and I'll answer you, Amanda."

He knew she would get out of here before then, or die trying. She had to. The amount of trouble her double could wreak with her clearances could devastate the nation. Amanda had access to all U.S. intelligence agencies—including those that didn't exist on paper. Every operative and mission around the globe was in jeopardy.

Kunz's double had taken over Amanda's life. Become her.

And for the moment, Amanda was doomed to sit and watch her live it.

# Chapter 10

Amanda returned to her apartment with more questions than answers and more worries than solutions. She grabbed a glass in the kitchen and walked straight to the fridge.

Joan had left a note in the ice bin—and had snitched most of Amanda's ice as a pretense.

Amanda palmed the note and dropped a couple cubes into her glass, filled it with water and drank heavily, then headed for the shower—the only place in the apartment, according to Joan, where Kunz prohibited monitoring equipment. Cranking on the water, Amanda stripped off her damp clothes, stepped into the tub and then shut the curtain behind her.

Then she read the note.

*S.Z. 11 P.*

Safe zone at 11:00 p.m. Joan was confirming their earlier conversation. It was about 4:00 p.m. now. Amanda could shower, eat, snoop around a little and then meet Joan. Anticipation rippled in her stomach like the water rippled over her skin. She needed to talk to Mark in a bad way. They had to somehow break down this machine Kunz had built—before it broke down the government.

She chewed up the note, swallowed and soaped, rinsed then soaped again, letting the delicate fragrance soothe her raw nerves. Being around Kunz had made her feel dirty, and she wanted to feel clean again.

Common sense warned she had only a narrow window of time to develop a plan. With Colonel Drake already accepting her double, a very narrow window of time. And the plan had better be the best created in her career. Failing was not an option. The costs were higher than even imagined. Bluntly put, they were astronomical.

If Kunz and GRID succeeded, they would decide the economic and political structure of the United States. And the United States fed a large share of the world, and provided grants for medicine and humanitarian aid essential to sustaining life. Kunz and GRID would effectively choose the quality of life for the entire world, and he would choose who lived and who died.

There was no way she could allow that kind of power to fall into the hands of a sadistic, twisted man like Thomas Kunz—or any one man, for that matter.

*All necessary means, Princess.*

All necessary means. She swallowed hard. Would her "all" be enough?


Overbite stood on the sidewalk and watched Amanda's bedroom window. She turned off the light. Minutes later, he sat down on the grass, leaned back against the trunk of the old oak in the front yard and lit a cigarette. He definitely considered her down for the night.

In the dark, she pulled on black pants and a long-sleeved top. The heat would be murder, but she'd have more protection than with her skin exposed to any light. According to

Joan, they were safe from night vision glare. Amanda hoped she was right. She tugged the sleeves down to her wrists, then covered her hair and most of her face with a black scarf she found in the top right dresser drawer. That gave her the hee-bie-jeebies; that Kunz even had duplicates of her things in the exact place she kept them at her real apartment. How many times had her home been invaded and she had not known it? Or had Kunz had all that done during her three-month ab-sence? Or by her double?

Unable to answer any of that, she slipped out the bathroom window and slid down the outer wall into the hedge. Taking cover from trunk to trunk, she followed the thicket of trees splattered throughout the yard toward the path to the golf course. It was pitch dark, no moonlight. If she could make it to the course, she could make it to the safe zone undetected.

The air was hot and heavy. She moved quickly to the sev-enth hole, to the safe zone, and was glad to see Joan's silhou-ette.

"Mark's with me at the lab now," Joan said without pre-amble. "At the moment, he's okay."

Amanda had to choose. She could trust Joan, believe that she wasn't working with Kunz to test Amanda, or she could try to do what needed to be done alone. Her odds for success in the latter case were slim to none, which left her with no choice at all. "Kunz showed me my double today," she said. "The woman's already inserted into my life. How many dou-bles are there?"

"I don't know exactly. I've been here less than six months. But in the last two months, Kunz and Reese have really ramped up the process."

Cold shivers slammed into Amanda and she rubbed her arms. "Listen, Joan. I'm not sure you're aware of the magni-tude of all this. If Kunz effectively manipulates U.S. opera-tives, he can effectively manipulate world events."

"I know."

"And I understand now how GRID is so successful at getting accurate intel to broker on the black market. There are fail-safe protections in place, security measures to prevent this type of thing. But his doubling scheme is so complex… Who could have anticipated that?"

"No one without an evil, diabolical mind."

"Problem is, it's working." Amanda scraped her damp forehead with the heel of her hand. "I—I don't know how pervasive it is, but my instincts are telling me every U.S. operative and mission worldwide is in jeopardy."

"I'd say that's a fair assessment."

"Exactly what kind of doctor are you?"

"I'm a psychiatrist with extensive experience in psychological warfare. Specifically, in memory manipulations." She looked haunted. "I wanted to help Alzheimer's patients. Instead, I got myself and my family hijacked by a sadist."

"How?"

"He threatened to kill my family."

Amanda shrugged. Threats against loved ones weren't uncommon. "And you caved on that?"

"Not at first," Joan admitted, her voice soft and thick. "Not until he killed my parents and my husband's parents on the same day, and told me Simon and Jeremy were next."

Revulsion raced through Amanda. "I'm sorry."

"Me, too." The sorrow in her eyes was a window to the wound in her soul that would never heal.

"Do you do the plastic surgeries on the doubles?"

Joan shook her head that she didn't. "He has a staff of surgeons, former Soviets, who are all experts. They do the surgeries."

"Why?"

"Money," Joan said. "And it's one of the last places in the

world where they can experiment on live subjects. The idea appeals to the twisted asses."

"Are they here?"

"No, they left about a week ago. I wasn't told where they were going."

Amanda gave Joan a level look, her face swept in shadow. "You know he gave me twenty-four hours to decide whether I'll train GRID operatives in S.A.S.S. operations or die."

"I didn't." Joan sucked in a sharp gasp. "You can't do it, Amanda. We've got to stop him. I don't know how or by what means, but we've got to do *something* to stop him."

"I was hoping you'd say that." Amanda stepped closer, dropped her voice lower. "Where are the records on all the doubles?"

"I don't know. He has sweepers clean off anything on the computer system and takes all the records out of the clinic before he inserts the doubles. I have no idea what he does with the files or disks. They could be in a vault here or in another compound."

"Do you know where the vault is? Or how many compounds there are?"

"No, I don't. Paul Reese might, but I sincerely doubt anyone else does. Kunz keeps everyone as much in the dark about operations as possible."

"Do you have any idea who the doubles are, or where they're inserted?"

"Only the thirty I've debriefed."

*Thirty? Oh, God. Thirty?* "If you had to guess, how many doubles would you estimate he's inserted overall?"

"Hundreds. All over, not just in the military. FBI, CIA, NSA, INS, Secret Service, OSI—everywhere. His goal is to infiltrate Congress, Amanda. Knowing Kunz, he won't stop until he's tapped into the White House."

Amanda's blood chilled to ice. "We've got to take him

down and find out how far he's gotten. But we need serious help to do it."

Joan looked down at the ground. "You know he'll kill us and Simon and Jeremy if we're caught."

Amanda held her steady gaze. "Yes."

"And Mark."

"Yes." A knot formed in Amanda's throat. "Mark has to come with us."

"That's risky. Really risky—"

"That's not negotiable."

Joan let out a deep sigh, resigned herself and stiffened, steeling herself for what she had to do. "Okay. Here's the deal. I'll manipulate Mark's debriefings. I won't drug him. You rescue Jeremy, Simon and me. We get out of here, and then we work from the outside to bring Kunz and GRID down—and that bastard Paul Reese."

"Did he hit you, too?"

"He raped me in front of my husband and son." Joan's voice trembled with anger.

Shock coursed through Amanda. "Paul Reese? The white knight?"

"So he claimed. I never saw any evidence of it." Joan's voice went flat. "I couldn't repair his face. So I had to be scarred, too."

Amanda had damaged his face. Guilt flooded her. He had raped Joan to retaliate against Amanda. "I—I'm so sorry, Joan."

"You didn't rape me, Amanda, he did. But I lived." She lowered her gaze. "I've been talking with Jeremy about it. I think he understands. It's hell to have to explain something like that to a child."

"Oh, God, Joan. I—I—"

"What?"

"I scarred him." Amanda's stomach roiled and knotted. "It's my fault."

"No. It's not. He's responsible, Amanda. Only him."

She swallowed hard, trembling with outrage. "Don't worry about Reese anymore. I'll handle him."

"How?" Joan parked a hand on her hip. "What are you planning to do?"

Amanda looked her right in the eye. "I'm going to kill him."

"Can you do that?" Joan sounded torn between horror and fascination.

"Yes, I can." Amanda didn't elaborate or justify.

Joan licked her lips. "I'm scared, Amanda," she whispered. "I mean, really scared."

"You'd be nuts if you weren't." A furrow formed, pulling at the skin between her eyebrows. "The question isn't if you're afraid—it never is. It's whether or not you've got the courage to do the right thing in spite of being afraid."

Joan paused, looked off into the distance. Quiet resolve slid down over her face. "I'm not a particularly brave person—I never have been. But I have to do this or I'll never again be able to look myself in the face."

"That's my standard criterion for taking on outrageous risks."

"We have to do this, and I know we can."

Glad to hear it, Amanda dragged her mind from Reese and the rape back to GRID. "Explain to me how things work in the compound—and tell me, where the hell are we? It's supposed to be the Middle East, but the humidity says—"

"The soil says Texas. South Texas, somewhere off the I-10 stretch. I'm not sure exactly where the nearest town is or what it is."

Amanda had been that route several times. You could drive all day and see nothing for miles and miles. Even gas services were a hundred miles apart in places. Egress out of here was going to have to be by air. Mark flew helicopters, so they were covered on piloting. But they'd have to steal a chopper—one with a full tank of fuel. "Where are the helicopter hangars?"

"Hangar Row," Joan said. "Two buildings down on the left from the one with the screening room you were at today."

"Where is Simon being held?"

"In the cabins off the third hole on the golf course. They're off to the right, about two blocks. There are several rows. All the detainees whose doubles have been inserted are kept there."

Detainees. Prisoners kept alive indefinitely to answer any questions or assist their counterpart doubles. Kunz was one sick puppy. And one damn smart one. "Is everything on the compound centered on the golf course?" That struck her as extremely odd.

"Yes, it is."

"Why?"

"Kunz and Reese are into golf." Joan shrugged. "Many of the operatives play as well, so the doubles have to practice and play. In fact, you played often while you were here."

Amanda stared in utter disbelief. "I don't play golf."

"You did when you were here before."

So this was her Middle Eastern complex, too. Unwilling to ponder what else she'd done while here, Amanda turned the topic back to Joan's husband. "Which cabin is Simon's?"

"The second one on the second row."

"I need access to Mark, in order to plan."

"Wait here."

Amanda stood in the clearing and heard more than saw Joan disappear into the night. Minutes passed. Almost too many. Then Mark joined her in the safe zone. His face was bruised, his hand swollen. He had been tortured during interrogation. Her heart hitched. "Joan said you weren't being tortured, but—"

"Shh, I'm fine." He hugged her to him, his heart beating hard and fast against her chest. "You okay?"

"So far." She stroked him, wanting to comfort him without getting maudlin, remembering too well how fragile she'd felt after the tomb, and how much she had resented that fragility. "You?"

"Pissed to the gills." He looked down at her. "They're inserting doubles, Amanda. Joan's explained the entire process to me. It's damn diabolical."

"Worse," she said. "It's working."

"One of the doubles for a CIA agent in Europe had seventeen plastic surgeries to perfect his appearance before he was inserted. That's why the absences. They need time to make the changes and program—for lack of a better description— the doubles."

"Mark, are you getting what happened with Harding and Sloan?"

He stilled, looked down at her.

"The doubles did the killing," Amanda said. "Kunz couldn't have a wife or significant other noticing details that a wife would notice. When Harding's wife, Sharon, made the appointment with the OSI to report something 'troubling,' Kunz had her killed."

"And then withdrew the double and reinserted Harding into his own life to take the blame," Mark said. "Harding really didn't have a clue what had happened to Sharon. He wasn't there. He was here."

"Or somewhere like here. There's more than one compound." Amanda said. "So why didn't Harding remember it?"

"Joan says it's a combination of amnesia-induced drug therapy and reprogramming. She used the analogy of erasing that sector of a person's hard drive."

Brainwashing? Amanda recalled a security briefing about

a new laser technology that destroyed neuron firings in the brain, which destroyed memory paths. This was technologically possible. The use intended had been to help trauma victims, but corrupted, it could be used to destroy healthy, unwanted memory. "If there are hundreds of doubles, Kunz can't go around killing off spouses and everyone tied to all of them to protect against exposure."

"Many of us don't have spouses or anyone tied to us. You and I don't have spouses."

His point hit her. "He's targeting loners. Only going for operatives with spouses or significant others when he must have them in position."

"Reasonable conclusion in my opinion."

One thing was patently clear. Kunz had resources and the ability to carry out high-level, extremely sensitive and difficult maneuvers. Stopping him wasn't going to be easy. He had far too much to lose.

She couldn't help but shiver. "You ready to get out of here?"

"Yeah. We can do what we need to do outside. But we'll have to move fast or Kunz will go underground and take all the detainees with him."

"We're not leaving them here." Harry could be one of them—if Kunz hadn't killed his ornery ass.

Mark softened his tone. "We can't rescue everyone, Amanda."

"How many detainees are on-site?"

"Shh!" Mark shoved Amanda toward the trees. "Look."

Amanda dived onto her belly, burrowed under a clump of some spiny, sour-smelling bush and watched the light on a golf cart shine on the ground. "Is this routine?"

"Not according to Joan." Mark peeked out from between thorny branches. "The course is typically deserted at night."

"Damn it." Amanda resisted the urge to grind her teeth. "They're looking for me."

"Meet me back here at 3:00 a.m.," Mark said. "We don't have much time. Kunz oversees Joan's work. She'll have to put me through the paces. We have two days at most."

"We have less than twelve hours," she corrected him. "Kunz gave me twenty-four hours to agree to train doubles as S.A.S.S. operatives or die. And that was ten hours ago. I could swear on my mother's grave I'd train doubles, but he'd know I was lying. He's going to kill me, Mark."

"He just inserted your double. He's going to make sure she doesn't hit a brick wall first."

"I'm not willing to bet my life on it," she said. "I pissed him off, taking down his guards. He knows I'm going to be a thorn in his side, and he doesn't want the bother."

"Then we'd better move fast." Mark thumbed her chin. "I'm not ready to lose you just yet," he said, then slithered on his stomach across the course and disappeared in the darkness

He hadn't had her yet, but Amanda knew what he meant. They connected. It was special. And she wasn't ready to forfeit that connection, either.

The light swept closer. She considered just standing up and walking back to the apartment, but if she did, Kunz's men would watch her like a hawk every minute. She had to get back without being discovered, to have the freedom to meet Mark later.

The light came closer, shone directly on her. Flat on the ground, her hands buried under her chest, she resembled a small black lump and nothing more. *Come on, light. Be too weak to expose me. Be too weak!*

"Whoa. Back up." Beefy's voice carried across the course. "Over there."

Amanda's heart nearly stopped. Her pulse thrummed in her head and she broke into a cold sweat. The light crossed over her back, just above her, and shone into the trees. A raccoon scurried through the grass, dodged behind a tree, hiding from the light.

"It's just a raccoon, man. I'm telling you, Frank said she's lights out in her bed. Why are you so paranoid about her?"

"She broke my freaking nose. She took down three of us, stole a car, nearly stole a chopper, and you're asking why I'm paranoid? Why are you stupid? She's going to try to escape. It's just a matter of when."

"So what if she does?" the second man countered.

"Mr. Kunz will kill us, you idiot."

"Try to keep up, okay? Say she escapes. Where's she gonna go? We're two hundred miles out in the middle of nowhere. Even she can't hike two hundred miles across desertlike land, man. Not unless she's got superpowers." He chuckled. "Does she have superpowers?"

Beefy belted the guy, and he fell out of the cart and onto the ground. He got up madder than hell and took a swing at Beefy. In seconds, the two were tumbling on the ground to the sounds of fists hitting flesh, breaths swooshing and bones crunching.

Amanda knew an opening when she saw one, and took it.

At 2:45 a.m., Amanda made a production of turning on her bedside lamp to catch the guard's attention outside. In front of the window, she slung on her robe, walked to the bath and flipped on the light. She doubled back to the bedroom and checked the window to see if the guard had noticed.

Gaston stood on the sidewalk just outside the shimmering rim of light from the street lamp, staring up at the bathroom window. Definitely watching.

She turned the bathroom light off, again in front of the window, took off her robe, then turned off the bedside lamp and waited.

Still dressed in concealing black, she pulled on her shoes,

then snagged the scarf and shielded her hair and face. Ready to go, she checked the window. Gaston had gotten comfortable on the ground under the tree.

Leaving once again through the bathroom window, she made her way back to the golf course, then to the safe zone at the seventh hole.

Mark stood waiting for her. "We only have about fifteen minutes before they come through to do a bed check." He shifted from one foot to another. "Have you done reconnaissance and developed a plan yet?"

"Not yet. Kunz kept me pretty guarded most of the day," she said, inhaling Mark's familiar scent. It steadied her and she wondered why. She'd faced formidable odds a million times on her own. Why did his scent have this soothing effect on her? Why did he?

She'd like to believe it was merely hormonal; a physical reaction to a virile man with a compassionate heart was acceptable. But the truth, like it or not, was that damn intimate bond intrigued and lured her. It was new and different and odd and terrifying and wonderful and coveted and hated all at once. She should just set her mind to hating it, keep a healthy fear of it, and shove it off. But she didn't. Couldn't. It tugged at her. At something significant she'd longed for as a child and had never had, and only now, with him, did she realize the true worth of what she'd been missing. That, plainly put, was irresistible.

"I'll take care of it once you go back for the bed check," Amanda continued. "Joan will relay the plan to you and any specifics I think will be of help. I'll check out the best means of retrieving Simon."

"And if I spot any gaps or loose ends, I'll relay them back to you through Joan," Mark agreed.

Amanda nodded. "Have you seen a guy named Harry?"

"He approached me earlier today, wanting to know if I'd seen you."

Relief washed through Amanda. "I thought he might be dead. His replacement said he'd been shot down over Iraq." A thought confused her. "Mark, if he's dead in his identity with the CIA, then why is Kunz keeping the real Harry alive?"

"He's an instructor pilot and a CIA operative. Training doubles?"

That made sense. "Okay. Can you still fly helicopters?"

"Yeah. I'll take care of jamming the surveillance, too. Joan says that Simon's located the master control room. It's just off the fairway near the second hole. He's created a loop feed of film to play through the surveillance system so our actions are concealed from the monitors as long as possible. That'll give us a little cover, trying to get out of here." Worry scudded across Mark's face. "Provided the guards don't immediately recognize they're looking at film and not at live shots. I have no idea of the quality of Simon's work."

"Considering his family's lives are on the line, I'd be willing to bet it's the best work of his life."

"Your mouth to God's ears."

She disclosed the location of the choppers and then added, "I'll liberate Simon and Harry and whomever else possible. We can fit eight in the chopper. Any others will have to make a run off the compound and hunker down until we can get help back for them."

"You hate leaving anyone."

God did she. "It could be us, Mark."

"Yes." He didn't flinch. "But this is national security, and that's every American. Considering we feed half the world, it's even more."

"I know, but still…"

He thumbed her chin, looked her straight in the eye. "We have no choice."

Blinking hard, she pulled in a steadying breath. "I know. But I don't have to like it."

"No, you don't," he agreed. "Neither do I. We just have to do it."

"Sometimes I really hate my job."

"Sometimes you're supposed to hate it."

She nodded, a hole spearing into her stomach at having to choose who stayed and who went. "You know those left behind will probably be dead before Rescue can get here."

Again, Mark held her gaze and didn't flinch. But his voice dropped rough and ragged. "Yes, I know."

They shared a look of painful resignation, and that bond strengthened yet again. Amanda stepped back and cleared her throat. "You be ready to jam that surveillance, run the loop feed and snag the chopper."

"Check. Don't worry. I'll be prepared. Joan's covering, giving me time to do some reconnaissance." He started to turn away and stopped, his eyes narrowed, worried. "Amanda?"

"Yes?"

"You have a double. From what Simon and Joan have said, it's virtually impossible to tell the real thing from the double. How do I know I'm really dealing with you?"

She pretended not to feel a little stab of personal pain that their connection didn't make it evident. But the truth was, men were historically less intuitive than women and he had a reasonable point. She thought a moment, then said, "Use standard operating procedure." That's why they had a code phrase. He knew that.

"Of course." Mark stroked her face, but he didn't whisper the phrase.

She paused. "You could have a double, too."

"I could," he confessed. "But I haven't seen or heard anything about one."

His three-month absence had occurred long before hers. Joan had only been here six months—nearly six months after Mark had been released—but she was going to start working with him now to get the information from him that Kunz and Reese needed to train a double. If they already had a double in place, they would have the information. "Maybe you don't have one—at least, not yet." But why wouldn't he? There would have to be a reason. Maybe faking his security level being lowered and his no longer being a member of Delta Force had quashed Kunz's interest in doubling Mark. Maybe he had no use for a lead investigator. Or—the phones in Mark's office were being bugged—maybe Kunz already had one. Both possible and, unfortunately, probable.

He brushed her cheek with a light kiss. "When do we meet here again?"

She inhaled deeply, savoring his scent to carry with her. "Let's touch base here at 10 p.m. and finalize any details, then take it from there." The plan would have to develop and process faster than she would like, but they just couldn't risk taking more time. As it was, she was going to have to delay Kunz beyond his twenty-four-hour deadline.

Nodding, Mark backed away from her. "I'll look for you in plain sight."

Amanda looked back at him; saw her worry and fear reflected in his eyes. "In plain sight."

As he moved away from her, her thoughts turned horrific. This mission contained too damn many variables and too few iron-clad answers. Doubles could be inserted all over the place—including Joan or even Jeremy. Kunz wouldn't refuse to use him just because he was a kid.

He'd stolen all of their lives. And that he had succeeded was chilling.

Mark's scent lingered on Amanda's skin. It reminded her of the stakes and helped her focus, which half irritated and half relieved her, but she couldn't honestly say which emotion she felt strongest or appreciated most. The idea of needing someone else had her bristling and edgy. That it was Mark, and that her head kept telling her she hadn't known him long enough to feel so strongly about him, had her irked. But her heart didn't seem to care what she thought about logic or intellect. It seemed it didn't care about her aversion to needing anyone else, either. Hell, it didn't even seem to care about anything she'd lived and breathed and believed inviolate for decades.

And that rattled her to the bone.

Maybe—she cut through a copse of mesquite trees hugging the edge of the course and left it near the second fairway—*needing* wasn't the right word. *Want*. Yes, *wanting* him fit better. She could deal with *want*. If the way he presented himself was real and not some act put on to sucker her in.

Two guards walked the perimeter of the cabins. She ducked down near one of the spiny bushes that smelled sour and watched the guards move through their routine. They crossed paths at the end of the row of cabins and worked from row to row. There were three rows of seven cabins in this area. She'd passed two other areas, though both had appeared to be deserted.

Mark had been right. They couldn't rescue everyone at once.

A third guard stepped out of the door of the last cabin on the row, sweeping the area with his flashlight. Amanda felt the light on her face and froze. *Damn it!*

He pulled out his gun, walked over and stopped out of her reach. "Come out, Amanda. Now."

She darted her gaze to the other two guards, her heart pumping hard and fast against her ribs. Both were four rows over, continuing their grid walk. When they crossed at the end of the fourth row, made the corner then took off down the fifth row, she scooted out from under the bush, pulled herself to her feet and stumbled into the guard, knocking him off balance. "Sorry." She shouldered his ribs, pushed his gun away from her, barrel up, skyward. With a flick of her wrist, she knocked the gun from his hand and turned. He caught her with a left hook on the jaw that set her ears to ringing. She kicked, slammed her foot into his stomach, twisted, captured him in a headlock and snapped his neck.

He slid to the ground.

Adrenaline shoved through her veins and her chest heaved. She dragged him into the trees, checked the sky. Another hour or so and it would be dawn. She had to find somewhere to stash his body. Somewhere he wouldn't be noticed for a day or so.

An idea formed.

Struggling under his weight, she hauled him back to the cabin she'd seen him leave. Fortunately, no one else was inside. Half dragging, half pushing, she got him in and onto his single bed. After stripping off his clothes, she covered him up with a sheet and thin blanket, fluffed his pillow, and then backed off.

To anyone who looked, he appeared to be sleeping.

Now, she thought. How to keep anyone from getting close enough to realize he wasn't going to wake up…?

"Got it."

She rummaged through the kitchen drawers, found a white cloth and a pen and, in the living room, a piece of paper. On it, she wrote the words guaranteed to keep a man from coming in. Few women here would bother.

DO *NOT* DISTURB.

Maybe QUARANTINE would be better. She tilted her head, stared at the sign. No, some macho jerk would think he was too strong to get whatever it was and come in anyway. If for no other reason than to bring food. And someone would likely send for a doctor to make sure no one else was at risk. Sex was her best bet. A man who deliberately interrupted a guy getting laid had better be ready to fight.

She pulled the curtains and shutters closed, dug around

more and found some tape, then left the cabin. After draping the white cloth over the doorknob, she taped the sign to the outside of the door.

Not seeing the other guards, she cautiously made her way back to the golf course, and then back to her apartment. When she closed the bathroom window, she swallowed a large glass of water, and heard the doorbell ring.

She peeked out and saw Beefy standing on the porch. "Just a minute."

Running upstairs, she ripped off her clothes and slung on her robe, then ran back downstairs to the door. She mussed her hair, cracked the door open and scowled. "What could you possibly want in the middle of the night?"

"It's morning," he said, obviously before thinking.

She hiked her chin, glowered at him. "Not to me."

"Just letting you know we're changing shifts out here."

"Whatever." She stepped back, slammed the door and went up to bed. Beefy had been verifying she was actually in the house. Why?

She was just rolling into bed, when she heard Beefy's voice carry up through the window from outside. "Gaston, what the hell is this?"

"I must have done it," he said.

Amanda slid out of bed, walked to the window and looked down. The shrubs outside the bathroom window. She'd done some damage going over them.

"When?" Beefy asked Gaston. "Why?"

"She got up to go to the bathroom a couple of hours ago," Gaston said. "I wanted to make sure she wasn't slipping out through the back, so I checked the window. I guess I screwed up the shrubs then."

"You're sure you did it?"

Amanda looked down from above, saw her own shoe print in the dirt below her. How could Beefy miss that?

Gaston saw it, ground his shoe in the print. "I'm sure. I checked it and then came back a second time just to double-check. I did it."

He was covering for her. Surprise rippled through Amanda.

No, he was covering for himself. If he admitted she'd gotten past him, Kunz would kill him. According to Joan, he had a zero-tolerance policy on errors.

Whatever his reasons, Gaston had covered for her. Amanda walked back to bed, totally exhausted and ready for a long sleep.

She pulled the covers up over her and caught a whiff of Mark's scent, lifted her inner forearm to her nose, breathed deeply. Later today, she could die. But for now, she would hold the moment. She would sleep, and she would hope Mark really was Mark because, like it or not, he'd gotten to her. Bad.


Just after ten, Paul Reese, Beefy and two other guards stormed into the apartment. Amanda heard them enter downstairs, jumped out of bed and took to the stairs to see what the hell was happening. Reese met her halfway down, and she stopped on the steps.

He let his angry gaze roll over her gray tank top and shorts. "You killed him, Amanda, and I know it. I only have one question. How did you get there to do it?" The white bandage protecting the wound where she'd bitten him and the failed reconstructive surgery to repair it that had gotten Joan raped in the presence of her family covered half his face. Its edges crinkled, fighting the tape with his every word. "I want an answer right now, or I'll beat you to death. I swear it."

He would. When they'd first met, he'd described himself to her as a white knight to women in distress. She'd soon come to learn that he was a sleazy, opportunistic manipulator who preyed on women's desires and fantasies of love. But she'd assisted that facade in shattering, and now he saw himself through her eyes, and all that was left in him was hostility, animosity and hatred that consumed. Evil had battled for him and won.

She'd seen it happen before, and dealing with the remnants never had been less than sheer hell. Reese had no limits on what he would do. Not anymore. And that made him an incredibly formidable enemy. "What are you talking about, Paul?"

"Don't play games with me." He took a step up, then stopped.

She didn't dare back up. Didn't dare. If she did, he'd know she was afraid. He'd own her. "I'm not playing games. You're the one raging. I have no idea why you're here or what you want."

"Rafe Batten. The GRID guard at the cabin. You killed him."

"Who's Rafe Batten? What cabin?" she asked, feigning puzzlement. "What the hell are you talking about?"

"You killed him!" Paul screamed.

*Stay calm. Stay calm and cool and unruffled. That's your advantage. Control. Go on the offensive.* She took a step down toward him and launched her attack. "Listen up, Paul Reese. If you can't keep your guards alive, don't blame me. I've been under lock and key and constant surveillance since I've been in this devil's armpit of a desert hellhole. If you screwed up, you take the hit." She jabbed a finger in his direction. "I take my hits because I deserve them. But I damn sure won't take yours to get Kunz off your ass because you're lousy at your job."

Paul's temper got the best of him. He raised a hand to hit her.

She didn't flinch or back up. "If you do it, you'd better kill me." She dropped her voice, calm and cold, and forged every word with resolve. "Because if you don't, I swear I'll kill you."

He hesitated. Clearly furious, and convinced she would carry through on her threat, he stilled with his arm midair and clenched his jaw.

Amanda held her ground. Glared into his angry eyes and dared him to try her, warned him he'd be a damn fool to do it. His throat was totally exposed and with one move, she could seize the advantage and he would lie dead on the steps.

Apparently, he realized it. He slowly lowered his arm, his pulse thrumming in his neck. "I hate you, Amanda West."

"I'm delighted to hear it." She peeled her lips back from her teeth in the coldest smile of her life. "If you didn't, I would hate me, and frankly, Paul, you're not worth it."

A muscle under his eye ticked and his red face paled. "I'm not through with you. But I'll choose when and where and how you die. Watch for me, Amanda. All the time."

"I look forward to it. Anytime." She hiked her eyebrows, inviting him to carry through on his threat. "In fact, I'll make it easy for you. I'm going to accept Thomas's offer. I'm staying, Paul."

"You're staying, all right." He backed down the stairs, afraid to turn his back on her. "Toes up in a coffin."

"Get out of my apartment." She started down the stairs. "Out!"

Motioning, Paul left, and his men quickly followed him out the door.

Trembling, Amanda followed, jammed the heel of her fisted hand against it and slammed home the bolt lock. "Sick bastard."

She took a steadying breath, ordered herself to calm down, then stumbled to the kitchen to make a cup of coffee. They'd found the body so quickly…

Not a single break. Not one. "Damn it." Couldn't they have waited just a little longer before finding the body? Just a few lousy hours?

Now every guard in the compound would be on high alert during their escape attempt.

Reese probably found the body himself. He was the only man she knew whose ego wouldn't be able to stand the thought of someone else getting laid while he went without. He'd ignore the Do Not Disturb sign and intrude.

Reese might have been fooled, but there was no way Kunz was going to believe she hadn't killed that guard. No way. He'd double the guards on her, which would make her checking out the helicopters before ten tonight even more challenging.

The intensity of that challenge would depend on who stood on the front lawn guarding her today. Gaston would be more amiable than Beefy. He was out for her blood. She needed to check the living-room window; see who was pulling guard duty. First, she poured herself a cup of coffee. When she turned, she nearly had a heart attack.

Thomas Kunz stood in the center of her kitchen.

# *Chapter 11*

Amanda splashed hot coffee down the front of her T-shirt. "Damn it."

She set the cup down on the countertop, pulled the fabric away from her skin, then snagged a dishcloth from the counter and dabbed at the spill, determined not to let Kunz see fear in her.

"Sorry." He took a few steps toward her. "I assumed your highly attuned instincts would warn you that I was here. Apparently they're a little rusty…or is it, overestimated?"

She frowned at him for that backhanded-slap-of-a-remark and tossed the cloth onto the counter. "You could've knocked."

"I own this place and control your destiny. I knock when and where I choose to knock."

Amazingly, he didn't sound or look furious, but there was no mistaking his vibes. Sheer outrage crashed through his pores and pounded into her in shattering waves. "So I've been told." She sighed and held it, making sure he didn't miss it. "Since you're here, would you like a cup of your coffee?"

He crossed his arms over his chest; spread his feet, claiming his ground. "I'd like for you to stop injuring and killing my guards."

"You didn't answer my question," she reminded him, pointing to her cup. "Coffee?"

"Why not?" His expression didn't soften; neither did his stance.

Not a good sign. Amanda reached into the cabinet, withdrew a cup and filled it from the pot. "Look, Thomas. I assume you're pissed off at me about this Batten guy."

"Oh, yes. Rafe had been with me for years."

"I'm sorry for your loss." How many losses had S.A.S.S. and other Intel groups suffered due to him and his projects? She passed him the coffee cup. "This is a courteous gesture. I don't expect to have to wear it."

He took the cup from her and nodded. "Détente on the coffee."

*Détente.* She hadn't heard anyone use that word since the end of the cold war.

Dipping her chin, she said, "While you're in an accommodating mood, you can point your poison darts about Rafe Batten elsewhere. I've already been through this with your sidekick. I was present and accounted for right here by your surveillance equipment and your men."

A flicker of surprise crossed Thomas's face. He quickly suppressed it. "Paul is convinced you killed Rafe Batten, Amanda."

She rolled her gaze toward the ceiling, plopped down into a kitchen chair. "Well, he would be, now, wouldn't he?" She set her mug on a sage green plaid place mat. "I scarred his face, Thomas. The man does not find me endearing. He'd blame me for anything he could—including rainfall, mechanical failures and the coming of the Antichrist." She grunted, shoved a hand through her ruffled hair. "Good grief, for a smart man, you're damn slow."

Kunz sat down, sipped his coffee. "Save your breath, darling. I know you killed the man, and I know you're hatching some sort of plan to escape. It would be totally alien to your inner nature for you to not be scheming." He set his cup down, leaned forward in his chair and lowered his voice. "You forget that I know you, Amanda. Probably better than you know yourself, and a hell of a lot better than any other living man knows you or ever will."

*Darling? Darling?* Her heart hammered. There was no misunderstanding the hazy look in his eyes, either. Dr. Vargus had said she'd had sex during her three-month incident and until now, for some odd reason, she'd assumed it had been with Paul Reese. But that look and the endearment out of Kunz had her wondering. Had she really had sex with Paul? Or had her partner been Thomas Kunz?

The possibility of Kunz touching her had her flesh crawling, her stomach rebelling and her chest tightening. "You're forgetting that I know you, too, Thomas."

Unprepared for that comeback, he stiffened on his seat. Uneasy. Anxious. Edgy. She capitalized on it. "What? You thought the drugs would make me forget what you did to me?"

He clenched his jaw, said nothing.

"Not a chance." She drank from her cup and walked to the pot for a refill. "I remember it all. Every bit of it." Should she risk pushing too far? Straining credibility? Hell, why not? What more could she have at stake than she already did. "In intimate detail."

"You remember only what I want you to remember." He smiled.

The warmth in it chilled her to the core. It seemed so genuine and sincere. So honest. Those were deadly traits in a corrupt man. "I remember you." She came around the edge of the table, stood close to him and hoped to hell she wasn't putting a bullet through her own head with this performance. "Did I so much as hesitate at calling you by name on seeing you?"

She hadn't, and he had realized it then, and again now. He looked up at her, serious and solemn. "You're a dangerous woman, Captain West."

*Captain West.* She had him on unsure ground. "Yes, I am." She smiled. "But you're a dangerous man, too, Thomas, and you do seem to have the momentary advantage."

"There's no seeming to about it, it's a fact. And it isn't momentary, Amanda. The sooner you accept that as truth, the better for both of us."

She brushed against his shoulder in a show of defiance and a lack of fear that was totally bogus and then returned to her chair. "What is your overall plan? Take over the world? Manipulate the economy? Destroy the country?" She shrugged. "The last is pretty much a given." She tilted her head, looked at him through a fringe of hair slipping over her eye. "Do you hate anything quite as much as America, Thomas?"

The light in his eyes died. They looked distant and gray and empty of any emotion. That absence terrified her most of all. She could deal with everything from joy to rage, but there was no effective way to deal with indifference.

"There's no need to disclose my plans. You'll be around to see them unfold." He thumbed the rim of his coffee cup with a blunt fingertip. "That is, unless you become more trouble to me than you're worth."

He'd regained his footing. More's the pity. "Well, that would take quite a bit of effort, don't you think?" She tilted her head, challenged him with her tone but not with her soft expression. "My double is new, and as I've said before, there's no way you could learn everything about me or the way my mind works in three months. You need me. Somehow, you have to convince me to help you." She wrinkled her forehead. "Frankly, I don't think it's possible, but I know you'll give it a shot anyway."

"You'll help me."

"I don't know, Thomas," she said, tilting her head, pondering. "Operatives have killed themselves for far less."

"But you're not one of them," he said. "You're a survivor. That's something we have in common."

"We have nothing in common, Thomas."

"Yes, we do. Surviving." He paused to sip from his cup. "If you were going to kill yourself, you'd have done it when your father brutalized you and locked you in the box. If you didn't commit suicide then, you won't now. None of the operatives I've chosen to double have, and none will."

Because he likely was right, Amanda frowned. "Speaking in absolutes is a dangerous thing. You usually end up eating your words."

"It's a given. A fact, Amanda." He rolled his shoulders, relaxed. "You see, there's a streak of idealism in all of you that makes you believe that as long as you're alive, you might find a way to save yourself and your country." He snorted. "It's truly amazing that a woman who's known your reality can still be an idealist."

Amanda squared off at him. "What's amazing is that someone who's lived your reality didn't choose to be an idealist." Genuinely curious, she prodded. "You were abused. I recognize the signs, and they're all over you, so don't bother denying it. You know what it's like to be small and helpless and hurt, and rather than protect people from all those awful things, you do worse—and actually enjoy it. You love to torture people. I don't get it. Why do you do that, Thomas?"

His eyes gleamed. "You never feel more alive than when you're about to die. Don't you remember the rush? The gasping for breath not knowing if it would be your last?"

Memories blasted out the door of the safe buried inside her, and her father's muffled voice ran through her head. She lay curled up inside the box in the dark. She'd been there at least two days. Realizing he'd forgotten she was in there, she had listened for his footsteps and, when she had heard them, she had beaten the box lid with her fist and begged him to let her out. *Please, Daddy. Please!* And all the while she'd prayed that if he did let her out he wouldn't beat her again.

More than a few times, she had prayed to either escape or die. It hadn't mattered which.

But that was then and this was now, and now it mattered. "I remember terror, not a rush. There was no rush."

"For me, there was no terror." His eyes gleamed. "The rush was like nothing I've experienced before or since."

"You're one twisted bastard, Kunz," she said from between her teeth. He was just like her father. Looking at him, she felt her stomach heave.

"Thank you." He smiled. "Idealist. You'll do what I want, Amanda."

"No," she said softly. "I won't. You consider me an idealist. I'm not. I lost any idealism the day I was born, and if I choose to die—"

"You'll be kept without any means to kill yourself."

She dropped her voice low. "I am never without means, Thomas."

"You are now. I control you. Everything, even your breathing is subject to my control."

"You're so wrong." She lifted her chin. "My will is my own, Thomas, and it's stronger than anything you can imagine."

"Keep consoling yourself with that nonsense, if you like,

but don't bother trying to convince me. Soon enough, I'll prove you wrong."

She glared at him, stood her ground. Her days of backing down were long over.

He ignored it. "You mentioned earlier that I need you—to confer with your double on any challenges that may arise. I confess," he said, "consultations between you two would eliminate incidental annoyances, but never delude yourself. I do not need you, Amanda. And if one more of my guards is injured or killed—whether or not you are responsible—you are going to die for it. So you had better invest in their health and well-being."

Her stomach curled. He thought he was smarter than she, and the hell of it was, he could be. "Ah, Thomas. Whatever am I going to do with you?"

"I believe that should be my question to you."

She gave him an indulgent look. "I had hoped you'd at least grasp the rudiments of civility during my absence. Yet here you are, threatening to kill me while sitting in my kitchen, at my table, drinking coffee. I'm deeply offended."

He gave her a sunny smile. "Then I shall remind you that this is my kitchen, my table and my coffee—all of which are provided for your use and benefit as a courtesy I extend to you, as is your life. Regardless, for now, I shall remove my offensive self from your presence." He scooted back his chair and stood up. "I've been extremely patient with you because, when we first met, I admired your courage and professionalism and, later, because you were delicious in bed. But even I have my limits, Amanda. Don't push me."

*Oh, no. No, no, no!* She had had sex with him. That she'd been drugged out of her mind at the time didn't do a damn thing to comfort her. That slime had touched her. He had dared to touch her.

*Oh, please. Please, tell me I didn't ask him to, or want him to. Please tell me it was rape.*

Ignorant of her internal debate, Thomas continued, "You are enormously headstrong, and I don't think you've gotten past your anger yet and to the point where you can make wise decisions." He gripped the back of his chair, eased it toward the table. "I'll extend your time until dusk tomorrow. By then, you must decide if you want to live here and work for me, or die." He took a step back, pointed a finger at her. "But if you attack another of my guards, the clock stops, and your freedom to choose vanishes. I will kill you, Amanda. And I'll take great pleasure doing it—and you'll suffer great pain. You have my word on that."

Icy inside, she held his gaze until he finally turned and walked out of the kitchen. Moments later, the front door closed.

When it shut, she ran to it and drove home the dead bolts. Shaking, her entire body in revolt, she forced herself to think. To go back to the kitchen and bag his coffee cup for lab analysis. The revulsion in her grew and she suddenly felt as small and helpless as she had as a child, only this time, the box was her body.

She charged up the stairs to the shower. Shame and guilt and filth and rage rushed through her, merciless, relentless, and the only thought she could hold was that she had to try to get clean.

Somehow, she had to try to get clean.

An hour later, when Joan knocked on her bathroom door, Amanda was still in the shower. Her lips were blue and her teeth chattering from the cold water. Her skin was red and raw, and still she scrubbed. "Go away!"

"I can't, Amanda." Joan said, then cracked open the door and walked into the bath. "They told me to come check on you. You've been in the shower for over an hour." Joan reached for the faucet.

"No!" Amanda shouted. "Touch it and I'll break every bone in your hand."

Joan jerked back. "What's wrong? What did Kunz do to you?"

"I don't know." The water pelted her in the face, on the chest and shoulder and ran down her stomach to her feet. "That's why I can't get clean. I don't know." She jerked the shower curtain out of Joan's hand and pulled it closed. "Get out, Joan. Just go. I have to get clean. Don't you understand? I have to get clean."

Joan left.

And returned within minutes with Mark. "I think she's been raped. She's exhibiting symptoms of it, but she denies knowing what happened to her. She's in some dark place, and I can't reach her, Mark."

He wiped his damp palms on the pale blue scrub pants that "patient" detainees wore, and then walked into the bath. "Amanda."

"For God's sake, get out of here. Leave me alone!"

"Amanda, it's me, Mark. I'm not leaving." He closed the door behind him. "I have to talk with you."

She hugged the wall; let the cold water pelt her. It stung, hurt. That, she remembered. The pain was clear and certain in her mind. That, she could feel.

"I'm coming in there," he warned her.

She flattened against the wall, huddled, trying to be small. So small he couldn't see her. Amanda knew what she was doing. She knew this behavior was irrational, erratic, maybe even crazy, but her emotions seemed to have snapped and they refused to let her control them anymore.

Mark eased the shower curtain aside and stepped into the shower, fully clothed. "Amanda." The water was beating on her. She was red and blue and yet her eyes were dry. No tears. "Come here. Please."

She stared at him. "I don't know what I did," she whispered low to keep anyone from overhearing her. "Did he rape me, or did I want to have sex with him? I don't know, Mark."

"Come here, Amanda." He opened his arms. "Please, honey."

"He's the enemy. He's everything I hate. Yet he touched me, and I swore I'd never be touched again by anyone I didn't want to touch me. I swore it." She slumped toward Mark.

He closed his arms around her. "It's okay. Shh." He pulled her head close to his chest. This was about her father. About his abuse and her being a defenseless victim. This was about Kunz making her feel like that helpless and hopeless child she had once been.

Rage burned in Mark's stomach. He talked to Amanda, whispered gentle words and reassurances, talked of nothing and everything; about their work and all the ways he knew her to be strong. Everything he could recall that proved her strength he related while holding her and rubbing small circles on her back.

Finally, she calmed down enough that he could reach behind her and turn off the water. They were both freezing cold. Her skin felt like ice. He snagged a towel from the rack in the back of the shower and wrapped it around her. "You're okay, Amanda. Kunz never touched you."

"He did!" She let her forehead fall forward, against Mark's shoulder. "He specifically said—"

"He lied," Mark insisted. "I swear he didn't touch you. He *never* touched you."

"How do you know that?" She looked up at him, her eyes haunted, pleading. "You can't know that."

"I can and do. I read your file here and I watched your tapes. Joan helped me," he whispered close to her ear. "I know where you were and who you were with. You slept with Paul Reese, Amanda, not with Thomas Kunz. With Reese. And you chose to do it. Not because you wanted to, but because you had to get closer to him to find out what was going on here. You chose."

She stared up at Mark. A little dazed. "You're sure?"

"Positive." He let her see the truth in his eyes. "I swear it."

"Kunz said…" Her voice cracked, and she tried again. "He made me believe—"

"Of course he did," Mark said. "He knew it would make you crazy. He knew it would hurt you. He's playing mind games with you, Amanda. He plays them with all of us."

*Mind games.*

Joan had warned Amanda of that. She lowered her gaze, suspicion taking root and pulsing through her until her knees threatened to fold. She looked back up into Mark's worried face and then whispered close into his ear, "How do I know who you are?" Did she dare to believe him?

He smoothed her dripping hair back from her face. "You're okay." He pressed a gentle kiss to her cheek and dropped his voice even more, so that even the extremely sensitive mike in the hallway outside the bath wouldn't pick up so much as a muffle. "In plain sight, baby." He kissed her cheek again and then pulled back to look into her face.

Fear and doubt raked her raw nerves. "But did I make that agreement with the real Mark Cross? How can I know?"

He stilled, stiffened against her, searched her eyes and let her see the truth in his. "Look at me. Not with your eyes, but with your heart and your instincts. You've always trusted your instincts."

She closed her eyes and let her instincts take over.

"I swear it on my life, Amanda," he whispered. "On Kate's life, and you know what she means to me. She's the only family I've got. I'd do anything to protect her."

And he'd die before hurting her. "Okay. Okay, I believe you." Everything in Amanda promised he was telling the truth. She buried her face against his chest, clutched her fingertips at his sides. "This place is making me crazy, Mark. Thomas Kunz is making me crazy."

"No, he's not. He'd like to, but he's not. You won't let him have that kind of power over you. No man will ever hold that kind of power over you." Reminding her of who she was, Mark dabbed her dry with the towel, and then moved toward the edge of the tub. "Come on. Let's get out of here."

She stepped out and he opened the door. Joan came in, holding a thick towel and fluffy pink robe, and something blue. "I thought you might have to go in to get her," she said. Looking worried, she passed the clean set of scrubs to Mark.

"Thanks." He shivered.

"Are you okay now, Amanda?" Joan helped slide her arms into the robe.

"Of course." She looked at Joan as if she had no idea why Joan was concerned. Completely in control.

Flummoxed, Joan looked at Mark, raised a questioning eyebrow.

"She's fine. Really," he assured Joan, then glanced at Amanda. "The truth has set her free."

"Oh." Joan backed away, relieved but perplexed and not bothering to hide it. "Okay, then."

"Okay, then." Amanda smiled at Mark and mouthed a silent thank-you.

He winked, and she thought she just might love him forever for that.

"We'd better get you back to the clinic." Joan motioned to Mark. "I'm supposed to have you into one of the detainee cabins by noon and if anyone notices you're missing, there'll be hell to pay."

Why *hadn't* anyone noticed? Amanda wondered. "How

did you get here without being seen? What about the guard outside? The monitors in the apartment?" Only the bathroom was clear of devices.

"Jeremy's occupying the guard outside," Joan answered. "I jammed the lead line into the house with aluminum foil. It gives us a few minutes. Any longer and someone will come to investigate."

"Resourceful."

Joan gave her a level look. "I have a lot to lose."

Her family. Amanda nodded. "Go, then. I'm fine now. Really."

Mark signaled "ten," referring to the time for their arranged meeting, and left with Joan.

Totally wiped out, Amanda flung herself across the bed, jerked the covers up over her, then huddled, thankful she and Mark had had the foresight to establish a code phrase and even more so that she'd learned to trust her instincts.

Without them both, she'd still be going insane. Not that she wasn't mortified by what had happened. She was, but she wasn't naive enough to believe her breaking down had been totally about Thomas Kunz. It hadn't been. Still, she never in her adult life had totally lost it like that. Never. Regardless of circumstance, she had maintained emotional control. That she'd lost it now embarrassed and terrified her. Why had that happened now?

Why, after all these years, and all that had happened to her—all the armor she'd given herself to combat feeling helpless or hopeless or like a victim—did her father still have that kind of power over her? It was he and the memories of his tormenting power that had made her snap. Not Thomas Kunz. But why?

*Because you give him that power.*

She did. Damn it, she did.

*So if you don't like it—*

"Stop it. Now. Just stop it and take the power back. I know." She did. It was her personal power and her choice.

Resolved to reclaiming it, Amanda snuggled into the covers and drifted off to sleep. When she awoke with a start, she was surprised to find that it was almost one-thirty. She tossed back the covers and got up. She ran a mental check, made sure she had centered herself, made sure she was totally convinced that Mark was indeed Mark, and allowed herself a shimmer of relief on discovering she had and she was. And so what if he'd viewed her tapes and he knew about her father and the beatings and the box? So what? She didn't like it, but it didn't change a damn thing—and if it did, then to hell with him. She could make her way ahead just fine alone. Hadn't she always done it?

Her mind-set again balanced and her attention focused, she looked through the window down to the lawn to see who was guarding her. *Gaston.*

Thank goodness. And he was in a suit and street shoes.

Better and better. She dressed quickly in running gear. If she warmed up and then ran full out, there was no way Gaston could keep up with her. She could check out the helicopters, the security system and guards, and Gaston wouldn't be any the wiser. He'd be grateful to see her doubling back on him, to end the run.

She bent down to tie her shoe and the truth hit her. She and Mark were working together to get out of a mutual jam, but he hadn't had to treat her with the respect and care and compassion he had shown her. He was the first man in her life who had treated her well and had expected nothing in return. Maybe these were simple courtesies to other women, but to her, they were nothing short of shocking. And once again, she felt that tug to him, that connection grow a little stronger.

A warm glow settled low in her stomach. She mulled over the unfamiliar feelings it aroused in her to be treated with dignity and respect. Oh, she had those things from men she worked with, but that was different. They respected her because she was good at her job; it wasn't personal. With Mark it was very personal. And the more she thought about that, the more uncertainty crept in. Here. Now. Under these conditions. Were her instincts truly that reliable? Could she trust judgments she made under these circumstances?

# *Chapter 12*

Amanda walked out the front door of the apartment. Jeremy was again playing ball on the lawn. She waved at him. "Hi, there."

He grinned at her. "Wanna play?"

"Maybe later," she said more for Gaston's benefit than Jeremy's. Let him think she was wrestling with a weighty issue and that's why she was running like the devil himself was nipping at her heels. "I have something I need to think about right now."

"My daddy did that, too." Jeremy twirled the blue ball in his hands.

"What?" she asked, afraid to assume anything in this bizarre place.

"He ran when he was worried."

"Yeah." She stretched out and toed the grass, a sad ache wedging its way into her heart. Jeremy talked about his father in the past tense, as if Simon no longer had a place in his life, and he hurt from the loss. Didn't he see Simon at all? Surely Joan arranged…then again, maybe not. Jeremy was young. He could easily slip and forget he wasn't supposed to see his dad. "Does he live here, too?" Amanda asked, telling herself she'd asked because it was wise to know how Joan was playing this, and not her own morbid curiosity, which of course, it was.

"No." Jeremy lowered his gaze and ground his foot into the grass. "I don't remember him all the time anymore. Sometimes I forget his face. But I still dream about him and then I can remember."

In her mind, Amanda saw Simon stepping up to Jeremy's bedside, greedily taking in the sight of his sleeping son, knowing that seeing him while awake was too risky for them both. How hard that must be for all of them, including Joan. "Dreams are good."

"Yeah," Jeremy said with a little smile. "He ran real fast. Do you run real fast?"

"Sometimes," she admitted. "It helps me think."

He bounced the ball on the concrete sidewalk. "My mom says nobody can run fast enough to get ahead of their troubles."

"Your mom's very smart." Because he looked worried, Amanda smiled at him. "I don't even try to get ahead of troubles. I just think better when I run. That's all."

"Okay." He dropped the ball to the ground and kicked it, then went running after it.

Gaston frowned. "You're going to run."

He looked so devastated she couldn't help but smile. "Afraid so." She looked at his suit and shoes. "Sorry."

"Not half as sorry as I am."

Amanda took off down the street. She'd already beaten Gaston in his mind. He wouldn't put his energy into keeping up. Not today, and not in this heat. It rippled up off the pavement in thick, heavy waves that sucked the breath right out of her lungs. Amanda adjusted her breathing and slowly escalated her pace.

Drenched in sweat, she passed the entrance to the course, doubled back as if she'd changed her mind, and took off down its edge, hugging the woods. Gaston stayed within sight but definitely fell behind. She had to push to get to the southeastern bend before he got to the next fairway. Otherwise, she wouldn't have enough time out of his sight to cover her moves. Pulling on reserves, she pumped her legs harder, until the muscles burned nonstop and she swore if she didn't back off, her heart would beat right out of her chest.

Risking a glance back, she saw Gaston go down, faking an injury because he couldn't keep up.

Fine with her. Made her job easier, not more difficult. He probably expected her to rib him about falling behind, but she wouldn't do it. She'd let him believe she bought into the injury.

Hooking left at the edge of the bend, she checked her watch—2:10 p.m.—and then cut through a thicket of oaks and mesquite trees to the row of hangars.

Ten minutes later, she was crouched low in a safe zone, watching the hangar that housed at least six helicopters. It stood in the center of a row of five separate hangars. For easy access, she would have preferred it be on the end, near the woods, but obviously Thomas Kunz or Paul Reese preferred placing the aircraft in the center hangar to make unauthorized access most difficult.

Three teams of men guarded the perimeter of the hangars. They moved in pairs, but their timing wasn't consistent. Their paths weren't consistent. There seemed to be no set pattern for their rounds or any other commonality. They actually wandered. How the hell could she send Mark into this to capture a helicopter? They needed patterns, consistency or arms to be successful.

*Click.*

Chills crept up her back.

A pistol cocked and a gun barrel tapped against the back of her head at the base of her skull.

Amanda's heart rocketed into high gear. Careful not to move suddenly and startle whoever stood behind her, she raised her hands. "Okay. You've got me. Take it easy."

She turned and saw Beefy drawing down on her. The only possible worse person to see standing there would have been Reese, or Kunz. "Go ahead," she told Beefy. "Do it."

"Mr. Kunz would prefer that I don't—unless I have no choice." Beefy let his gaze drop down her body to her feet, then lifted it back up to her eyes. "I'd just as soon shoot your skinny ass."

Something moved in the trees behind Beefy. She raised her voice to cover the noise. "Then go ahead. Have a party. But remember, I can only die once."

"Once will do just fine."

Mark stepped out of the woods carrying a baseball bat. He swung and it collided with the back of Beefy's head. His knees folded and he collapsed onto the ground.

"Go on and get back," Mark said. "Gaston's hobbling this way."

"How did you get out?"

"Joan didn't lock my cabin. I told her I needed to do a little recon."

Amanda looked down at Beefy, saw no signs of movement or consciousness. "Is he dead?"

"No. I'm going to get Joan and we'll get him to the clinic. Joan will give him a knockout shot and keep him under wraps for a while. At least, until we can get out of here."

"Okay." She started to leave, stopped and turned back to Mark, then placed a chaste kiss on his cheek. "Thanks."

Tenderness flickered in his eyes, and he motioned for her

to go. "We're on plan. I've got a fix on getting the chopper. Joan's worked out a cover to relay messages between us and her and Simon, so he's aware of what's going down and prepared for it. Hurry, before we get spotted and shot."

Amanda ran back to where Gaston sat on the fairway. He'd walked for maybe two minutes after she had seen him stumble and fall. Stopping at his side, she bent down. "Gaston, are you okay?"

"My ankle's out." He clutched at it. "Twisted the damn thing."

"Do I need to carry you back?"

He looked mortified. "No way." He swallowed hard and pulled himself to his feet. "I'll call for backup."

If that backup was Beefy, she had a problem. "I'd appreciate it if you didn't. Thomas Kunz has threatened to kill me if one more of you guys get injured due to me."

"You didn't injure me. I twisted my ankle."

She pretended fear. "I don't think he'll make the distinction. He said if any of his guards were injured for any reason, he was holding me responsible."

Gaston frowned. "Okay. Okay, we'll walk. But your run is over, Amanda. My damn leg's throbbing."

"I'm sorry." She tried to sound affable. "Whenever I'm worried, I always run full out. I meant to slow down because you're not dressed for a run, but I got lost in thought, and well, I forgot."

"It's okay. I should have grabbed a golf cart." Gaston sighed, sweat rolling down his face in steady streams. "I know what you mean. There've been times here when I'd like to run fast enough to transport myself to China."

"Hard decisions?"

"Yeah." He swiped at his face with a folded white handkerchief.

"Have you ever refused?"

He looked at her as if she had lost her mind. "No one refuses Thomas Kunz." Gaston shoved his handkerchief into his slacks pocket, swept his short-cropped hair back with a broad hand. "Well, no one refuses him more than once."

"Why not?"

Gaston stared straight into her eyes. "Because the second time you want to refuse, you're already dead."

"I thought it might be something like that." She dabbed at the sweat beading on her face with the flat of her arm. "That takes a lot of the decision making out of one's hands, doesn't it?"

"It did mine."

"I'm not ready to die, so I guess I'll have to agree to train his people." She glanced over at Gaston. "Those are my choices."

"I know," he admitted. "We all do."

"It really sucks." Her sincerity came through in her tone. "Were your choices any better?"

"Frankly, not a bit." He glanced off to the left, beyond the fairway and into the rough. "Fortunately, I wasn't married, so I only had myself to worry about. But that was more than enough."

Amanda followed with her gaze and saw the red dot on the camera reflect in the sunlight. They were back in the monitoring zone.

As if on cue, they both stopped talking and walked in silence.

Amanda looked at her watch. She had almost seven hours until 10:00 p.m. and their escape. Seven hours. It was a solid plan. Sort of. They had communication provisions to make any necessary changes. Simon was prepared with the loop feed that would tell the monitors all was well during their escape. She and Joan would get themselves and Jeremy to the right place at the right time and Mark had a plan for getting the chopper. In any operation, the unexpected could happen and everything could go south on a dime. One seemingly insignificant thing could happen or change, and in a blink of an eye the best-laid plans could become obsolete. No one, no matter how skilled or perceptive or smart, could prepare for every eventuality. Not them, and not Thomas Kunz. So maybe best-laid plans weren't so great after all!

Amanda and Mark had done the best they could, utilizing the resources available to them. Now they were down to the wire and she wondered:

In the end, would any of them still be alive?

## Chapter 13

Darkness fell and Amanda watched the clock tick off minutes with a mixture of anticipation and dread. She and Joan had gone for a short walk that evening to the safe zone to finalize their plan. Joan had finally talked to Mark late in the afternoon and he had taken care of the helicopter. Amanda had the guard patterns down pat at the cabins. Beefy was the wild card. Joan had to keep him quiet until after they'd gone or they were all screwed and Amanda was dead.

Hell, they probably all were. Kunz wouldn't allow a conspiracy against him to go unpunished. He couldn't afford to open the door to rebellion within the ranks.

Amanda dressed in black: slacks and long-sleeved top, socks and shoes, and grabbed the scarf, again wishing she had her headgear. But she didn't, and the scarf would have to do. She checked the front window and cringed. The bad news was the man who was standing guard wasn't Gaston. Well, that was good news for Gaston. He could save his skin. It was bad news for Amanda. This guard wouldn't give her cover.

The worst news was she hadn't seen this guard since he'd held an M-16 on her in the warehouse where she'd scarred Paul Reese's face. She knew nothing about him. That made him extremely dangerous and her extremely uncomfortable. But there was no help for it. If he proved to be a problem, she'd have to eliminate him and remove the risks by whatever means proved necessary.

She checked the back of the house; saw no movement outside. Easing through the kitchen window, she dropped down into the shrubs beneath and paused in a familiar crouch, waiting for her eyes to adjust and for her ears to attune to the sounds of the night. She checked the sky. No moonlight. Finally, a break.

Hoping that would be indicative of the escape effort, she slowly made her way through the bushes and trees to the golf course. Hugging the edge of the trees, she stayed low to the ground and worked her way to the seventh-hole safe zone.

Joan stood waiting beside Mark, her arm around Jeremy, whose eyes sparkled with excitement. "Are we set to go?" Joan asked.

"I'm good on my end, so long as Simon is in place," Amanda whispered.

"He is," Joan told her.

Amanda nodded, then looked at Mark. "You set?"

"We're good." He nodded.

Amanda's heart calmed. He had the chopper ready. "What about Beefy?"

"Beefy?" Joan looked confused.

"The guard who hit his head," Mark said.

"He's out for the night—maybe for the next twenty-four hours." Joan swiped at her forehead, pulled Jeremy closer. "I had to report his accident to Mr. Kunz. But it's okay. He wasn't suspicious or anything."

"How do you know that?" Amanda asked, bristling.

"He didn't come to the clinic," Joan said. "Whenever he's uneasy about a development, he comes to the clinic. Instead, he kept me busy all day with some silly report."

"Just in case, let's not linger." Amanda looked at Mark. "You get them to the chopper. I'll get others and meet you where we met during the recon. Then we'll claim the chopper and bring everyone on board."

"Everyone?" Joan asked, her voice shaking.

"Everyone we can. As many detainees as we have room for," Amanda said.

"No, Kunz will know." Joan's voice elevated a pitch. "They're too closely guarded."

"Lower your voice, Joan," Amanda said. "Listen, I know it elevates the risks, but the ones we leave behind…" Seeing Jeremy, she hesitated.

He didn't. "They'll get dead, Mom."

Amanda hated seeing a kid that little have the frame of reference to deduce such dark and ugly things. "He's right. Before we can get back…. Mark's been passing the word for the detainees to use the first opportunity to get out of the compound and head east. Tonight there's going to be an opportunity. Our escape will provide them a little confusion cover. As soon as we can get Rescue here, they'll pick the detainees up. But there will be a delay. And it might not be soon enough."

Mark frowned. "It's the best we can do, Joan. But taking who we can with us is better than leaving them here."

"We have limited space on the chopper and no means to communicate outside. At least not at the moment." Amanda's emotions burst through and the old feelings induced by her father surged through her. Helplessness, outrage, praying for help she knew wouldn't come in time to save her—all of it, in vivid, excruciating detail. Her heart wrenched, a tremor invaded her voice, and her stomach felt full of stones. "We've been detainees, and we're feeling it, too." She swallowed hard. "But a nation is at risk."

"Yes, it is," Joan agreed, a tear leaking from her left eye and splashing on her cheek. "I understand. Of course we have to take as many with us as possible. I didn't mean to sound so selfish."

"It's okay," Amanda comforted her. "We're all scared, and we're all human."

Mark picked up on Amanda's emotions and stepped closer, pulling her into a quick hug, and she felt their connection, pulled it close. His heart thundered against hers, and for the first time she didn't feel vulnerable or afraid. She felt comfort. Reassurance. Shared pain. "We're doing our best," he whispered.

She dipped her head against his chest. "Sometimes our best isn't good enough."

He gave her a little squeeze, then looked into her eyes. "Sometimes it isn't."

His turmoil flooded her, reflecting all the conflicts gnawing at her inside, and knowing her feelings were shared calmed and stunned her. But she didn't shun any of it. She needed that knowing to do what she had to do, and grateful for it, she grabbed hold and stashed it in her heart.

Mark stroked her hair back from her face. "Be careful, okay?"

"I will." She stepped back. "You just jam that surveillance and run the loop feed of film for me."

"Consider it done."

Jeremy snagged Amanda's hand and tugged. "Are you going to get my daddy?"

That surprised her. Jeremy had led her to believe that he didn't know his father was here. "Yes, I am."

He looked up at her, his eyes too serious and old for such a little boy. "Don't let him get dead."

Amanda felt a hard hitch in her chest. "I won't."

"Thank you, Amanda," Joan said, tears shimmering in her eyes. "You, too, Mark." She passed Amanda a syringe. "In case you run into trouble."

"Is it lethal?"

"No. It immobilizes."

Amanda took the syringe, slipped it into her waistband. "Thanks."

Mark spoke up. "Amanda, go—22:15. Hack ten."

She checked her watch. He'd need ten minutes to get the surveillance jammed and the loop of film running. Then she could move around more freely. Target time: 22:25—10:25 p.m. "Right."

"Be careful." He winked.

She held his gaze a moment, and then another. Some of the best promises were those made without words. "You, too."

He guided Joan and Jeremy along the edge of the fairway toward the helicopter hangars. Amanda turned and headed down the course to get to the cabins where Joan's husband, Simon, was being held prisoner.

Flat on her belly in the dirt, Amanda peered through squat, spiny bushes at the cabin. The guards worked their grids, moved predictably along their paths. Happy to see that, she checked her watch: 10:22. In three more minutes, Mark should have the surveillance jammed and the loop of film running so the monitor minders would consider everything normal. The guards walking the grid would be two rows over on the cabins. She'd have enough time to get Simon and the others out before the loop feed ran out and began repeating itself.

At that mark, the danger increased rapidly and it would continue to increase until the chopper flew outside the compound's antiaircraft artillery firing range. How much Triple-A Kunz had available, Amanda wasn't sure. If Mark knew, he hadn't shared that information with her, but Amanda would bet Kunz definitely had more than enough to bring down one chopper.

She stole through the darkness, tree to tree, to Simon's cabin. There were two windows in the back wall. She risked a glance inside. Two guards. Heavy arms. Simon was sitting at a rickety wooden table in the center of the room.

"No one is coming here." Simon's voice carried through the glass. "Can't you at least go outside so I can get some sleep?"

"Shut up." The larger of the two men walked from the back to the front of the cabin, then looked out the front window beside the door.

"I think we're wasting our time, too," the second guard said. "She's asleep in her bed. You heard the report just like I did."

The large man scowled. "We don't get paid to think. Mr. Reese said guard him, so we'll guard him." Speculation gleamed in his eyes. "Unless you want to tell Mr. Reese otherwise?"

"No." The second guard answered too quickly not to reveal his fear of Paul Reese.

Amanda knew then she could take them. She scratched lightly on the window, and then backed out of sight.

The large guard walked across the floor to the back of the cabin, looked out into the darkness through the dust-smudged window then stepped back away from it. "Did you hear that?"

"Yeah, I did," the second guard said, sounding as uneasy as he looked.

Pulling a gun out of his shoulder holster, the large guard headed to the front door. "I'm going to check it out." He motioned toward Simon. "Don't let him out of your sight."

Amanda watched from the corner of the cabin for the guard to walk outside. Moments later, the boards on the front steps creaked under his weight. He stepped down into the grass and, when he rounded the corner to the rear of the cabin, she approached the front door. Watching for a minimal-risk opportunity, she seized it, letting Simon catch a glimpse of her.

Picking up on his job in this rescue, he claimed the second guard's attention. "I don't understand why you're all over me," he said. "What's going on? Is my wife in danger?"

"What detainee in this compound isn't in danger?" The guard grunted. "Hell, yes, she's in danger. So are you—especially if you don't just be still and shut up."

Amanda crept forward at the guard's back, caught him in a headlock and twisted. He slid bonelessly to the wooden floor.

Simon paled. "Is he…?"

"Dead." Experience had proven to her that there was no easy way to say it.

Simon recovered quickly. "There's another one. He's out—"

"I know." Amanda motioned for Simon to get behind the door and stay flat against the wall. She put the dead guard in the chair Simon had vacated. "When he comes back, your job is to get out that door. Walk straight ahead into the trees and wait for me there."

He nodded, blinking fast. He was a small man, very gentle and bookish-looking. "Watch out for Krebs—the other guard. He's mean."

She nodded. "I'll be right there." She lifted a fingertip over her mouth, shushing Simon, then snagged the dead guard's weapon. He sat slumped over the table, as if he'd dozed off.

Krebs came back inside, shoving his gun into its holster.

He took one look at the guard seated at the table, and whipped the gun back out. Amanda kicked his wrist. The gun flew out of his grip, skidded across the floor.

He turned on her. "West." A low growl ripped out of his throat. "I'm going to wipe the floor with you."

Amanda smiled, stepped in. He caught her with a right hook that knocked her off her feet. She scrambled upright, took one to the ribs. Finally, he left himself open. Stepping in to close the distance between them and screwing up his swing, she straight-armed him, shoved the heel of her hand into his nose. Blood sprayed out and he bent double, cupped his face. Any more force behind the blow and she'd have driven bone into his brain and killed him. Instead, she took him down with a fast blow to the back of his neck that wouldn't kill him but would leave him with a hell of a headache when he woke up. He hit the floor with a resounding thud just as Simon cleared the doorway.

She made sure Krebs was out, then injected him with the syringe Joan had prepared to immobilize. All too aware of Gaston's remarks that many were in the compound under duress and not because they wanted to be working for Kunz, she opposed killing these men—except when given no choice. Some were fighting for their survival just as she was, but determining who worked for Kunz by choice, and who'd been drafted by him and had no choice, was a complicated process.

The first guard clearly had enjoyed flaunting his power over the detainees too much to be doing it under duress. She didn't waste a breath regretting having to kill him.

Krebs sounded meaner but did what he did out of fear. His distaste shone in his eyes and in his moves. In all fairness, she couldn't even take his hitting her personally. He struck out against the enemy to sustain life, unlike Paul Reese, who had hit her to punish her for defying him personally.

Double-checking her watch, she shoved Kreb's gun into

her waistband and moved to the door. She had three minutes and then the perimeter guards would run a pass. The loop-feed time Mark had used to jam the surveillance monitors had elapsed. They'd either be repeating now or they would shut down and the monitor minders would see what was actually happening in real time. She didn't know which was taking place, but either carried significant concerns.

She swallowed hard, steeled herself. She made her way into the woods to Simon. He sat stooped in the dirt. "Where are the others?" she asked. All the cabins were dark and empty.

"Gone. They moved most of them out today. A couple of choppers landed a little before two, I think. They loaded up quickly and took off again."

A sinking feeling pulled at her stomach like concrete anchors. That must have been what woke her up earlier. Kunz knew she'd be planning an escape. She had anticipated that, but not that he would prepare so soon. "Gone where?"

"To one of his other compounds, I would imagine. He has several." Simon rubbed his head. "Just before nightfall, Krebs and some of the other guards handcuffed and chained the rest of the detainees, and took them out of the camp. I couldn't get to Joan to let you know."

The sinking feeling in the pit of her stomach expanded and her chest went hollow. "Damn it."

Simon blinked hard, squinted, having difficulty seeing in the dark. "There are two others still here."

The news kept getting worse and worse. "Where are they?"

"Next cabin over. I warned them to be ready. We don't get to talk with each other much, but the guards were busy, and I took a chance. One of them was a pilot. They left him behind in case Kunz needed to evacuate. We're too far out in the middle of nowhere to evacuate by ground."

*Harry?* Amanda's heart raced. "Wait here," she told Simon,

and then checked her watch for the placement of the guards. When she had clearance, she moved out into the long shadows.

Hugging the rough cabin wall, she heard voices and peered into the window. Two men—Harry and a second man she didn't recognize—sat bound to chairs with ropes. Paul Reese stood in front of them, impeccably dressed in black, talking on a phone. She strained to hear him clearly.

"You pulled a visual check and you're sure she's in that bed?" he asked someone on the other end of the phone.

He paused to listen, and the tension loosened in the set of his shoulders. Apparently he was talking with Amanda's guard and had been reassured that she was in her apartment and sound asleep.

Actually, the guard must have seen the body of Rosalita, Joan's nanny, who wanted only for Jeremy and his family to get away from here and live a normal life. Amanda admired the old woman's strength and sacrifice. She'd made Amanda swear not to tell Joan what she'd done to help them, and Amanda would keep that confidence. Joan would have refused to let Rosalita sacrifice herself, and knowing she had would only make Joan feel guilty forever.

Reese turned his back to the window. "Fine," he said, his voice carrying through the window screen. "Make sure she stays there. Mr. Kunz doesn't want any trouble tonight and I've given him my personal guarantee that there won't be any." He disconnected the phone, spoke to Harry and the other prisoner. "Well, it appears your guardian angel has taken the night off." Paul smiled, lifted a hand. "No rescue."

"Are you going to untie us?" Harry asked.

"No. No, I'm not." Paul walked to the door of the cabin. "But I am going to leave you to the guards."

A raccoon ran across Amanda's foot. She jerked and bumped against the cabin wall.

Reese stopped in his tracks, looked toward the window. Amanda broke into a cold sweat, flattened herself against the cabin wall and prayed he couldn't see her. She slowed her breathing, stood statue still, glimpsing the bandage on the side of Reese's face at the window. He looked out, moved from side to side and listened intently. Amanda didn't move, didn't breathe, afraid he'd hear her.

Finally, he backed away and she dropped to the ground, hugged the dirt and slid on her belly around the cabin wall to the back, fully expecting Reese to come out and check around outside.

She took cover under a thick bush, took aim with the guard's gun and waited. Seconds later, Reese moved through the grass, his footsteps heavy, crunching on leaves and twigs.

Amanda weighed her options. She could expose herself and take him down. But then the entire compound would be alerted. Paul Reese had to die for hitting her; that record *would* stay intact. Yet the timing was hers to choose, and killing him right now wasn't in her best interests. Not if she wanted to get Harry, Simon, Mark, Joan and Jeremy out of here alive. And she did. So she stayed put, nestled the gun, saving it as a last resort.

Reese took the corner at the back of the cabin. Amanda put her nose down into the dirt to avoid any potential light reflection off her exposed skin. He moved cautiously, gun raised, sweeping the perimeter, stopped not a foot in front of her.

Her heart pounded against her ribs, but she didn't move. He sensed her there—she could feel it—but he hadn't pinpointed her location. She waited, sweat beading on her skin, adrenaline pumping through her veins. If he found her, great timing or not, she'd have to kill him.

The raccoon raced by, brushing against Reese's foot.

"Damn it!" He jerked and jumped a foot off the ground, took aim at the raccoon. "Get the hell out of here." He shouted, but he didn't shoot.

Reese blew out a shaky breath and walked back the way he'd come, clearly convinced the raccoon had made the initial noise that had set him on edge.

Amanda watched him walk away, turn the corner and walk over to the guard's cabin and close the door. Having no choice, she stayed still a long minute, in case he was baiting her to expose herself.

The clock ticked constantly in her mind, reminding her that for every second that passed, the danger and risk of them getting caught increased.

Reese didn't come back out. The guards didn't alter their routine. Convinced he'd blamed the raccoon, she moved.

Showing her face at the cabin's window, she hissed.

Harry looked over. His eyes crinkled and he gave her a slight nod, and then looked at the man seated beside him and winked. When the man winked back, the cycle of messages had been completed. They knew she was coming in after them.

When the guards passed the cabin and walked on, Amanda let out a ragged breath. Soon, they took the next row, and finally disappeared out of sight. Amanda sneaked inside, eased the door shut and pressed a fingertip over her lips. Quickly, she untied Harry and then the other man and motioned them to follow her. Rather than going out the door, she led them to a window at the back of the cabin, popped off the screen and climbed out.

Harry followed her, and the second man brought up the rear. Amanda motioned and led them into the woods. When hidden by the dense leafy trees, she glanced back at the cabin. Two guards now stood watch outside at the bottom of the steps to the front door.

Paul Reese, damn him, had trusted his instincts. They didn't have much time. At any moment, those guards would enter the cabin to pull a visual check and they'd sound the alarm. "Hurry," she whispered, leading them to the spot where she'd stashed Simon.

"God, I thought you'd never get back."

"Later, Simon," she said, heading to the golf course fairway—the closest route to the helicopter. She checked her watch. Mark should be in position now with Joan and Jeremy and ready to move in. "We have to move fast. They're on to us."

She and the three men cleared the woods and hit the fairway in a dead run.

Sirens blared.

Spotlights flooded the course with blinding light. "Get to the trees," Amanda motioned, seeing half a dozen guards run onto the fairway and several others coming at them in golf carts from different directions. "Simon, take them to the safe zone by the hangars. Tell Mark to go on. I'll hold them off for you."

Harry frowned. "No, we're not leaving you."

"If you don't, you'll be dead," she said bluntly. "And no one will know what Kunz is doing. The truth will die here, Harry. I won't let that happen. Now haul your asses to Mark and tell him to get that chopper airborne and get you out of here."

"Okay. Okay." Harry frowned. "Thank you, Amanda."

"SAIC Marcus Brent, ma'am." The second man spoke softly. "I appreciate the assist."

SAIC—Special Agent in Charge. FBI. Great. Just as Joan had said, Kunz had infiltrated beyond the military. Obviously, at least as far as the FBI. "You're welcome." Amanda nodded, seeing the golf carts and men on foot running closer. Pulling a quick count, she tagged about a dozen of them. They hadn't yet spotted Amanda's group, but it would be seconds, not minutes, until they did. "Go!"

Simon, Harry and Brent ducked into the trees, ran parallel to the fairway, heading to the helicopter safe zone. Amanda moved behind them, close enough to provide them cover but not enough to jeopardize them being caught if she went down.

A bullet whizzed past her ear. She dropped to a crouch, spotted the shooter and returned fire. The man fell to the ground. Amanda kept moving, clipped an ancient oak, bumping her winged arm. Pain shot through her, stealing her breath. She slumped against the rough trunk and waited for the initial streaks of pain to pass, then focused on burying the pain and getting a lead on her pursuers. Wincing, she leaned out to peer under a low-slung branch to see what was happening.

*Oh, man.* Everyone was now speeding in her direction; the shooting had snagged their attention. She sank deeper into the woods. The carts couldn't make it through the dense underbrush. That maneuver took out part of her opposition. Swinging wide, she worked toward the safe zone.

Lights swept the trees—ankle- and then waist-high, flooding through even the squatty bushes. She flattened her back against a tall pine. Her lungs air-starved, she drew in deep breaths, her mind racing. Enemy footsteps crept closer and closer.

She squeezed her eyes shut, determined not to fire unless absolutely necessary. They'd be all over her in seconds. Three men moved within striking distance of her.

One stepped in front of her, saw her. She chopped at his windpipe, and when he bent double, she followed up with a second blow with her foot. His knees folded, and she knocked him out.

Killing them nagged at her relentlessly thanks to Gaston's "not of their own free will" comment. Everyone had breaking points and Kunz, the sadistic son of a bitch, was a master at exploiting them. Yet under these circumstances, how did she quickly determine who was here by choice or by force?

In a split second, she made an executive decision on policy. Given the opportunity, she would let them live. Anyone who pushed to kill her died.

She wiped the sweat from her palm, freshened her grip on the pistol. A second man nearly stumbled into her. Amanda hit him from behind. He plunged forward into the dirt, not knowing what had hit him. Avoiding the third man, a burly redhead with shoulders the size of mountains, she moved again, closer to the safe zone.

Something flickered and caught her eye. A team dressed in covert gear was headed her way. She counted five of them, armed to the teeth with rifles with high-power scopes. Certainly they were night-vision equipped.

So much for lucky breaks. Her stomach knotted. She was screwed.

In the distance, she heard the plop of chopper blades. Mark. He'd gotten them off the ground. Relieved by that, Amanda focused fully on evading the approaching team. She couldn't avoid them forever, but she had to avoid them long enough for Mark to clear out with the detainees.

*Why weren't Kunz's men firing the Triple-A?*

There could be only one explanation: they thought their own guards manned the chopper. They didn't know yet that Mark had appropriated it. Nearly giddy that he wasn't dodging bullets, she dived into a little ravine and hunkered down to catch her breath. She had a good two minutes, maybe three, before the covert team would get to her grid. They swept methodically, thank God. These guys were professionals. From them, she knew what to expect.

Breather time over, she moved again, using stealth tactics.

At first, she outmaneuvered them and made decent progress. But within minutes, the team began closing in on her, tightening the perimeter circle to the point that she had no safe out. She assessed her position on the run. Her best odds were to hit the fairway and run full out. That was her only hope of evading them a while longer and keeping their focus off Mark and the chopper.

She took off like a shot, blowing past two men on foot and one driving a golf cart. Bullets fired behind her, speeding past her ear, lodging in tree trunks too close for comfort and raising stinging clouds of dirt and leaves. Dodging, she ran a zigzag pattern to up her odds of not being hit. The bullets kept coming, sending dirt flying near her feet, pinging dirt against her slacks legs and shoes. Close. Too close.

The sounds of the chopper grew louder and then deafening. What the hell was Mark doing? He was *supposed* to be headed *out* of the damn compound, not *into* it!

Mark swooped, dropping the chopper lower to the ground twenty yards in front of her. Someone—Harry maybe— dropped down a rope ladder. Glimpsing a slim shot at survival, she ran full out toward it, pulling on every ounce of reserve she could muster. Shots rang out from the chopper, aiming over her head at the men firing on her. Harry? Brent? Simon? Probably not Simon; she couldn't see him with a gun in his hand. But Kunz had messed with his family. Probably Simon, too.

The covert team rendezvoused with the guards. Bullets cross-fired all around her. Pulling up her last threads of energy, she pumped her legs hard. Her muscles burning, throbbing, her chest threatening to explode, she extended as far as humanly possible and lunged for the ladder.

A rung slapped against her palm. Half-surprised, she grabbed hold, locking on, and looked up the rungs. Harry stood in the door, looking down at her. She signaled him to haul it out of there. He cupped his hand at his mouth, yelling something she couldn't decipher, then whatever he was saying was lost under Brent's rifle fire as he leaned farther out the door and blasted the ground steadily.

In a momentary pause, she heard Simon shout, "We got her, Mark! Go, go, go!"

Amanda looped an arm around the ladder and returned fire on the men shooting up at her. Men on the ground ducked for cover, lay belly down on the grass.

The chopper lifted with a swoosh and made a jerky, sharp turn that sent Amanda swaying in a wide arc and had dragonflies swarming in her stomach. Swinging wildly, dangerously close to the trees, she took the ladder rungs as quickly as she could, dived into the chopper then tugged the rope ladder up after her.

Heaped between Harry's and Joan's feet, Amanda caught her breath and then looked up and over at Mark. "Thanks."

Mark smiled. "I never leave my partner behind."

Amanda fought the urge to smile back. "Coming back for me was a stupid thing to do, Cross. I'm questioning your judgment again. You could have lost everyone."

"Could have," he admitted. "But didn't."

She grunted. He was adorable and incorrigible, and that was that. And as partners went, he was a pretty good one.

"Oh, hell," Brent said.

"What?" Amanda moved to the front of the chopper. "Mark?"

"Triple-A."

Antiaircraft artillery. Kunz's men had discovered that the chopper had been stolen. Tracer bullets streaked through the sky toward them.

"I can't pinpoint the source location." Harry shouted. "I can't find the freaking source!"

Amanda grabbed the rifle from Harry, moved to the door and prepared to take aim. The scope wasn't equipped with night vision. Their luck was holding for catching minimal breaks. "Everyone, grab hold. Mark, drop fast and hang right. Standard evasion tactic."

He did. The chopper bucked and groaned and the tracer bullets rose harmlessly into the sky above the chopper. Amanda tracked the trajectory and fired in rapid succession.

The Triple-A ceased.

"We should be getting out of range," Harry said, sliding a look at Brent.

Simon sat in back, one arm around Joan. They both held Jeremy. Rather than the scared kid she expected—being shot at was no picnic even for an adult—Jeremy was smiling. "You okay, buddy?"

"It's an adventure," he told her. "Mom said."

Amanda laughed. "It is that." She moved up to Mark, planted a kiss on his cheek and dropped into the copilot's seat. "Thanks for doing the stupid thing for me." She reached for the radio, putting her headgear on and tuning to the emergency frequency monitored by Intel 24/7.

She'd nudged his headset, knocking it askew. Mark adjusted it. "Wouldn't have it any other way."

"This is Alpha Tango 135812. Please verify and secure communications."

A moment later, the tower chief's voice crackled through the headset. "Alpha Tango 135812, identity verified, communications secured. What's your situation, ma'am?"

"Code three," Amanda said, assigning a value on the standard one-to-five scale for rating emergencies.

"Code three recorded." The chief's voice took on a tense edge, befitting a Code three. "How can we assist, ma'am?"

"I need a secure patch to the Puzzle Palace, Tower Chief," she said, giving the slang term for the Pentagon. "OSI, S.A.S.S. action officer."

A moment elapsed and then the tower chief said, "We're ready to transmit your message, ma'am."

"Seven," she said, revealing the number of passengers on board. "Returning critical load. Arrange immediate transport."

"Roger, ma'am."

Amanda took special pleasure in her next transmission.

"Arrest and detain Captain Amanda West's double, and if one is there, Captain Mark Cross's." Mark's double, if he had one, could be at Providence wreaking havoc. She pondered on disclosing more, but decided that even with secure measures activated, she didn't dare. No communications were totally secure, and the last thing they needed was for this to show up on *Fox News* before they located all the doubles. "Please track signal and guide us in."

"Order verified and confirmed, Chief." Amanda felt beads of sweat trickle down her chest and soak her bra between her breasts.

Moments later, the chief fed in coordinates. Mark heard them through his headset and locked them in on the chopper's control panel. "Could you give us an ETA, Chief?" Mark asked for an estimated time of arrival.

No response.

Amanda interceded. "That's my pilot making the request, Tower Chief."

"ETA is in thirty-seven minutes, ma'am. The S.A.S.S. has been patched, notified, and the message delivered. Transport has been scrambled and awaits you on the flight line, ma'am. Do you require an escort?"

Amanda looked at Mark, Harry and Brent. Between them, they had four sharpshooters on board and adequate ammunition to fight a small war. "Negative, Chief. We're covered."

"Roger that, ma'am." He sounded relieved. "If you need anything else, we'll be monitoring on secure standby status."

"Thanks, Chief. Alpha Tango 135812 over and out."

"Tower Chief out."

Mark raised an eyebrow at her. "The lady has enormous clout."

"No more so than you," she said. He had a hot wire to Secretary of Defense Reynolds. "Actually, I would guess you have more." So why hadn't he used it? Underestimated again? She'd thought they were past that.

"Actually, if I had more, I'd order you to come kiss me. I've been worried about you. I would have been extremely upset if my lead partner hadn't finished her job."

Oddly touched, she smiled. "Me, too." She leaned over, pecked a kiss to his jaw. He was letting her get the glory for this one. Seeing the truth for what it was, she brushed off the tiny niggle that something wasn't right. Mark looked at Amanda. "They're bringing us into Lackland Air Force Base."

San Antonio, Texas. Lackland was well known for its medical facilities. "Great." Feeling guilty for doubting him, she kissed his cheek, sniffed gently, and was surprised by the difference in his scent. Was it the change in his diet while detained? Or just his favorite body soap that was missing? "Did they feed you?"

Sensing her fear that he'd been starved, he looked over, his eyes tender. "I didn't go hungry, Amanda." He smiled.

Not just with his mouth. He smiled with his eyes, and starving people didn't usually smile much. He was okay. They were okay.

"Will they follow us?" Joan asked, her voice shaking.

"Not immediately," Mark said. "The hangars were empty. I stole Kunz's emergency ride out."

## Chapter 14

Mark landed the chopper at Lackland Air Force Base.

A flat-blue bus sat parked at the edge of the landing pad, waiting for them. A lieutenant—Amanda didn't see his name tag—ushered them from chopper to bus and, once they sat loaded inside it, he signaled to a base police car that then escorted the bus directly to the flight line. A C-5 had positioned to taxi out and take off, its lights on and engines running.

The seven escapees boarded with little fanfare and took their seats. Amanda clicked her seat belt into place and saw a ruddy-faced pilot step out of the cockpit.

Wearing a major's rank, he approached and then addressed Amanda. "Captain West?"

She stood and nodded, half expecting to get reamed for her slovenly appearance. Old habits died hard. She looked as if she'd been doing exactly what she had been doing—running hard through the woods—and half the leaves and grass on the compound still clung to her clothes. "Yes, sir."

The major nodded. "We'll be taking you to Providence."

"Providence?" she asked, surprised enough to question him without first thinking. "Why not the Pentagon, sir?"

"Colonel Drake's orders." He shrugged, looked her over, and understanding flitted through his eyes. "Mine is not to question why, Captain." He put a lilt in his voice and turned back toward the cockpit. "Mine is to but fly the C-5."

She smiled and sat back down beside Mark. Across the aisle, Jeremy sat between his mom and dad. Harry and Brent sat directly behind them. "Unless I miss my guess," Amanda told Mark, "Colonel Drake will be at Providence waiting for us when we get there. Probably General Shaw, too."

Mark grunted his agreement. "And unless I miss my guess, Colonel Gray will be with them. He won't be able to resist the opportunity to strut his stuff and make Colonel Drake ask for his help on everything he possibly can."

Amanda hoped not. The last thing they needed was the pissing contest going on between the two colonels. At least if General Shaw was on-site, he'd keep them both toeing the line and their energy focused. She rolled her shoulder. The wound where she'd been winged had started to seep, and fresh, wet blood stained her shirtsleeve.

Mark noticed. "We better put a patch on that." He got out of his seat. "I'll get a first-aid kit. Be right back." He headed to the cockpit.

Amanda watched him move, appreciated his long lines and sturdy build, the confident set of his shoulders, the thoughtfulness in his tending to her wound.

He returned with a kit and nodded for her to move to the back of the plane. She walked to the tail section and sat down in the aisle seat.

"Pull your arm out of your sleeve." Mark set up directly across the aisle from her.

She shrugged her shoulder out and exposed her arm, pretending she hadn't also bared the left half of her bra and a lot of skin. Her cheeks heated and she felt like a fool. Why this bothered her, she hadn't a clue. It was beyond ridiculous. She'd been on missions where she'd had to strip naked in front of an entire team, who also had had to strip naked in front of her, and she'd never given it a thought—neither had the team—and that was the problem.

In a professional or clinical situation, anyone looking at her breast didn't strike her as any different than them looking at her ankle. But this wasn't anyone else, it was Mark, and while it was a clinical situation, it didn't feel clinical. It felt damn personal, and Mark would notice. He'd notice her breast, the swell of her breast, the turgid nipple pressing against the fabric cup of her bra. He'd notice the color and texture of her, and the sweaty dirt smear streaking down from her throat to the valley between her breasts. He'd damn well notice it all. Her face heated hotter, threatening to catch fire. Totally absurd, but she was damn breathless, too. Shy and breathless. It was appalling.

Pretending not to notice any of it, Mark kept his emotional distance and dabbed peroxide on the wound. "It's not deep. You must have skinned it again during the escape."

Damn. Was he totally unaffected? How could he sound so calm and detached? And why, when she should be on-her-knees grateful, was she disappointed and to-her-earlobes ticked? "Actually, I collided with an oak." She frowned. "It won."

"Gotta watch those twisted puppies—especially the monster roots. They'll jump out and grab you every time."

She smiled in spite of her snit, and watched him finish up with some antibiotic salve and a new bandage. His fingertips felt so gentle on her skin, almost caressing. Stretching her neck, she glimpsed his eyes and saw that he wasn't so unaffected after all. Innately pleased by that, she smiled again, wider.

Now he looked irritated. Obviously, he hadn't wanted to be caught noticing her, and that pleased her, too.

"There you go." He looked from her arm to her face, his eyes a little hazed. "That should hold you until we get to a medical facility."

The intimacy in his tone, the warmth in his eyes, had her breath hitching all the way up her throat. "Thanks. I'm sure it's fine now." A medical facility couldn't have done a better job. He'd been field-trained in medical procedures when he was with Delta Force and it showed. She eased her arm back into her top, and then stared at him.

"What?" He closed up the kit, wadded the trash in his hand and squeezed until his knuckles turned white.

"Nothing." She gave him a negative nod, then swept at her hair, getting it out of her face. "It's just that…" Her voice trailed. She shrugged, then tried again. "It's just that I like you, Mark."

"Good." His expression softened. "Because I like you, too."

"No, you don't get it." She felt her skin crease into a frown between her eyebrows. "I'm not happy about this."

"You're not?" He looked bewildered then motioned for her to slide over so they could sit next to each other and talk this through. "Interesting. I'm not, either."

She slid over a seat, and when he sat down, she added, "Good God, how could I be happy about it? You saw my films at Kunz's. You know exactly why this is awful. Sex, being physical, connecting that way is one thing, but I don't want to *like* any man."

"You think we're all like your father?" To his credit, no censure or judgment etched his tone. He simply wanted to know and so he had asked. It was a refreshing reaction, to just be asked anything straight out.

"No, I don't," she said, and she truly didn't. "But until I

met you, I hadn't allowed myself to get close enough to a man to actually like him—as a person, I mean."

"So you've slept with men you didn't like?" He sounded almost amused.

"I meant 'like' as in 'emotionally endearing' to me. Lust and/or desire is human, but you don't have to find someone emotionally endearing to experience either of those things. It's a physical and chemical and hormonal reaction, you know?"

"I know, but when you make soup—put all of those things together, Amanda—sex becomes lovemaking, and lovemaking is emotionally endearing and a lot more pleasurable than sex." When she sent him a skeptical look, he added, "More levels of involvement equates to more intense heat."

Doubtful about that—she'd had some pretty hot sex in her life—she shrugged. "I'll take your word for it," she said, though she wasn't sure she should, considering his record on judgment calls. "I've deliberately limited my investment in men to the physical."

"So you used them—for sex."

"No one used anyone," she said, then felt a flush of guilt. "Okay. Okay, so once I did. But only once. Otherwise, the terms of my relationships were mutually agreed upon by both parties, and they worked for both parties until they didn't work anymore, and then they ended."

"They worked for you," Mark countered. "Did the other half of these relationships have any choice?"

"Of course."

"Really? It wasn't your way or no way?" he speculated, his eyes far too seeing.

"Look, Cross." She bristled. "They worked for me, okay? That's the only way that's worked for me." She gave herself a mental shake. She was what she was and that's the way it was. He could accept it or reject it, but she would not apologize for it. She wasn't a victim, damn it. And she'd never be a victim again. A woman didn't apologize for refusing to be a freaking victim. Not in her world.

"Anyway, all of that is beside the point. This—us—we're the point." She wagged a pointed fingertip between them. "I'm not going to insult either of us by pretending I don't have feelings for you. I'm not going to pretend that this is just about the physical. I want you to know that." She had no idea what she was going to do with those feelings, but that was another conversation best saved for later—after she tried talking herself out of having those feelings, burying them, or stomping them to death. She wasn't picky. She'd settle for whatever worked.

"I'm glad, Amanda. Because I have feelings for you, too." Mark kept his hands on the seat's arms, but his knuckles were white. This was hard for him, harder than she'd at first imagined. "I damn sure won't pretend otherwise, and I won't let you pretend, either. But I'm fighting it, too, for what it's worth."

How could she be relieved and disappointed at the same time? "Fighting it, in what way?"

"I don't want to let you get inside me. I know you don't want to let me get inside you. Relationships work out best when people open the doors, not when chemistry between two people knocks the doors down. I'm trying to give the people in us time to catch up with our chemistry."

"But chemistry is good." It'd always been enough. It was a known entity. Not threatening or unfamiliar. Chemistry didn't breach her comfort zone.

"Can it lead to open doors?" He posed that as a question, but there was no missing the challenge cloaked in it. "Well, can it?"

"Anything is possible," she said, suddenly irritated.

He stared at her, waited, and when it became apparent he

wasn't going to move or say another word until she got more specific, she did. "It never has, but that doesn't mean it can't. I said I have feelings for you and I do. That's new to me, and I have no idea what to expect. But I can say that I'm not comfortable with it—at least, not yet. It makes me feel…"

"What?" His voice softened. "What does it make you feel, Amanda?"

She glared at him. "Vulnerable."

"And you hate feeling vulnerable."

"Yes!"

"But you don't hate having feelings for me?"

How did she respond to him when she couldn't get a fix on her reaction to him herself? "Hate? No, no, I don't," she said, realizing it was true. "But I'm not overly thrilled with the prospect because I do hate having my back exposed." Her father had taught her well the dangers of that. He always attacked her from behind, so she didn't see him coming.

The look in Mark's eyes turned gentle and totally enamored. "If you'll open your heart, I'll cover your back, honey."

She swallowed hard. Men had looked at her with desire, in sensual hazes that could set fires rivaling four-alarm blazes, but never before had she been looked at with such tenderness and indulgence and…and she didn't know what else it was, but she liked it. She really liked it. "Okay, then." That was about all she could manage. Pretty neutral. She didn't want that look to go away. It was addictive, worse than crack cocaine, her instincts warned. And having seen it once in a man's eyes when he looked at her, she'd never again be satisfied to not see it.

"Okay, then." Seeming extremely content with his progress, Mark stroked her cheek. "You'd better catch a few winks. It's going to be a long night that I figure will run over through most of the day—once they start debriefing us."

Amanda had about maxed on this emotional business, and

Mark clearly knew it. That he had suggested a reprieve from
it without her having to ask for one, much less insist on one,
endeared him to her more. And yet her instincts warned her
that there was only one way to honestly face this thing between them. The same way she had faced everything else in
her life: head-on and full throttle.

She leaned over, put her head on his shoulder and closed
her eyes. "It's going to be a longer day still *after* the debriefing—possibly extending well into tomorrow night."

He arched an eyebrow at her, his gaze speculative and
warm. "Is that a fact?"

"If you can adequately explain that six-date rule you're so
fond of implementing, then yes, it is a fact."

"Why is that?" A teasing light shone in his eyes.

"Because unless you object, I'm going to jump your
bones."

"I see." He didn't look at all opposed. Actually, he looked
damn pleased with himself. "And what if I don't adequately
explain it?"

Heartened because he hadn't objected, she grunted. "Then
I predict you'll have an even longer night. One with nothing
for company but cold showers."

That knocked the grin right off his face and planted one
squarely on hers.


Shortly before 4:00 a.m., Amanda and Mark finished briefing Colonel Drake, Colonel Gray and, via teleconference, Secretary of Defense Reynolds. The debriefing had included an
accurate description of Kunz. Everyone was now as worried
as Amanda about not knowing the number of doubles currently
active in U.S. intelligence agencies. Her double had been successfully inserted and no one had suspected a thing. That chilled
all of them down to the marrow of their bones. So far, there was
no evidence of Mark having a double. Hers had been arrested.

Early on in the discussion, the defense secretary had called in Special Operations, and later during it, he'd summoned the director of the FBI.

Now, the two were scheduled to pull a joint-forces coordinated mission to take down Kunz's Texas compound in a predawn raid.

Kate had flown down to Providence with Colonel Drake. While the secretary and Drake coordinated the Texas-compound mission, she had a brief reunion and a cold drink with Amanda and Mark in the break room. Colonel Gray had been present since their return, as predicted, but fortunately he was keeping his mouth shut. He might ride Colonel Drake's back and test her patience, but he wasn't stupid enough to give her grief with Secretary Reynolds up to his armpits in this and his team of special assistants on-site. It'd be career suicide and jeopardize his retirement pay.

A team comprising intelligence forces, OSI agents, Kate (representing the S.A.S.S.) and one of Reynolds's special assistants heard Joan give a full accounting of each of the thirty doubles she'd worked on at the Texas compound. As well as information she had on a second compound, this one actually in the Middle East. A similar second team debriefed Simon, Harry and Brent, and Jeremy met with a child psychologist, who specialized in hostage and war trauma.

By 5:00 a.m., the separate briefings were over and everyone came together in the conference room to compare notes. Finally, at 5:30 a.m., Colonel Gray arranged protective lodging for Simon, Joan and Jeremy and for Harry and Brent, and everyone called it a night.

Shortly thereafter, Colonel Drake dismissed Amanda and Mark. "Be back here at 10:00 a.m. for an update briefing and further instructions," she told them. "By then, Kate will have a CAA Report prepared and we'll know what we've got and what we need."

"CAA Report?" Mark asked, unfamiliar with the S.A.S.S. acronym.

"Compilation, Assimilation and Assessment Report," Amanda said. "She'll pull updates and status reports from everyone remotely connected to the GRID case, digest it all and give us a fix on the big picture."

"Great."

Dead on her feet, Amanda didn't have to be told twice that she could leave. She caught Mark by the arm and led him to the door. "Let's get out of here before we get recruited to do anything else tonight—today—whatever it is."

Smiling, Mark walked beside her outside to the Hummer, which had been impounded when they'd gone missing from the jail.

"It's nearly 6:00 a.m., but it's still dark." Mark opened the door, and when she slid onto the seat, he added, "Let's keep it easy and call it a night."

"I'm all for easy." Amanda clicked her safety belt into place.

They drove to Mark's subdivision. At the security gate, the guard waved them through and Mark drove on around, and finally pulled into his garage. He stopped the Hummer and just sat there, staring straight ahead at the wall through the dust-smudged windshield.

"Something wrong?" she asked.

He chewed at the inside of his lip, pondering his words carefully. "Maybe." A few silent beats passed. "I'd say after that conversation on the plane earlier we've gone beyond being partners and friends." He put the gearshift in Park, turned off the ignition then looked over at her, his expression as sober as she'd ever seen it. "It is personal, Amanda."

Definitely personal. He was driving the point home because this mattered so much to him. Looking at him proved beyond a shadow of a doubt that it was personal. Everything about him rammed her hormones and her emotions into overdrive.

She reached for the door handle. "So it's personal." Could that actually have been her voice, sounding so ambivalent? What did he want from her? "Okay, Cross. Are you looking for declarations of undying love, promises of some sort, or what? Last I knew, we were waiting for the doors to blow open."

He leveled her with an uncompromising gaze, signaling this was a make-or-break point with him and not negotiable. "I'm making sure you understand that I don't sleep around and I'm damn particular with whom I share my body."

Fair enough. It was the second time he'd told her this. Great news actually, but not at all surprising. He had that monogamous look. The kind that when women saw him on the street, they did a double take because envy shot right through them. That sexy kind of monogamous look every woman craves having someone say they see in her man. "Point taken." Her palm grew so clammy she lost her hold on the door handle.

He draped an arm over the steering wheel and another on the gearshift. "I think the odds are high we're going to end up in bed together and I don't do one-night stands."

"No, you do six-date stands. And you haven't yet explained that." She settled back against the seat, listened to the engine ticking. "I think that was part of the bargain."

"It's the job. Just like it is for you." He dragged an impatient hand through his hair. "It's being asked too many questions I can't answer. Having no choice but to tell lies to cover up the truth. It's apologizing over and over for too many unexplained absences. Catching hell for missing birthdays and special events and holidays. You know exactly what it is, and what I mean. It's easier to just cut it off after six dates—before anyone can start to think of you as a couple."

"Does that include the woman?"

"Especially the woman."

Amanda did know what he meant, and she agreed with him. It was easier to be alone than to be asked to explain that which couldn't be explained without violating oaths, breaching security and jeopardizing missions and lives. "Any other allergies besides peanuts?"

"No."

She unsnapped her safety belt, turned toward him in her seat and propped her arm on the seat's back and tilted her head to it. "Hmm, that explanation might do."

He paused, then slid her a look torn between accusation and elation. "You get to me, Amanda."

Her stomach hollowed and her chest swelled. For some reason she couldn't begin to sort out, that pleased her immensely. "Well, there is a bright side to this, Cross." She scooted over the gearshift and wedged herself between him and the steering wheel. Wrapping her arms around his neck, she whispered against his mouth, "Together, we don't have those pesky job-related dating problems, now, do we?" They both knew not to ask questions that couldn't be answered.

"No, I guess we don't." His breath warmed her face.

She slid her hand along the straight of his shoulder, around its curve and down his arm, then across his chest, following ridges of honed muscle. Rubbing their noses, she looked into his eyes. "Does this mean you're ditching your six-date rule?"

He caught her head in his hands and whispered against her lips, "Absolutely abolishing it. Effective immediately."

She pulled back and smiled, not quite satisfied with that response. "Women everywhere will rejoice and thank me."

"Apparently, I wasn't clear." He drew her back to him, and the look in his eyes stole her breath. "You're the woman in my life, and I'm abolishing the rule for you."

She smiled. "You do know how to charm a woman."

"Shut up and kiss me, Amanda. I'm dying here."

They kissed hungrily, greedily, tugging at buttons and sleeves and barriers keeping them from touching skin to skin.

Breathless, limbs heavy, and bodies in need, they initiated, inspired, indulged, consuming, not exploring so much as laying claim. Amanda separated their mouths, her blouse and his shirt hung open and loose, her bra bunched on one side, exposing an aching breast. Her voice ragged and rigid and rushed, she shuddered. "Inside, Cross. Hurry."

Mark opened the driver's door, pulled her out of the car and lifted her higher. Breasts to chest, she tightened her legs around his hips and her arms around his shoulders. "I'll get the alarm. You keep doing what you're doing to my neck. I think I love that."

Mark moved close to the panel and she punched in the code, then snagged the doorknob. He shoved the door open with her backside—their lips locked, their hands greedy—kicked the door shut behind them, and then made his way through the den to the hallway.

"Damn it, Amanda," he gritted out between clenched teeth. "If you touch me like that again, I won't guarantee we'll make it to the bedroom."

She snuggled closer, feeling his erection through her clothes at her stomach, and stroked him again. Harder. "Who cares?"

His shirt hit the floor.

Her blouse followed.

They cornered the hall into his bedroom—a huge suite as masculine as he, decorated in deep burgundy and navy and gold and full of gleaming dark woods and rich, robust fabrics, and his musky smell that she was drawn to. She didn't have to ask. She knew that she was the first woman he'd brought into his private domain, and the knowing unleashed a powerful prowess in her, a seductive magic that swept everything from her mind but this man. This gorgeous, surprising, amazing man.

He set her on the bed. In a heated rush, they stripped, came together, and lost themselves in blinding passion that seared and soothed, stoked and simmered, stole and saved. The intensity of their coupling surprised Amanda, and Mark obviously hadn't expected it, either. When they had satisfied their bodies and lay spent, Amanda still shook inside from the sheer force of it.

"That was…" Mark's thready voice trailed.

"Intense?" she suggested, too liquid-boned to actually move. Lost in a sensual fog, she couldn't grasp a more explicit descriptor. *Intense* didn't begin to describe what had happened between them, but nothing else did, either.

He turned on the pillow, stroked her hair, her face. "I was thinking *explosive,* but *intense* will do."

"For me, too." She snuggled closer to him, eyed her gun on the nightstand. "Do you think the adrenaline push of the escape had anything to do with it?"

"What escape?" he said, telling her succinctly it hadn't mattered a whit. "I wish I could say it did, but I'd have to lie, and I swear I'll never lie to you, Amanda."

"I didn't think so, either, but I'm a little fogged. Thought I'd better check with someone in their right mind."

"Don't look this way, honey. Not yet."

She smiled against his chest. "You know I'm crazy about you."

"Are you really?" He curled an arm around her, held her close.

"Yeah." She rocked back and looked up at him. "But break my heart and I'll cripple you."

Mark smiled. "You really know how to capture a man's devotion."

"Okay, so I'm a rookie at sweet talk. I haven't had much

practice." She pecked a kiss to his chin, then to each of his eyelids. "But I could have said I'd kill you, and I didn't."

"Cripple, kill." He laughed. "Yeah, I see the distinction."

She walloped him on the shoulder. "Well, damn it. Don't you have something to say to me?"

His eyes twinkled, but he didn't smile. "You cripple me and I'll kill you."

"Now, there's a real sweet-talking pro." She feigned a sigh. "Cross, you leave me breathless."

"Not yet—" he rolled over and caressed her "—but I intend to."

Amanda laughed and dived under the covers.

The Office of Special Investigations hummed with activity.

Colonel Drake sat at a desk in the center of the wide room, issuing orders to Kate and talking on two phone lines at once. Amanda knew that one was a secure-link teleconference with several Middle Eastern ambassadors. Amanda surmised the colonel was looking for or receiving information on potential GRID-compound locations.

Colonel Gray, Mark's commander, had taken up a station at the desk by the only window in the room—prime real estate, windows—and was relaying information from Joan to a Special Operations officer, apparently in the field in Texas. The commander had put the thrust of the raid on hold for Intel coordination, and the joint forces pounded the dusty dirt in wait mode, anticipating further orders any moment. From the chatter, it was going to be a while.

Mark sat in his cubicle on the far side of the operations center. He, too, was on the phone, trying to get the two men in his unit charged with murder cleared. General Shaw had agreed that Sloan could be released from jail and the charges against him dropped. And while M. C. Harding had participated in Mark and Amanda's abduction at the jail, his actions had been under extreme duress. Since M.C. was dead, General Shaw had agreed, and Secretary Reynolds had concurred, that Harding's daughter be told that her father had not killed her mother, that they had found the man guilty of the murder, and though his name couldn't yet be released, she could rest assured that he would be tried and convicted for the murder. It was a compassionate act on Secretary Reynolds's and General Shaw's part.

Kunz would be convicted of those murders. Amanda took immense satisfaction in knowing and believing that.

"Amanda," Kate called out from her desk. "You need to take this call. He says he's Paul Reese."

Her skin crawled and her stomach tightened. She walked to the nearest desk, which happened to be the one next to Mark's, and reached for the phone. Before lifting the receiver, she looked over at Kate. "Trace it. See if we can pinpoint his location."

"All of the calls are being traced," Mark reminded her. "We have a leak in the office, remember?"

She did remember, and picked up the phone, doing her best to keep her voice steady. "Captain West."

"I'm impressed, Captain. I would have bet against you on escaping."

*Kunz.* Her heart rate doubled. She flagged Mark, mouthed that it was Thomas Kunz on the phone. "You knew I'd try, Thomas. You even said you did."

"Try, yes. Succeed, no." He let out a little laugh. "But just how successful have you been? Do you know? How many doubles have been inserted? Where? And for what purposes? Ah, you don't have any idea, do you?"

"It's easy enough to figure out the ultimate purpose," she said. "You want what you've always wanted—to destroy America. It's not a big mystery, Thomas."

"They'll tell you that you've won. I'll let them all believe it for a time, until other matters occupy their minds and their focus shifts. But I want you to know that you haven't won, Amanda. I have. You can't stop me anymore. None of you can stop me anymore."

"Everyone can be stopped," she insisted, "including you."

He laughed, deep and rich and so full that she knew he was genuinely amused. In his mind, he couldn't be stopped, and he planned to prove it and to make a fool of her for trying to stop him.

"I wanted to share that with you," he said. "So you never have a false sense of security about where we stand." He dropped his voice, hot and sultry. "I own you, Amanda. I'll always own you."

The hell he did. The hell he would. She fought to keep revulsion out of her voice. He'd just feed on it. "Thanks so much. I can't tell you—"

"I'm not done yet," he cut her off, his voice flat and cold. "I wanted to share something else with you, too."

She leaned a hip against the desk, stared out Gray's window onto the street. "What is it?"

"This," he said. "I'm sure you'll recognize the sound."

Silence followed. Amanda frowned, every instinct warning her this wasn't a bluff. Thomas was about to do something god-awful. She could almost taste the terror of it.

And then she heard it, and knew she'd been right.

A massive explosion rocked through the phone. It nearly blew out her eardrum, and then the phone went dead. "Oh, Jesus." She darted a gaze to Mark. "He blew up something. Something huge."

Everyone stopped, turned their focus to her.

The room went silent.

Within twenty seconds, beepers began sounding. Cell phones began ringing.

Breaths held, everyone hung suspended, waiting, dreading to find out what Kunz had blown up. Amanda had to remind herself to breathe, to blink; had to block out horrific images of innocents being murdered.

*Stop it. Stop.*

There would be time to regret and to mourn when they knew the damage. Until then, she had to stay centered and focused on Kunz. *Damn him. Damn him straight to hell!*

The dreaded call came to Kate. As she listened, her face paled to the gray of ice, and she swallowed hard repeatedly, trying to retain her composure. Silently, she hung up the phone and looked at Amanda. Her voice staggered. "He's blown up the Texas compound."

"Wasn't it clear from the predawn raid?" Mark rose from his desk.

"They delayed it for further reconnaissance," Kate said. "They were transitioning from raid to rescue when Kunz blew everything up."

A warning tingle crept up Amanda's backbone and settled in the base of her skull. "What about the forces we left behind? The guards, etcetera?"

"Field command says it doesn't look good." Kate's solemn eyes mirrored her sober expression. "They don't yet have a report on casualties, injuries, or damage assessment."

Colonel Drake shot a hand skyward. "Well, what the hell *are* they reporting, Captain Kane?"

Kate lowered her voice, subtly reminding Colonel Drake not to give Gray ammo to use against her to prove to Shaw that he and not she had been the right person to command the S.A.S.S. "Special Ops is saying Kunz used enough explosives to leave twenty-foot-wide craters. There isn't a building in the entire compound that hasn't been reduced to rubble, ma'am. It's been obliterated."

"What about Kunz and Reese?" Amanda asked.

"No visual confirmation Reese was at the compound. Kunz was observed. The team leader had a bead on him seconds before the explosion. He's presumed dead. They'll look for fragments, but it could be quite a process. A second team member has verified identification on Kunz and says there's no way anyone got out or survived the blast. Percussion alone would have killed them."

"Reese will be his natural successor," Colonel Gray said.

"He will be if Kunz is dead." Amanda tried to absorb it. Kunz hadn't sounded like a man about to commit suicide. He had sounded like a man with a diabolical plan. She wasn't buying it. He'd never kill himself. He thought he was too smart to be beaten. The team members' sightings complicated things—the honchos would consider him dead and no longer a threat—but Amanda wouldn't be convinced until she saw his lifeless body. Especially not after that phone call.

Colonel Gray let out a sigh that heaved his shoulders, and confronted Amanda. "Damn it, West. The field just confirmed with dual visual verifications. Kunz is dead."

She didn't believe it and she refused to agree and say she did. She looked Gray right in the eye. "I heard, sir."

"Well, why the hell are you saying *if* he's dead?" Gray's face mottled red. He didn't like Amanda and didn't bother hiding it. He didn't like anyone who didn't fear him. "He's human, not a demon, and he's dead. The subject is closed."

"Colonel Gray." Colonel Drake's voice sounded like tempered steel and her expression made steel seem soft. She was highly pissed, and her anger was about to erupt on Gray's head. "I need to see you in the break room."

Seemingly oblivious, he turned on her. "Now?" He grunted. "This isn't the time for one of your bitch sessions, Sally."

She walked up to him, stood so close that with his every breath, her chest bumped into his, intentionally dominating his personal space. She dropped her voice. "I said now, David. Now means now, or the next person I speak to about this will be General Shaw."

Colonel Drake had intended for her comment to be private, but everyone in the office had seen the sparks and knew the ceiling was about to cave. Everyone pretended to be otherwise occupied when in fact they were waiting to see who'd win the battle.

"Fine." Colonel Gray said, then walked out the door and into the hallway.

"West!" Colonel Drake looked at her with daggers. "You're in command until I return. Proceed at will." She strode to the door, her body wiry and tense, then paused and whispered to Kate, "If I'm not back in ten call the base police. He'll be dead."

Not sure if she was kidding or a hundred-percent serious, Kate nodded. "Yes, ma'am."

Amanda put her money on Drake, then her thoughts turned right back to Kunz. The deaths of his own men. He really had no regard for human life. None.

Shaking, her knees weak, she sat down at the desk she'd been using and drew in three deep, stabilizing breaths. She had to get a firm grip on her emotions. She took in three more gulps of air, filling her lungs, then slowly exhaling.

Calmer, she looked over at Mark. He was on the phone again—they were all working the phones again. He reached into his desk and pulled out a bag then ripped it open. Peanuts? *Peanuts?*

A horrible, sinking feeling washed through Amanda and smothered her like a tidal surge. It couldn't be possible. *It couldn't!* She stared at him and, as if sensing her gaze, he looked up at her and smiled.

Amanda was torn between ripping his throat out and screaming. Her heart ached, broken. Shattered. But that was nothing compared to the sense of guilt swamping her. She was drowning. Drowning in guilt and betrayal. This man she had dared to trust, had given so much to last night and again this morning, had betrayed her. She'd honest to God risked caring for and about him, and he had used her. *Used* her!

Fear swelled and joined the guilt and anger and other cascading emotions tumbling inside her. She had to get out of here.

Leaving the desk, she walked out of the office and into the rest room, then over to the sink. She bent double, doused her face with cold water. Her hands were shaking, her stomach bitter and churning.

The door swung open behind her. "Hey." Kate came in. "What's wrong, Amanda? You look like the walking dead."

She forced her emotions down, buried them deep inside that safe where she'd always buried them. Where they couldn't hurt her. "Get Joan in here. Be discreet."

"Okay, but why—"

"Damn it, just do it now, Kate! Only Joan." She swept a hand over her skull, turned back to the sink and squeezed her eyes shut. "Please," she said, forcing her tone to be civil. "Please, just do it now."

"Sure." Kate left, and minutes later returned with Joan.

"Amanda, are you sick?" Joan asked immediately on entering the rest room.

"Yeah, but not the way you think." She leaned back against the sink. "Did you disclose Mark's allergies in your briefing tapes?"

"No. I held back that information so I would know I was dealing with him and not a double," she admitted. "If you recall, he had a three-month absence before I got to the compound. I considered it highly possible that Thomas Kunz had already doubled Mark. I checked the medical records that came over with him and they didn't list allergies. I asked, and he told me he was allergic to peanuts. I didn't post it."

"Well, the one in the office out there—*the one I slept with*—is eating freaking peanuts, Joan."

"But he can't—"

"Mark can't eat peanuts," Kate insisted. Reality dawned. "It's his double?" Kate gasped. "Then where's Mark?"

Now Amanda understood Kunz's call. He had intended to torment her, and he'd known how to do it. Take the one man she's dared to trust and arrange for her to discover that he is not the man she believed him to be. That the man she trusted and cared for was...

"Oh, God. Kunz has Mark, doesn't he?" Joan's face leaked out its color. "Oh, Amanda!"

"Was he at the compound?" Kate blinked hard. She and Mark were friends and surrogate family.

Shaken, Amanda fisted her hands at her sides. She wanted to kill the man posing as Mark, but he was her lead to finding the real Mark. Her Mark.

She headed to the door.

"Amanda, what are you going to do?"

"I'm going to kill that son of a bitch," she said. "But first, I'm going to find out from him where Kunz has Mark."

"So he wasn't at the compound," Kate said, running to keep up with her.

"No. That would be too easy." Amanda stormed down the hallway, damning herself for not listening to her instincts. She'd known by his scent something was different. Why had she let her emotions cloud her judgment and override her instincts? She *knew* they were sound.

"Kunz wants Mark to die," she said. "But he wants me to feel responsible for his death. He wasn't at the compound. I'd bet on it."

"So where do you think he is?"

"I don't know." Amanda couldn't think. Her mind was racing yet numb. "Kunz loves mind games, Kate. He always plays mind games with everyone. He's playing one with me about Mark. I have the information I need to find him. I just have to figure out what it is."

"Well, you'd better hurry," Kate said, worry and fear etching her tone. "Otherwise, by the time you find him—"

"I know." Amanda's stomach flipped. Never in her life had she been this pissed off and scared at the same time. "He'll be dead."

Kate didn't insult her by denying it. "Where do we go from here?"

"Go get Colonels Drake and Gray out of the break room and have them and Joan meet me in the vault ASAP. I'll go straight there and wait. If our fake Mark asks where I am, tell him I started my period and I'm in the rest room cleaning up." Men had an aversion to discussing periods. Mention them and they cease all questioning, if not all conversation—fast.

"You got it." Kate paused near the corner, checked to make sure she wouldn't be overheard. "I'm sorry, Amanda." Kate dropped her voice low. "I know how hard it was for you to trust him...."

"I don't trust him. I trust Mark." Amanda thought about that and her insides went hollow. "At least, I think I do." If Mark was Mark and not Mark's double. Irritated and off balance, she dragged her hands over her face. "Just get them to the vault, will you?"

"Sure. Just one thing," Kate said, her short blond curls framing her face. "You really going to kill him?"

"I don't know yet." The uncertainty had Amanda even more upset. "If he was forced to take on the role, then probably not. But if he took on doubling for Mark by choice, you can count on it."

*When? When had he taken on doubling for Mark? After they'd been captured and taken to the Texas compound? Or before?*

The office leak.

A bleak certainty settled in on Amanda, weighed down on her shoulders. The double could act in Mark's stead during his absences from the office; by telephone, when Mark was otherwise occupied. He could—and had—substituted himself for Mark at convenient times and never aroused suspicion. He had been doing all that and more, intermittently ever since Mark's three-month absence. Mark's double *was* the leak in the OSI office.

# Chapter 15

The vault was buried in the bowels of Building One.

It had no windows, one door that was time-locked. To enter required top-secret or higher security clearance, an authorized ID badge scan, a biometric iris and fingerprint scan, and successfully crossing the threshold without setting off alarms for carrying metal—including watches and keys—recording devices, or anything, including pens, pencils or a sheet of paper, in your hand. To exit required the same rigid ritual.

Inside, there were four workstations separated by three-foot-high, tabletop dividers. Workers were visible at all times to security monitoring and surveillance, but maintained privacy from any other person in the vault. That was essential to the level of classified information accessed in the vault.

A conference table for secure meetings sat in the center of the room. It was scratched and well used; it's finish dull and dark. Six chairs surrounded the table. Two people sat at one end, having a private conversation.

On the far side of the vault, a half door was open. A guard stood there, protecting the sensitive files kept on his side of the opening. They were stored in individual, locked safes. Only persons with specific clearances to view the material contained within each safe had the ability to open it. The guard assured no one tried opening one without proper authorization or access. A failed attempt to open any safe resulted in that individual being detained and questioned by agents from the Office of Special Investigations and Intel. There was a zero-tolerance policy in full force and effective at all times. No exceptions.

Amanda looked around at the half-dozen people currently inside the vault. "Everybody out." She said it twice more, and no one in the vault questioned her. They got up, stowed files in their respective safes, locked them down then filtered through security and left the vault.

Amanda then retrieved Joan and her authorizations to enter from out in the hallway and brought her inside. The guard was instructed to close the top half of his safe room, which sealed him with the files in a soundproof room. Minutes later, Kate came in with Colonels Drake and Gray.

"What the hell is this about, West?" Colonel Gray asked, clearly peeved at being summoned by an officer of lower rank.

"You got something to say to one of my people, Gray, you come through me." Colonel Drake's temper had flared as hot as her spiked red hair. She turned to Amanda. "What the hell is this about, West?"

Amanda grunted. "The man in the office isn't Mark Cross." Softening blows wasn't possible under the circumstances, so Amanda bluntly took care of business. "Mark is allergic to peanuts. This guy is eating them. Dr. Foster—" she nodded toward Joan, standing across from her "—withheld that information from Mark's files when he and his files were brought to her so she'd have a way to determine whether she was dealing at any time with the real Mark or his double."

"You programmed his double?" Drake asked.

"No, but I suspected he had one," Joan said. "So I didn't note that information. I always do that—keep some individual key fact to myself so that I know if I'm dealing with the actual person or one of Kunz's doubles."

Amanda was glad to hear that. "You've done this on each of the thirty cases you've handled?"

Joan nodded.

"Excellent." Finally, a decent break.

Colonel Drake frowned. "We can interrogate this guy, but I doubt he's going to give us anything."

"He won't," Joan assured her.

"We have methods you can't begin to understand, Dr. Foster." Colonel Gray lifted his chin, his legs spread in an arrogant, authoritative stance. "We'll get what we need from him."

"You have methods that won't work," Joan said, disagreeing with him. "No disrespect intended, Colonel, but Thomas Kunz knows your methods and he's designed his own to counter them. If you want information from Mark's double, then there's only one way to get it and that's Kunz's way."

Colonel Drake interceded. "What exactly is Kunz's way, Dr. Foster?"

Joan shifted her weight from her left to her right foot, clearly uncomfortable and probably fearful she'd be judged harshly for her part in this. "Drug therapy."

"What kind of drug therapy?" Kate asked.

Lifting her chin, Joan let her regret shine in her eyes, but also her acceptance that she would be held accountable for her actions. "The kind I used routinely at the compound clinic to feed facts directly into the subconscious minds of detainees and doubles so those facts would be recalled by them as genuine memories. You see, if the programming was effect-ive, Mark's double doesn't know he's a double."

Like everyone else in the vault, Amanda knew S.A.S.S. had this technology. But there were other factors to be consid-ered—the moral and ethical consequences of actually using that technology. If she hadn't known Kunz and hadn't con-fronted the sadistic side of him herself, she would have been hard-pressed to believe anyone would violate another human being to this extent. But she did know him and she had con-fronted him, and unfortunately, she had no doubt whatsoever that he had the willingness to use the technology. "This guy honestly thinks he's Mark?"

"Yes, he does." Joan assured her. "If he was prepared prop-erly and programmed effectively. And Kunz wouldn't have inserted him for Mark if he hadn't been both."

Colonel Drake pondered for a long moment, her hand on her hip. "So you use this drug therapy and you can get into his real mind and find out—what? What's there?"

"His real identity, for one thing. His real memories, and any information he has relating to GRID. The double knows what classified information he or she has passed on to GRID and to whom he or she passed it. From what I've discovered, intelligence passes directly to either Kunz, Paul Reese, or if its classification is merely top secret or lower, to a select group of subordinates."

"His double could know where Mark is now?" Amanda asked, her hope igniting despite her warning herself not to let it.

"He could. Some have only minimal information on the GRID organization. It depends on the assigned mission and what the double needs to know to do the job. But a few of them have intimate knowledge of the GRID organization. That's how I discovered there was a Middle Eastern com-pound in the tribal area of Afghanistan near the Pakistani border, and that the compound where we were detained was in Texas."

Colonel Drake nodded to Kate to see if Intel had yet found the exact location of that compound. She moved to security to leave the vault to take care of it immediately, and Colonel Drake turned her attention back to Joan. "What do you need to do this? To find out what he knows?"

"The drugs." Joan shrugged.

Colonel Gray stepped up. "Dr. Vargus can get you whatever you need. Kate," he called out to her. "Can you locate him and have him call Joan—secure line?"

"Yes, sir." Kate snagged control. "Right away."

For once, Colonel Drake didn't take exception to Colonel Gray's interaction with her S.A.S.S. operatives. Amanda was glad to see it.

"Do we need to put guards on Mark's double?" Gray asked.

Joan looked peaked. Certain she was reeling, Amanda answered for her, to give her a minute to come to terms with everything and her place in the situation. "Not if he thinks he's really Mark. We do need to covertly monitor him, his calls, anyone he interacts with—everything he does—until we can find out what he knows. He could lead us to some of the others, if he's given the opportunity to have contact."

Amanda shifted uneasily on her feet. "Injecting him with drugs falls outside acceptable interrogation boundaries, Colonel Drake. We should get legal in on it."

"Can't do that," she said. "National interests."

Gray's eyes gleamed. If Drake didn't seek higher authority, he would definitely use it against her.

Colonel Drake picked up on Gray's gleam. "But we can seek counsel," she relented. "Get General Shaw and Secretary Reynolds for me, Amanda."

"Yes, ma'am." Relief shimmered through her. Both men

far outranked Gray. He wouldn't dare to tangle with either of them. Silently lauding Drake as a strategic wonder, she linked up the call.

Gray muttered under his breath, clearly disappointed. Amanda didn't spare him a glance. The man had started out low on her respect scale and he was now so far down he had to look up to see a ground-level pit.

Half an hour later, the group had cleared the vault and moved to the infirmary down the hall from the office they'd appropriated in the OSI facility. Dr. Vargus had spoken with Joan, received her instructions and arrived at the infirmary with a black medical case, which he passed to her.

"Dr. Foster." He nodded. "I prepared three injections to your specifications."

"Thank you, Dr. Vargus." Joan took the bag, set it on a cabinet near the sink then opened it. Inside, three syringes full of a milky serum stood in a padded protective sheath. Otherwise, the case was empty. Tension flooded Joan's face. "What if he refuses to allow me to inject him?" She shot a worried look at Amanda. "What do I do then?"

Amanda tried to reassure her. "Don't worry. He won't object. If he does, just back up, and stay out of the way. We'll neutralize him, and deliver him to you." She slid a look at Kate, who nodded her agreement.

Colonel Gray cleared his throat, warning them he was coming down the hallway with Mark's double.

Moments later, the two men walked through the door. Colonel Drake stood to the right of the opening and, after they walked in, she filled the doorway, preparing to block any attempt to exit.

Mark's double looked at Amanda, more curious than concerned. "What's going on?"

Joan shot Amanda a look of pure panic.

Amanda stepped in without missing a beat. "Joan thinks we

might have been chemically contaminated while we were at the compound. She's testing us to see. Harry, Brent, Simon, Jeremy and I have had ours. Now it's your turn." Amanda grabbed him by the arm and led him to the patient table. "Sit here."

He sat down on the table's edge. "What kind of test?"

"One we need to make sure we haven't been contaminated with anything that affects our security clearances," Amanda lied. "Quit being a pain and just bare your arm."

He rolled his eyes at her and whispered, "Pull in your claws, honey, your PMS is showing."

"Up yours, honey. This isn't PMS, it's my normal sweet disposition." She smiled and sent Dr. Vargus a conspiratorial look, since he had been gracious enough not to report her memory lapses. "Roll up your sleeve."

Mark's double sat down, and Joan injected him in the right arm.

When she pulled out the needle, both colonels quietly left the room, and Amanda sent Joan a look as clear as if she'd spoken the words. *Now what?*

Joan responded to it, recalling that Amanda should already be familiar with the process. "We wait ten minutes, Mark, and then run the samples. It's totally painless." Joan cooled her look and her tone, pivoted to Amanda. "I'd prefer you not be in the room during testing."

"Why not?"

"You and Mark have a close relationship— I'm sorry if that was supposed to be private, but you did ask," Joan reminded her. "Outside stimuli can negatively impact the test results."

"How could her being in the infirmary skew the results?"

"Think hormones, Captain Cross," Dr. Vargus said, looking at Mark's double over the glasses parked on the tip of his nose.

"Oh." He had the grace to blush.

This, Dr. Vargus would report. Colonel Drake would be panic-stricken at finding out there was a personal relationship involved in this already complicated mess.

Amanda's stomach soured. "I'll be in the corridor."

Minutes later, Kate walked out of the infirmary and joined her. "Joan's ready for the colonels. I'm going to get them." Kate walked next door and stepped into the office and out of sight.

Amanda took in a sharp breath. Both Colonels Drake and Gray insisted on being present during the double's questioning.

When Kate returned, she glanced back to make sure they were alone in the corridor then whispered, "Dr. Vargus is going to tell Colonel Drake about you two, Amanda. Mark asked after you left the room and Vargus said he would disclose everything revealed to him." Kate looked worried. "I thought you'd want to know in advance."

"Figures." Minimal breaks. Absolutely minimal. Seemed she couldn't catch one with both hands and a net. "I appreciate it, Kate."

"No problem."

Colonel Drake walked past them and entered the infirmary. Colonel Gray followed her, then shut the door. Kate cooled her heels in the hallway next to Amanda, who hadn't had time to sort through her feelings on all this. Exactly how should she feel about Mark? About having had sex with his double? How would the real Mark feel about it?

She imagined, positions reversed, it'd go over about as well as a lead balloon. But she'd honestly believed he was Mark; that should count for something. It was damn humiliating was the problem. She'd never once dared to trust a man, and the first time in her life she made an exception, it was not only a mistake, it was a colossal, deep-and-serious-consequences mistake that had national-security-threat implications *and* drove her nuts.

*When you screw up, Princess, you really do it right.*

"You okay?" Kate asked, her foot propped and hands pressed flat against the wall behind her.

"Freaking fabulous." Amanda tried but failed to keep the sarcasm and bitterness out of her voice. "In my position, who wouldn't be?"

Thirty minutes later, Joan, Colonel Drake and Colonel Gray joined Amanda and Kate in the hallway outside the infirmary. Mark's double had been left inside under the care of Dr. Vargus.

Colonel Gray asked the first question. "Is he helping us only because I've threatened to have him tried for treason, or because Kunz has set a trap for us?"

Joan schooled her expression, feigning patience. "He's cooperating because he has no choice. It's part of his programming. With all due respect, Colonel, your threat was useless, and if there's a trap involved, he doesn't know it."

Colonel Drake absorbed that information quietly, then asked, "When he comes out from under the drug, will he remember that he's a double and all of the real information about himself and GRID?"

"If I want him to, he will."

"You want him to," Drake said, her lips compressed, her body held stiff and straight as a metal rod.

"Yes, ma'am."

"Is the tactical team in position in Afghanistan?" Colonel Gray asked Kate.

"Yes, sir. Awaiting orders."

He looked at Colonel Drake. "We should have them move in and level the compound."

Amanda gritted her teeth, but she couldn't neglect to voice her opposing opinion. Gray probably wouldn't get over a subordinate's having the audacity to disagree with him, but that was just another unfortunate item he'd have to add to his list of her infractions, because she did disagree—strongly enough that she had no choice but to speak her mind. "Colonel Drake, that course of action isn't consistent with assuring our success in the overall mission."

"Overall mission?" Gray asked, his jaw ticking, his hands fisted and stuffed in his slacks pockets.

"There are other compounds. There are other doubles, sir," Amanda said, keeping her voice level and her tone tightly controlled. "We know about those Dr. Foster treated and we've got Intel resources dedicated to locating them. But we don't know the identity of the others. We do know they've infiltrated all domestic and foreign U.S. security forces. If we level the Middle Eastern compound without first examining the contents kept there, we might destroy the only records that will prove where and with whom Kunz has infiltrated."

"Kunz is dead, Amanda," Colonel Drake said. "We can't hold off too long on taking over the compound or it'll be deserted and all the records destroyed. That or we'll walk into a turf war between factions battling for controlling power of whatever is left of GRID."

"All true, ma'am," Amanda said. "I don't disagree."

Drake caught her intent. She didn't disagree but felt they were moving down a destructive path. "Then what do you suggest we do?"

"That depends, ma'am." Amanda turned to look at Joan. "Do we know where Mark is?"

"No, we don't." Regret stole into Joan's voice. "But his double made a cryptic reference to you having forty-eight hours to save his life."

"Mark has to be at the Middle Eastern compound, Amanda," Kate insisted. "Harry said they took all the detainees to it. At least, according to Gaston they did. He passed Harry the message before he evacuated with the other detainees, and said, if you were still alive, to make sure to give it to you."

"Colonel Drake," Amanda said, "I request permission to covertly infiltrate the Middle Eastern compound before tactical takes it down."

"Fine. But infiltrate with the tactical team. There's no logical reason for you to go in again without backup. Brief the team on what assets to protect before going in," she said, and then added, "I'm giving you forty-eight hours, Amanda. That's all I can get from General Shaw and Secretary Reynolds. I'm out of favors to call in. After that, we elevate this to a Code Two crisis and take the compound down."

A Code Two mandated completing the mission by any and all necessary means, and that meant regardless of who was inside the compound—including their own. Including Mark. "Yes, ma'am."

"And take Kate with you," Drake said. "She's the best explosives expert in the business. I want her boots on the ground at the site."

"Yes, ma'am." Amanda turned to Joan. "Thanks."

"You're welcome." She motioned Amanda aside and dropped her voice so only the two of them could hear. "If it helps, he thought his feelings for you were genuine. There was nothing fake about them."

Should that make her feel better or worse? "Do you know if he agreed to be a double for Kunz willingly or under duress?"

Joan didn't meet her gaze. She fidgeted with her pen, clicking it rapidly and watching its point extend and retract. "I haven't asked that."

She didn't want Amanda to kill him, so she'd avoided asking the question she didn't want answered. "I see."

Joan sighed. "Amanda, you know what Kunz is like. You know what he's capable of doing."

Amanda hadn't forgotten that he'd sanctioned Paul's raping Joan in front of Simon and Jeremy. "Tell me you know when Mark's double inserted." Sheer force of will kept Amanda's voice level and her expression serene. Inside, everything twisted and stabbed and she had as much trouble breathing as the time a guard twice her size had fractured four of her ribs in a knock-down, drag-out bust. Then, every indrawn breath forced ragged rib edges into her punctured lung. Now, it stabbed into the ragged edges of her heart. This mattered. She might hate it, but this really mattered. *He* really mattered. "It's important to me, Joan."

She stilled the pen, met Amanda's gaze openly. "I know, and I did ask. But I can't give you a date. He inserted on and off since Mark got back from his three-month absence. But it was Mark, the real Mark with you most of the time at the compound. When he was switched out there I don't know for sure."

"Why not?" No, this couldn't be left unanswered. It couldn't.

"Because that isn't how he framed his response," Joan explained. "He said that you noticed the difference between him and Mark immediately."

Surprise streaked up Amanda's back. "I noticed?"

Joan put her pen in her lab-coat pocket. "Mark's double said you noticed something different about him almost immediately."

"That he smelled different. I thought it was his diet or his soap."

"That change in scent wasn't due to diet, it was body chemistry, and that Kunz couldn't change," Joan said.

So Mark had been Mark until the night they'd made their escape. In plain sight…it had been Mark in the shower. But she suddenly remembered the hangar and the kiss she'd given Mark after he'd walloped Beefy for her. His scent had been different then, too. It just hadn't registered in the quickness of the moment. Sometime in those few hours, when Joan had thought Mark was guarded in his cabin, he'd been replaced. Relief washed through Amanda, sudden and sweeping. But fear for Mark's safety snapped fast at its heels.

"I'm glad you fell for the man and not the facade of him, Amanda." Joan didn't smile, but her words were sincere.

"Me, too," she confessed, confused at having slept with that facade. Confused and angry and used. Violated. She felt all that, but also took solace in knowing that Kunz, who was really responsible, unlike her bastard father, would be held accountable. And the price for what he'd done would be his life.

She should feel guilty or angry toward Mark's double, too. But he hadn't known he wasn't Mark, and neither had she.

Mentally smacking herself for being distracted, she put her priorities in order. "So where is Mark?" she asked Joan.

"So far as his double knows, he's at the Middle Eastern compound with the rest of the detainees, like Harry said."

"And Harry *is* Harry, right?" Amanda needed a pilot.

"Absolutely."

Colonel Drake had given her forty-eight hours before Special Forces went in to attempt a rescue of the detainees and records retrieval. The only survivors then would be those high-ranking within GRID, if any were found on-site at the time of the raid. But Amanda wasn't a fool and experience told her what would actually take place. Tactical and Special Forces would do what they could in the way of rescues, captures and evidence gathering, but within minutes of infiltrating, they'd raze and burn the compound. It was in hostile territory; they had no choice but to follow that protocol.

Never had forty-eight hours seemed like such a short period of time. Amanda feared a second to even blink. She didn't just want to find Mark.

She wanted to find him alive.

"Amanda, time to suit up." Kate had approached them. "We're due on the flight line in fifteen minutes."

Fear widened Joan's eyes. "I wish you weren't personally going to the compound. Reese wants you dead, Amanda. You know that."

"A lot of people want me dead," she said. And until she saw his lifeless body for herself, that included Thomas Kunz. "I have to go. It's my job. I'm going to rescue Mark, and the others, and to find out as much as I can on how pervasive Kunz's twisted project has progressed so we can weed out the doubles before they cripple the government."

"If Reese doesn't kill you, Kunz will."

Joan was worried for Amanda, not being judgmental about her activities. It touched her. Kate and she worried about each other. But an outsider being concerned about her welfare was new and it engaged untapped emotions because it was so totally unexpected.

And it was telling.

What Joan had said proved she didn't believe Kunz was dead, either. "Yes," Amanda said softly. "If either Reese or Kunz can, they'll kill me."

Joan blinked hard three times, and her chin, while held taut, revealed a telltale quiver. "But you have to do this, anyway."

"Would you leave Simon there?"

Pondering the question, she hesitated, clearly striving for honesty. When her expression crumbled, it became apparent she had found it. "No." Worry put back the tension that had been in Joan's face before her family's rescue. "I admire your courage, Amanda, and as one you're trying to protect, I'm grateful to you, but…"

"But?" she prodded.

"But I have too few friends to lose even one." She clasped

Amanda's hand in both of hers and squeezed hard. "Don't let them kill you, okay?"

The bonds of friendship enveloped her. First Mark, and now Joan. Friends outside the S.A.S.S. Amanda was hardly a loner anymore, and frankly, she had no idea how to feel about that. It would take a little time to get used to, and a little more time to let her emotions rise and not automatically tamp them. Lifetime habits—good or bad—were hard to break.

Joan's request also struck a familiar chord. She sounded exactly like Jeremy had when he'd asked Amanda not to let his daddy get dead. "I won't," she said, making the same promise to the mother she'd made to the son—and hoping she again lived to keep it.

# Chapter 16

Colonel Drake issued the necessary official orders and Amanda, Kate and Harry assembled their covert gear and hitched a ride on a C-5 heading to Ramstein Air Force Base in Landstuhl, Germany. There, they were transferred to a C-130 Hercules attached to the 731$^{st}$ Airlift Squadron at Peterson Air Force Base, Colorado, that was in theater, participating in a massive training exercise. It flew them to Saudi Arabia.

From Saudi, they were transported on a supply flight to Afghanistan and, there, Harry turned over the authorization order and took delivery of an Apache Longbow armed to the teeth to affect an attack in thirty seconds with everything from an M230 that fired six hundred twenty-five rounds a minute to radar-jammers and Hellfire missiles that were loaded under each wing. Harry looked like a kid cut loose in a candy store—exactly the same way Kate looked on taking delivery of C-5 explosives and, as she put it, "a host of other incidentals."

Amanda wasn't an explosives expert or a bomb-squad specialist, but she knew enough to know Kate's "incidentals" could flatten a small country in a matter of hours. As team commander, Amanda received Intel update and reconnaissance briefings from the tactical team leader, Lieutenant Douglas.

Amanda's team had slept as much as possible on the planes. It was nearly 9:00 p.m. locally by the time they had gathered all they needed to carry out the mission and rendezvoused on the flight line, ready to board the Apache. Tactical would follow in the team's own transportation, which also gave both teams access to a secondary means of egress to extricate, if need for it arose.

In the distance, the headlights of a bouncing jeep spread light across the rock-strewn ground and it became apparent the vehicle was heading for the Apache. Kate, Harry and Amanda went on alert. "Friend or foe?" Kate asked.

Harry shook his head, backed toward the aircraft. "No idea."

Amanda and Kate took a defensive stance, armed with AK-47s. Harry got into the chopper and fired it up. The props thumped and plopped in the night air, stirring up a breeze that carried a fair amount of dust.

The jeep stopped, and a lean colonel with a sour disposition etched into his face crawled out. "Stand down, Captain West." He looked at Amanda.

Amanda pointed the nose of her weapon to the ground, but didn't alter her stance. *Anyone can put on a uniform.* Mark's words came back to her.

"I'm Colonel Grant, theater Intel commander." He stretched out a ham-fist to shake Amanda's hand. "I got some new recon reports on the compound. I thought it best to keep your presence low-key. Only the tactical team and I know why you're here."

That explained the strange looks and unfriendly attitudes they had encountered from the moment they set foot on the ground. She'd put it all down to the wicked desert heat. Instead, it was resentment because they hadn't been told who Amanda's team was but they viewed it as encroaching on their turf. "Leaks?"

"Like sieves." He frowned. "We're heavily dependent on locals for a lot here. Outside forces have different perspectives on what is good and right and what is treason. At times, that makes for challenging complications."

That was a nice way of saying the place was crawling with spies. Amanda nodded and kept her mouth shut.

"I can't even guarantee my secure quarters are secure." He shoved a brown envelope of papers into her hand. "Here's everything we've gotten on the GRID compound since your briefing with Lieutenant Douglas."

"Thanks." Amanda took the envelope, passed it to Kate and gave her a nod. She would pick up on the unspoken order to get in the chopper with Harry and review the contents so she could debrief Amanda ASAP.

Dawn waited on no man or woman or mission. With their technology and equipment, they owned the night, but the night would soon be giving way to day. Kunz and Reese were professionals with a lot to lose; Amanda couldn't afford to forfeit any advantage.

"Colonel Sally Drake instructed me to put that info into your hands myself. STAT," he said with a slight sneer. He pulled a cigar from his pocket and lighted it, blowing a puff of smoke downwind. "I can't say I'm overly fond of being issued orders by an officer of equal rank—especially when she didn't try a friendly asking first. She came out of the gate making demands, which really pissed me off. The woman isn't much on diplomacy, is she?"

Amanda looked right at him and said nothing.

When it became evident to him that she wasn't about to touch that lightning rod, he went on. "Whatever." He let out a huff and exhaled a plume of smoke with it. "Considering what we found at that compound, I'm willing to make an exception and overlook it. But next time you talk with her, tell her not to issue me orders again or there'll be hell to pay."

"Yes, sir." She'd never deliver that message, and they both knew it. "What did you find at the compound, Colonel?" Amanda watched his expression carefully. He had a macho demeanor and he was a big guy with an "I own the world" attitude. He wouldn't rattle easily.

"It's in the report." He bit down on the cigar and squinted to avoid a stream of spiraling smoke from getting into his eyes. "Captain, I hope you two are as good as Drake says you are, because otherwise you're going to get killed."

Amanda stiffened. "We're professionals, sir."

"You better be. We're depending on it." He turned toward the jeep. "Good luck, Captain."

She saluted when she really wanted to knock him on his pompous ass. "Thank you, sir." Because she couldn't resist a dig at him, she added, "We appreciate the assist."

Sufficiently ticked that the Pentagon had sent her and Kate in to execute the mission rather than assigning it to him and his troops, he glared at her, his hackles raised to the rafters at the chain of command. That soothed her temper. She smiled and watched him climb back into the jeep and speed away.

Amanda got into the copilot's seat in the chopper. "Kate?" She strapped in and glanced back at her. "What've we got?"

Kate looked up and there was no missing the fear in her face. "A freaking fortress."

Harry waited on the chopper, ready for a fast extraction.

The compound region was rocky, mountainous and steep-ledged, but the compound itself sat dead center in a barren, flat section of ground that had been leveled and scraped clear in what Amanda estimated to be a radius of about three kilometers. Nothing and no one was going to approach from any direction undetected.

Amanda and Kate lay facedown in the gritty dirt, decked out in covert gear, their faces smudged black and backpacks loaded down with an assortment of tools and arms. Looking through her night-vision distance gear, Amanda visually swept the compound proper from her vantage point about a hundred yards out. Aside from a couple boulders, only three single-story buildings slightly larger than outhouses were visible, which meant the majority of the compound complex was built underground. Not good news.

The perimeter fence was charged, topped with razor wire, and Colonel Grant's reconnaissance team had detected and mapped dozens of land mines outside the fence. They hadn't breached the perimeter, which could mean it was mined, as well. The tactical team recommended following mined operating procedures because it deemed it improbable that Kunz wouldn't have mined the area. Three, no—she spotted another—four GRID patrol units prowled the perimeter fence. "What do you think, Kate?" she whispered into her lip mike. "Can we get in?"

"Sure." Kate's transmission sounded crystal clear in Amanda's earpiece. "We've got enough C-5 to take the top off the mountain. Getting in is no problem." Kate looked away from the compound to Amanda. "It's getting out that's going to be a bitch."

"Let's get to it, then. Level the playing field." Amanda crept on her stomach up to the fence. Keeping an eye out for the patrol teams they'd spotted, she examined the system.

"You could short-circuit it," Kate suggested.

"No, I don't want them to notice anything unusual. That'll give us more time to avoid any mines." Pulling out her tool bag, Amanda created a loop in an arch wide enough to slip through, then reached for her wire cutters.

"I've got it." Kate cut the wire. "There's a trip wire about four inches below the ground."

"Is there enough play to bring it up out of the dirt so it can be seen?"

Kate checked. "Yeah."

"Do it." Amanda put her tools away. By the time she finished, Kate had the trip wire aboveground and flagged. "Ready?"

Kate nodded.

They moved into the outer perimeter and within minutes spotted the first of the four patrols coming their way. "They're breaking the pattern." Amanda's adrenaline spiked. "Take cover."

They dropped to the ground, snaked to a large boulder and slid behind it. The three-man patrol unit came closer. Then closer.

"We're going to have to take them," Kate whispered. "They're going to see the hole in the fence."

"No guns unless we have to use them." Amanda dropped her extra gear, pulled out her knife, glanced over and saw Kate had done the same. "Go left. I'll take the two on the right."

"Do you need assistance?"

Amanda recognized Lieutenant Douglas's voice. The tactical team riding shotgun was in place. "Not at this time, but thanks."

Kate interceded, ending the interruption and getting back to business. "We asking questions?"

"Not a viable option." Amanda didn't even consider it. "Take them out."

"You sure you don't need backup?"

Douglas again. "Not yet, thanks." Amanda's voice was a little more firm, carrying a warning for Douglas to pace the sidelines but stay out of the way. She barely restrained herself from sniping at him.

Kate didn't bother. "Damn it, Douglas, stay off the freaking channel. You're cramping our style."

"Fine, Wonder Woman. Handle it, then."

"That's 'Wonder Woman, ma'am, Lieutenant." Kate pulled rank on him.

"Ma'am, damn it."

Amanda smiled. Kate was smitten and being her typical ornery self. "Flirt later, Kate."

"But he's cute—for a tactical guy, anyway."

Amanda imagined the tactical team sputtering and giving Douglas a hard time. Why was it when danger ran highest, operatives teased and joked and ribbed each other most? Stress reliever? Because death was so close and taking joy in life pushed the fear away?

Whatever it was, Amanda had seen and felt it a million times.

The guard on the far right peeled off. "Heads up," Amanda warned Kate. "They've made us."

Simultaneously, she and Kate rose to a crouch and watched the remaining two men continue to move in. "Steady." She signaled Kate. "Steady."

When they were within striking distance, Amanda issued the kill order. "Move on three."

The pair moved closer. The third made a wide swing to Amanda's right, away from Kate. Amanda would have to take him simultaneously, and hoped she had the strength to do it. Normally, she'd feel pretty confident about her odds— the men were loud and lumbered; not slackers by any stretch of the imagination, yet definitely not Delta-trained—but she was running on sheer adrenaline, and they appeared well rested. That gave them a hell of an edge.

"One." She began the count. The tension of mentally preparing for battle set into the men's shoulders, into their steps. "Two." They were creeping now, moving with stealth and unfortunately, skill. Widening the gap between them, the women turned back to back. "Three."

Seconds later, Amanda engaged the enemy. He, too, had a knife and his reach was longer. She assessed him in the first ten seconds of combat. No slouch. Stronger. Six-inch and fifty-pound advantage. Fast. But—she parried and whipped a flurry of snapped thrusts—she was faster.

Cursing, he dropped a sweeping kick and knocked her feet out from under her. She hit the rocky ground with a hard thump, heard her own grunts and groans and Kate's. From the corner of her eye, she saw him advancing, setting up for the kill. She waited…waited…waited…then surged to her feet and slammed into him, shoulder to gut, with a forward momentum that knocked him on his ass. A swipe with her knife and his throat lay wide open. Blood flowed out, soaking his shirtfront, and he collapsed on the ground.

Breathing hard and heavy, Amanda darted an assessing look at Kate. She was still battling the guy, but she was gaining the upper hand. Where was the third guy? He'd seemingly vanished into thin air.

Amanda spun to look behind her—and took a hard blow to the face. Pain blasted in her jaw and she saw stars. Shaking her head to clear it, she tumbled onto the ground to get out of striking distance then rolled up and onto her feet.

He lost his composure, roared, "I'm going to kill you, bitch."

*Overbite.* She recognized him from the Texas compound. Luckily, he had a ferocious temper and it controlled him. Determined to use that against him, she smiled, hoping it would throw him off guard long enough for her vision to clear. "Hope you're better at this than your sidekick, honey, or you're doing nothing to me."

Letting out a growl, he dived into her, knocked her sprawling on her back, his knife blade arced above his head, gleaming in the moonlight. She rolled out from under him as he positioned for a powerful down thrust intended for her chest. The knife blade sank into the dirt up to its hilt.

That was the one moment Amanda needed, and she seized it, kicking him in the head. From where she stood, she heard his neck snap. He sank into a heap, dead before he landed facedown in the dirt.

Her chest heaving, her lungs craving more air, she checked on Kate, who delivered an uppercut to the man's chest that drove the blade through his heart. He fell forward against her. Staggering backward from his dead weight, Kate shoved hard and rolled her shoulder. He fell into a heap on the ground, raising a little cloud of dust.

"You two okay?" Douglas asked.

"Fine." Gasping for air, Amanda swiped at the sweat burning her eyes, rolling down the sides of her face.

"Yeah, Douglas," Kate said. "Nicked my thigh, but it's nothing that can't be kissed and made better." She blew out a shuddery breath, retrieved her knife and swiped at the blood dripping from the blade on the man's jacket. "You married?"

"No."

"Glad to hear it."

"Kate…" Amanda put a warning in her tone.

"What?" she objected. "I'm multitask proficient."

"Fine. Multitask your ass on moving." Amanda retrieved her gear. "Tactical, we're going in. Radio silence from here on out."

"Yes, ma'am," Douglas said, his disappointment obvious.

Kate bit a laugh from her voice. "We'll play later, Douglas."

"Looking forward to it, ma'am."

Amanda gritted her teeth and took the flirting between the two of them in stride. Kate was good enough to get away with it, and apparently Douglas was, too. Not for a second should anyone be fooled into thinking Kate wasn't keen on every aspect of the mission. That would be a lethal underestimation. She genuinely was proficient at multitasking, and flirting relaxed her, making her more proficient. It wasn't Amanda's way, but whatever worked, worked, and she was a smart enough team leader to respect that.

Long before they reached the first of the three buildings, a man intercepted them, whispering loudly enough for anyone within fifty yards to hear him. "Amanda West? Amanda West?"

"Gaston?" Amanda whispered, recognizing his voice and his gait. She picked up her speed, stopped before him. "What the hell are you doing here?"

"Kunz evacuated me with the others."

"How did you know we were here?"

"He brought Mark here. It didn't take a genius to figure out as soon as you could, you'd come after him and then settle the score with Reese and Kunz."

"No," Amanda said. "I mean, how did you know Kate and I were here now? Are there monitors? Cameras?"

"Don't need them here. We're on the top of a mountain. Nothing comes into the compound unseen." He grabbed a breath, then went on. "I've been waiting for you since the recon team first showed up. I knew you wouldn't be far behind them." Gaston spared Kate a glance and winced when he saw blood on the knife in her hand. "Don't worry, Amanda. No one knows they've been here. I didn't report it, and I made sure the other guards stayed outside the perimeter and didn't see anything."

"Why?" Kate asked, blunt to a fault.

Gaston glared at her as if she were a bug. A stupid bug. "Because I'd like to get the hell out of here and get back to my life."

His tone didn't sit any better with Kate than his glare. She put a stiff bite in her voice he'd have to be dead to miss. "Which is—what?"

"Who the hell are you?" He pulled no punches with the verbal smack. "I'm trying to help your ass. Don't give me grief over it."

"Kate, this is Gaston." Amanda introduced them to give them a minute to let the level of tension between them diffuse. "He saved my backside when I was in the Texas compound."

"Sorry," Kate said. "We didn't expect any friendlies."

"No problem." He bristled but gave her the benefit of the doubt and let his hackles lower.

"How many of my guys are being held here?" Amanda asked. "And where are they being held?"

"Seven," Gaston said. "Belowground. It's a maze, Amanda. I'll have to take you there."

"Whoa, wait," Kate objected, ignoring the fact that Gaston could overhear every word she said. "This smells like a trap, Amanda."

"It isn't." Gaston glared at Kate.

Amanda looked from Kate to Gaston. He looked sincere. His body language rang true to what he was saying, and she knew he wasn't with Kunz by choice. At least, that's what he'd told her repeatedly. Once again, she opened her sensors and relied on her instincts. "Is this a trap, Gaston?"

"No, but there is a condition."

"Of course." Kate huffed a sigh.

Amanda sent her a squelching look. "What is it?"

"You have to take me with you. If I stay here, I'm dead."

"What's your affiliation?"

"I'm CIA," Gaston admitted. "That's all I'm free to tell you."

It was enough. "How long have you been with GRID?"

"Two years, one month, twelve days."

And he'd quite obviously hated every one of them. She

nodded. "Okay. I'm going to trust you, Gaston. Don't make me regret it."

"Not a problem. I've seen what happens to people who cross you. That was a real number you did on Reese's face, Amanda."

She didn't respond. What was there to say? She certainly had no intention of apologizing, and Reese had deserved worse. He was going to get it, too, just as soon as the opportunity presented itself. He'd hit her, trying to incite fear and dominate her. She hadn't forgotten that.

Her silence spoke volumes to Gaston. He turned and began a stealth ascent toward the second building. "Give me five minutes. I'll take care of the guard and, if we're lucky, you can walk right in."

Amanda nodded, backing against the concrete building.

Kate hit the wall beside her. "I don't like this. We're totally exposed."

"If you've got a better idea for getting into this fortress, I'm all ears."

Soon Gaston returned and signaled for them to follow him. Weapons drawn, they entered the building, took the winding corridors through the bowels of the underground system. Kate covertly dropped markers so that if push came to shove, they could follow them out—and, Amanda suspected—so that if Gaston took them in a circle, she could take him down without Amanda opposing.

They paused at a T in the tunnels. "It's a straight shot from here," Gaston whispered. "All seven are in a cell midway down. Guard's drugged at his desk at the other end. I'll run interference from here."

Amanda got an uneasy feeling in the pit of her stomach, but they didn't have a lot of choices, so she and Kate took the hallway, foot by foot, passing two openings, checking in front, behind, above and below for signs of any trouble.

Finally, she saw a door of steel bars and identified the men inside as Americans. None of them was Mark. Disappointment flooded her.

Kate rigged one of her incidentals and blew the door. The men were all capable of traveling, though a few were pretty bruised up. "Where's Captain Cross?" Amanda asked.

One of the men, sporting two black eyes and a busted nose, answered, "They took him out today in the helicopter."

"Where?"

"Don't know. No one knows, ma'am. But they did leave the compound with him. The guards were glad he was gone."

"Why?"

He looked at her as if she were a brick short. "He was Delta Force. They're scared shitless of Delta Force."

Mark wasn't here. Damn it, he wasn't here. "Wise of them." Why hadn't Gaston told her that? Now where did she look for him?

First priority had to be to get the detainees out. "Stay close between us." She motioned from herself to Kate. "Everyone can walk, right?"

"Yeah," the same man said. "We're all mobile."

Amanda took the lead and worked them back toward Gaston at the T in the tunnels. But when she got there, an unwelcome surprise awaited her that had her muttering curses under her breath and her finger itching on the trigger of her gun.

Paul Reese and not Gaston stood there, waiting for her.

"Where's Gaston?" she said.

"Sorry, who?" Reese smiled. The bandages were gone on his face, and the red scars were prominent. "Captain West, I'm so glad to see you again."

She just bet he was. "Let's go, Reese. You're outmanned and outgunned. Don't fight me on this. Just turn around and start walking."

"Of course." He turned and a metal plate dropped from the ceiling to the floor behind them, forming a wall.

They couldn't regress. Her instincts shoved her to push hard—hard and fast—and so she did. Drop-kicking Paul Reese in the face, on the same side as the scars she'd given him. He fought back. They were well matched, but she got lucky, landed an uppercut to his jaw and heard the bone crack.

He turned and fled, and suddenly disappeared. One second he was in the hallway; the next, there was no sight of him.

They backtracked out of the maze, following Kate's trail of markers. About halfway, Gaston lay in the dirt. Amanda paused, dropped down beside him.

"Is he dead?" Kate asked.

"No. Unconscious." She began lifting him, determined to find out why he hadn't told her Mark had been moved out. "Somebody help me here."

"We'll take him," one of the men said. A second one stepped forward, grabbed Gaston's free side. "You're armed. You lead us out."

Amanda again took the lead, moved swiftly and sure-footedly toward the entrance. She expected all hell to break loose at the mouth of the building. But it didn't.

It waited until they were out of the building in the middle of the open stretch of land between the building and the Apache. No place to take cover. No barriers. No protection. Nothing but scraped land. "Straight ahead," she told the men. "There's a chopper waiting. Haul ass." They scurried in the direction pointed.

Lights flashed, sirens wailed, and a flurry of men came running out of the third building.

Moving quickly, Kate rigged a line and planted explosives. "Call in tactical."

"No," Amanda said. "They'll be mown down." Lieutenant Douglas no doubt heard that transmission through his headset. "Stay put, Lieutenant."

"But, ma'am—damn it, ma'am—"

"Stay put!"

"Yes, ma'am," he responded, sounding disgruntled but resigned.

Glad to hear it, Amanda moved into position behind the line and warned Kate, "Hurry. You've got less than a minute."

The guards ran closer. And closer. Sweat popped out on Amanda's skin and trickled down her face. "Thirty seconds… Twenty… Getting close, Kate."

"Done!" Kate sprang up from a crouch.

Amanda took off running. Kate followed, close on her heels, allowing a reel of wire to freefall unwind from its spool.

"They're gaining on us." Amanda said, pumping her legs harder and harder until her knees were about to break from the jarring of hitting the rocky ground.

"Run faster."

The men were there at the chopper. Harry was hauling them inside. "Twenty seconds out." She glanced behind them at the guards following.

"There!" one shouted. "Ten o'clock."

Bullets rang out. Amanda and Kate ran in random patterns, making them more challenging targets. Finally, the bastards stepped into the kill zone.

Kate depressed the detonator, counted backward. "Five… Four…Three…Two…One."

A massive explosion shook the ground under their feet, sent dirt and rock and fire fifty feet into the air.

"Get us the hell out of here, Harry." Amanda hopped into the helicopter. Kate rolled in, landed beside her.

"Nice job." Amanda smiled.

"Yeah, it was, wasn't it?"

Amanda laughed. "You're taking a little too much pleasure in blowing stuff up, Kate."

"Hey, that's why I became an expert—so I could do it without going to jail for it."

Amanda spoke into her lip mike. "Lieutenant Douglas?"

"Yes, ma'am."

"Intel is light. Cover every inch of that rat maze and the grounds with thermal detectors. Reliable source says no doubles or other prisoners are on-site. See if he's in the know or blowing smoke. Also, check for anything that reveals locations or identities of detainees or doubles. If you recover a body that appears to be Thomas Kunz, verify it by DNA analysis. Visual isn't good enough."

"Yes, ma'am."

"Notify me of anything you get on him."

"Direct, ma'am?"

Typically, he'd satellite link to Intel at Langley. "Add me to the list."

"Yes, ma'am."

"Proceed at will."

"You heard the captain," she heard Douglas tell his team. "It's time to rock and roll."

Amanda glanced over at Gaston. He was coming around. Moving through the chopper, she stooped down beside him. "Where the hell is Mark? You said he was here."

"He was here. You didn't ask if he was still here, you just wanted to know where the detainees were. He'd been taken out earlier in the day. I didn't intend to offer unclear info."

What he'd said hit her. Her heart shattered. "He's dead?"

"No. No, not dead. Not yet, anyway." Gaston rubbed his throbbing skull. Reese had sacked him a good one. "Kunz sent him out just before dark tonight."

Fear loosened its grip, and relief about Mark washed through her. Anger at Gaston chased its heels. "Kunz is dead, Gaston," she said, putting him to the honesty test. "We have visual confirmation that he died in Texas." She grabbed him by the throat of his shirt. "Quit jerking me around."

"Whatever you say, Amanda. I'm telling you, Kunz was here today. You believe what the hell you want."

Maybe a double did the visual verification in Texas, or maybe the ID was simply a mistake. She paused. It verified what she already knew, instinctively. "Where did he send Mark?"

"I don't know." Gaston slumped against the wall of the chopper. "But I heard Reese say that sooner or later you'd figure it out. No doubt later. And Kunz said that was the plan. You'd be devastated and feel guilty forever. He'd have the ultimate revenge, hitting you where you live. That it was equitable payback for the resources you've caused him to lose." Gaston looked her straight in the eye and more than a little flicker of fear passed to her. "Kunz really hates you, Amanda."

"The feeling is mutual," she assured him. "You know, Gaston, you sure heard a lot for a man on our side."

Gaston frowned. "I'm supposed to hear a lot. It's my job and I'm damn good at it."

"Apparently. How did you manage to hear all this without being detected?"

"We have tools, Amanda. Just as you do."

He'd bugged either Kunz or Reese, she surmised, and put her odds on Reese.

"What did he have in mind—specifically?"

"He wasn't specific. But I took it that you'd find Mark, but he'd already be dead, and you'd blame yourself for it."

"Captain West?"

Amanda looked up to the pilot's seat at Harry. "Just got a patch from Colonel Drake, ma'am. Kunz's remains weren't found at the Texas compound. Drake's orders are to return to home base immediately. The tactical team is moving in to lock down the compound. Colonel Grant's called in Sweepers to mop up."

"Fine, Harry. Let's head home."

* * *

Hours later, Kate and Harry were sacked out on a C-5 heading for the States. Amanda was exhausted but couldn't sleep.

A flight attendant stopped at her side in the aisle. "Captain West?"

Amanda looked up at her.

"The captain says for you to tune in to frequency 129.8 on your headset."

"Thanks." She changed the frequency and waited.

"Captain West?" It was Secretary Reynolds. "Where's Cross?"

"I don't yet know, sir." Amanda had been racking her brain for hours, but couldn't imagine where the hell Kunz would put Mark.

"You have to find him."

Amanda's heart raced. "I intend to, sir." For personal and professional reasons. She knew what was coming and, God, but she didn't want to hear it.

"He's too skilled, his expertise and knowledge too valuable to be loose and in enemy hands."

Dread filled Amanda's stomach. But it didn't stop the inevitable.

"Damn it, I hate this," the secretary grumbled.

He hated it? She was about to lose it. Yet, here it came.

"Extricate or eliminate him, Captain West."

The order every operative with high-level security clearances knows is standard operating procedure in the interests of national security, but prays never to hear.

She had to talk around a fist of bitterness stuck in her throat. "Yes, sir." She swallowed hard, prayed harder that she wouldn't be put in the position of having to eliminate Mark. Her stomach flopped over and a vinegary taste of rebellion flooded her throat to her mouth. The idea alone had her nauseated and coming unglued. God help her, even in the case of national security she wasn't sure she could kill him.

"Hold on, Amanda," Secretary Reynolds said. "You've got a patch coming through from tactical. I'm monitoring."

Lieutenant Douglas. She stiffened. "Yes, sir."

"Captain West?"

"Go ahead, Lieutenant."

"We have a visual confirmation on a corpse who appears to be Thomas Kunz."

"Great."

"No, ma'am, not so great," Douglas said. "The field surgeon's pulled a quick exam. This Kunz has evidence of a number of plastic surgeries, including having the shafts of his leg bones shortened. He's a double, ma'am."

It figured, damn it. "What about detainees or other doubles?"

"Sensors picked up four detainees buried in a box on the grounds. We got them out and they're dehydrated and hungry but otherwise unharmed. No doubles have been retrieved."

Buried in a box? Hope lighted in her. "Was one of the detainees Captain Cross?"

"No, ma'am. I'm sorry."

Disappointment rippled through her and settled in. "Anything else to report?"

"Intel is going to remain light, ma'am. Every scrap of paper in the compound has been burned. A team's seeing if there's anything they can recover now."

"Thanks, Lieutenant. Keep me posted."

"Yes, ma'am." Douglas signed off.

Secretary Reynolds spoke up. "You have your orders, Captain."

Mark wasn't there. She had orders to extricate or eliminate him. Panic seized her stomach. *Okay. Okay, stop. You can't afford this, Princess.* She'd figure out later what *this* was. Right now she had to think. *Think like Kunz.*

She refused a beverage offer from the flight attendant. Amanda had met Kunz, talked with him, and had more insight on him than anyone else in the government—except maybe for Gaston. But Kunz didn't fear Gaston. He did fear her and he hated that fear. Kunz had to get rid of her and he would use Mark as bait. Payback for injuring and killing his men, while escaping with his chopper—as he had wanted her to do. If he hadn't, he would have nixed the plan, since he certainly knew about it courtesy of Mark's double. Kunz would play on her emotions and use them against her to destroy her. Not just her emotions, but her fears, too. Her *fears.* He would put Mark in a situation that would somehow reflect *her* darkest fears.

She thought about it all the way back to New York, then to Washington, and even more on her way to Providence Air Force Base in Florida. Somewhere over Carolina the obvious smacked into her. She didn't fear situations. She feared a place. Or at least Kunz thought she did.

A place he believed she wouldn't think about until it was too late.

Suddenly certain where Mark was, she got out of her seat, rushed up to the cockpit. "I need your radio, Captain."

"You have clearance?"

She reeled off her authorization number. "Tower Chief," she said, then followed with her ID information. "I need an emergency secure patch to Colonel Sally Drake, action officer, S.A.S.S." She reeled off the number, knowing it'd be relayed to the colonel at Providence in Florida.

Within two minutes, the patch was in place. "Go ahead, S.A.S.S. Higher headquarters is monitoring."

The colonel and either General Shaw or Secretary Reynolds. Maybe both. "Request emergency landing at the nearest airport to off-load all personnel aboard. I need the aircraft to get to North Carolina immediately, ma'am."

The pilot glowered at her as if she'd lost her mind. "Did you say you intend to commandeer my aircraft?"

"Yeah. Shut up, will you?"

Colonel Drake's voice sounded. "Purpose?"

Amanda shuddered. "Essential to extricate-or-eliminate order issued by Secretary Reynolds, ma'am." She would already have been notified that the target was Mark Cross.

"Scale?"

"Ten, ma'am." Drake's worst ranking. Honesty forced Amanda to add, "if not higher."

"Then you need backup."

"No, ma'am. No backup."

Drake hesitated. "Are you sure?"

"Positive, Colonel."

"Permission granted. Report your coordinates and estimated time of arrival as soon as possible."

"Yes, ma'am. The captain of this aircraft opposes surrendering possession, ma'am," Amanda said in what had to be the most colossal understatement of the year. The man glowered.

A man's voice interceded; one Amanda recognized. "Put him on the horn."

The captain was monitoring the conversation through his headset. "He's on, sir." Amanda lifted a hand.

"This is Captain Barnard Whitmore," he said, ignoring her rolling her gaze toward heaven at his formality. "To whom am I speaking?"

"Secretary of Defense Reynolds." He rattled off his security code, which sent Whitmore into a lathering tizzy. "Park the damn plane and turn it over to Captain West immediately. That is an order, Captain. Do you have any questions?"

His face turned green in the cockpit lights and it had nothing to do with the reflection of the soft glow beaming from the instrument panel. "Yes, sir. No, no questions, sir."

"Fine."

Colonel Drake returned to speaking. "Amanda, Thomas Kunz isn't dead."

"I know, ma'am. He was sighted at the Middle Eastern compound earlier today. He must have bugged out. What's supposed to be his corpse isn't. No idea where he is now."

Captain Whitmore intervened, his gaze fixed on the instrument panel. "You might want to take your seat, Captain West. We're about to land."

Amanda signed off and returned to her seat.

"What's up?" Kate asked.

"We're dropping you and the detainees off at the nearest airport. Colonel Drake is arranging transportation."

"Okay." Kate looked at her, gauging what to say and what not to discuss. "I'm sorry about Mark."

"He's still alive. At the moment, anyway."

"How do you know that?"

"Kunz wants to kill us both. Or to kill Mark and make me feel it's my fault—because I failed to save him. Unless I'm totally off, Kunz has only one way to accomplish that."

"How?"

"By stashing Mark in the place Kunz thinks I fear most." It'd be his final "in your face, I won" act. Actually, it was the only sensible possibility she'd been able to think of. If she proved wrong, she would feel as if she'd killed Mark.

"Guilt is a bitch, and Kunz does love playing mind games. If Mark, God forbid, is dead, you will take it personally and, I suspect, hard."

Amanda nodded. "So will you."

"I love him. You're in love with him."

Was she? Hell, she probably was, but it might take wild horses and a syringe of Sodium Pentothal to get her to admit it.

Kate's blue eyes went from sober to haunted, proving she had her own demons to face and fight. "Where is that? The place you fear?"

"My box."

Bewildered, Kate frowned. "What box?"

"My tomb, Kate."

Her mouth flattened into a grim flat line. "I'm going with you."

"No, you're not. He's probably got Gaston outfitted with a satellite tracker. You have to get him disconnected and get the rest of these people back to Providence unharmed and debriefed so Special Forces can start tightening the noose on this maniac. I can handle it alone."

"Can you? Really?"

"Kate, we're survivors, you and me. We do what we have to do to protect total strangers. We always have."

"True, but—"

"But nothing," Amanda interrupted. "It's who we are and what we do. So how much more will I be able to do for a man I'm crazy about—whether or not I want to be crazy about him?"

Kate stilled and looked deeply at Amanda. Finally, she answered. "Gauging on Drake's one-to-ten assessment scale, I'd say about forty-seven."

"At least forty-seven. Frankly, I'm not fond of the feelings, so I'm shielding."

"Honey, if this is shielding, you're hovering at the hundred mark."

Amanda issued a frown meant to freeze out further comments and then checked her weapons. Her instincts said that if Mark was still alive inside that tomb, Kunz had no intention of letting her just walk up and dig him out.

He'd have a surprise waiting for her. No doubt about it. And if she wasn't careful, it would be a deadly surprise.

## Chapter 17

Alone on the C-5, Amanda put through a secure radio patch to Colonel Drake. After the initial information exchange, she asked for the location of the nearest landing strip with C-5 capability.

"It's too far from the drop zone, Captain," Drake said. "I've contacted our friends who man the zone. They recommend you use the highway."

It was an isolated area, traffic would be minimal or nonexistent.

"If you'll verify your ETA, we'll have that section closed off."

"No, ma'am. Not necessary." Amanda adjusted the flaps, banked right twenty degrees, following the flight plan. "The area could be wired or crawling with company."

"So you're going in solo in a C-5. That'll make quite an entrance, Captain."

Drake's disapproval was evident. "Back-dooring it, ma'am."

"I'm sending in backup."

"If you do, I guarantee Captain Cross will be D.O.A." Dead on arrival got Colonel Drake's attention in a huge way. Her husband had been D.O.A. after a home invasion three years ago where she, and not he, had been the intended target. "I know the enemy, Colonel, and in this case, it isn't me."

"Scale?"

"Ten, ma'am. But more manpower won't affect the value rating or the odds for success."

"Anticipated survival rate?"

"Fifty percent." Amanda felt sweat bead on her neck, roll down her nape and soak her collar.

"Anything we can do to increase it?"

Amanda paused and decided to be totally candid. "Only one thing comes to mind, ma'am."

"Name it."

Amanda licked her lips, then said softly, "Pray."


Black clouds drifted between Amanda and the waning moon, and the humidity hung in the air as thick as honey.

She'd landed the plane on the highway in the recommended stretch, disembarked, and disappeared into the woods. The cemetery was about two kilometers due north. Whomever Kunz had waiting for her would expect her to arrive from the drop zone. Hopefully, the shift in ingress would give her a small advantage, however short-lived.

About a quarter kilometer out, her night-vision gear failed. She removed it, checked the compass on her watch and kept moving. Without clear sight, she had to move more slowly than she liked and to rely heavily on her other senses.

Smells were potent and plentiful: earth and decaying leaves, trees and wet grass. It had rained earlier that day. Maybe Mark had been able to punch through the wall of the tomb enough to get water. But it seemed unlikely Kunz would copy Reese's mistake and bury an arrow with Mark to show one-upmanship.

Did Kunz collect anything he would bury with Mark?

She mentally reviewed his dossier and found the only things he collected were intelligence to black market and the lives of other people. Lives he stole and destroyed, like Harding's and Sloan's and the women they had loved.

Mark flooded Amanda's thoughts.

Poor guy would be dehydrated, obsessed with wanting a drink of water. Remembering that thirst had her reaching for her canteen and taking only a small sip. When she rescued him, he would need it all, and coming from this direction, she wouldn't pass the artesian well for a refill.

Finally, she made it to the edge of the cemetery. All was quiet. Normal night sounds: an owl's soft hoot, crickets chirping, frogs croaking, the light wind whispering through the leaves. No scents of skin or soap or sweat or anything people-related that didn't belong here. No unnatural visuals apparent in an intense, though unassisted-by-technology scan conducted in the dim moonlight.

The absence of signs of a trap had her edgy and hyperalert. Kunz had something in store for her here. *Something, somewhere.* Had he rigged the tomb itself? When she punched through the wall, would it detonate a bomb that would kill Mark? That would be a coup de grâce for Kunz. He would love to see Mark dead and her survive to carry the guilt for killing him the rest of her days.

*Mind games.*

The bastard loved them. She eased from tomb to tomb. Utter stillness surrounded her and doubt attacked. What if she was wrong? What if Mark wasn't here at all? She'd been so sure, but he could be somewhere else, dying because she'd made a mistake.

Her stomach coiled in knots, her throat bitter and tight, she lifted a hand and touched the brick of her tomb, let her fingertips glide over its rough surface, unsure whether to hope that she was right or pray that she wasn't.

The mortar was wet.

A flood of emotions coursed through Amanda: relief, fear, joy, anger, confirmation, vindication and stark terror. All were intense and all simultaneous, sending supercharged adrenaline rocketing through her body, electrifying every nerve, every cell.

She pulled in three slow, even breaths and centered her emotions, then let her training kick in.

A visual inspection of the tomb netted no signs of explosives, wires or anything else that could cause lethal consequences. Remembering Kunz's trip wires four inches below the surface at the Middle Eastern compound, she dug into the soft earth with her bare fingertips but found nothing.

Still, her instincts warned her that neither Kunz nor Reese would ever make the rescue this easy.

*Unless Mark was already dead.*

But her same instincts told her both of them would see to it she did the killing, if at all possible. The guilt would be a bigger burden for her to carry than just being too late. At some distant point in time, a woman could forgive herself for being too late. They would want to insure she never forgave herself, and that she never forgot what she'd done wrong.

Dropping to a crouch, she pulled her tool bag out of her gear, removed a hatchet. The blade gleamed in the moonlight.

She smelled cloves.

The hair on her neck stood on edge. Paul Reese smoked clove cigarettes. She hadn't seen any cigarette butts on the ground around the tomb, but the scent was distinct, pungent and unmistakable.

She stood up—and a man leaped from atop the tomb, knocking her off her feet. The hatchet slipped from her grasp and landed in the dirt with a muffled thud. He landed on top of her, nailing her shoulders to the ground. His elbow jabbed into her ribs. Her breath swooshed out on a painful groan, and before she could recover, he straddled her and pinned her arms in the dirt above her head. Her heart bouncing off her ribs and into her throat, she looked up into a face she had learned to hate. "Reese."

"I'm going to kill you, Amanda. You're too late to save your lover, and now I'm going to kill you and bury you with him."

Mark couldn't be dead. He couldn't. Damn it, she'd dared to risk caring about him, loving him. He couldn't be dead!

Emotions poured through her, as hot and heavy as lava. She couldn't lock them away. Not this time. "How amorous—and typical of you, Paul." She crimped her fingers, clawing in the dirt, seeking the hatchet, but it was too far away. Disappointment rippled through her, and she fought down a wave of panic. "But you're a liar. I don't believe you have the balls to go one-on-one with Mark, much less to do what it would take to kill him."

"A .38 is a hell of an equalizer."

"Not in a liar's hands."

"Stop calling me a liar. Do you hear me?" A muscle under his eye ticked. He raised a fist and punched her in the jaw. "Stop it."

Pain exploded in the entire side of her face. Even her eye seemed to throb.

"You slept with me to get inside GRID. What does that make you?"

"Desperate to stop you before you destroyed any more lives." She bucked and he lost his seat atop her. She twisted, slammed a foot into the back of his head at the base of his skull. His head jerked, but he'd been braced, ready for the blow, and that prevented his neck from breaking.

He rolled, caught her by the arms and seized the advantage. She fought back, doing her damnedest to reclaim it. They tumbled in the dirt, slammed fists to flesh, traded punches and jabs and kicks until both were huffing, winded and covered in sweat and blood.

Amanda couldn't sustain hand-to-hand combat against him much longer. He was well trained, larger and stronger. More importantly, he was intimately familiar with every survival technique she'd been taught and some she'd never before seen used. The longer this played out, the greater the odds Reese would win, and she and Mark would wind up dead.

Marking her time, she backed off, parried, and finally got an opening. She stopped, dropped and rolled, snagged her hatchet and then bounced to her feet. Knowing he expected her to come at him with the hatchet, she feinted and thrust hard with a series of kicks that had him sprawled in the dirt. He hit his head on a rock and from the way he shook it, she knew he was seeing double. Before he found his balance, she had him pinned. "Where's Kunz?"

He smiled, his mouth red-rimmed with blood. "He's not dead, Amanda. He'll be along after you soon."

She'd be along after him sooner. He'd deliberately allowed her to escape with Mark's double so he could fake his own death then disappear until the heat on him cooled and he could rise like a phoenix to press on with his slimy business of selling and stealing other people's lives. "I asked a question and I want an answer, Reese. You can respond or wear a Mohawk. I don't give a damn which, you sorry excuse for a human being."

Reese laughed and groaned simultaneously. His right wrist was broken and, gauging by the gurgle in his breathing, he'd suffered a few broken ribs. "You thought you had him. He never evacuated, Amanda. He was there all the time."

"In Texas?" She couldn't believe it. "Do I look stupid,

Reese? The FBI has crawled over every inch of that com-pound. There's nothing left to it."

"Apparently, you're all stupid. He isn't *in* the compound, Amanda. He never was." He laughed again, deeper. "He's *under* it. None of your ace investigators looked under it. You, of all people, should have thought of that. You ran the maze of tunnels yourself in Afghanistan."

Oh, hell. She had to warn Colonel Drake. But first, she had to secure Reese. Her legs were shaking now; she didn't have the stamina for another round with him. Amanda stood up. "Move and I'll kill you." She moved to her gear to get some rope. He was going to die for hitting her, but he was going to tell her every damn thing he knew about GRID and Thomas Kunz first.

Prone on the ground, Reese eased his left hand to his waist, pulled out a snub-nosed .38 and drew down on her.

Amanda caught the flash of the metal in the moonlight, re-acted instinctively, and threw the hatchet. It sank deep in the center of Paul Reese's chest.

The gun fell harmlessly to the ground. Reese slumped for-ward, chest to knees, and then swayed to the side until he lay bent on the ground.

Shaking, Amanda retrieved her hatchet, checked for a pulse and felt nothing. Reese was dead.

Mark.

She returned to the tomb, hacked away at the mortar and soon punched through a small opening. "Mark? Mark, are you there?"

"Amanda?" He sounded afraid to believe.

Her throat went thick and a hitch caught in her chest. "It's me," she said, her voice a husky rasp. "I'm here." *Oh, God. He was still alive. He was here and alive!*

"Water."

Remembering, again feeling that insatiable thirst, she swallowed hard. "I know. I'm hurrying." Tears flooded her eyes and she swung harder, faster, with renewed force. Mark was alive. "Get as far away from the hole as you can. I'm using a hatchet."

"Don't miss."

She laughed through her tears, her vision blurred, her nose still stinging. "I won't."

Finally, the hole was large enough and she passed the canteen through to him.

"Thank God." He snagged it, and the sounds of him chugging down water echoed.

A lump in her throat, she worked with renewed fervor. Finally, the hole was large enough and he climbed out.

When he stood on the ground before her, she stilled with the hatchet in hand and just stared at him. In an odd twist, her first thought was to wonder. Was he really Mark? Or was he another of Mark's doubles?

Kunz had been good enough at mind games to pull off a double-switch. Of course he had been.

*But had he done it with Mark?*

Her nerves wired tight, she opened her mouth to investigate. Yet before she could say a word, Mark smiled and it touched his eyes. "In plain sight," he said, then opened his arms to her.

She dropped the hatchet, stepped into his arms and curled hers around his waist, then breathed in deeply. The familiar scent of his skin filled her, melted the fear of his being anyone else, and it drained away. She smiled and hugged him hard, relieved and happy from the heart out. "In plain sight, baby," she said, passing him back the canteen without drinking from it.

He drank deeply, then found her mouth and they kissed without restraint or pretense, ignoring the pain of bruises and battles, the dirt caking skin, the sweat and the thirst for water, taking total joy and heart in quenching their thirst for something longer-lasting and more real: the first touch of the reunion they had feared would never be.

# Chapter 18

They walked along the edge of the highway in the dark, and rounded a bend in the road. The C-5 came into view, and Amanda glanced at Mark.

His jaw hung loose, stunned. "Hell of a parking place, hon."

"We use what we've got." She smiled and clasped his hand, oddly content to be touching him.

He squeezed her fingers. "I thought about you a lot while I was in that tomb, Amanda." His voice turned sober. "And while I knew you were with my double."

She wasn't ready to tell him what had happened between her and his double, but it looked as though she wasn't going to have a choice. And, being honest with herself, if their positions were reversed, she would want answers now, too. She could hardly ask more from him than of herself. But, oh, man, would she like to. "Mark, you know how I feel about men—because of my…"

"Father."

She nodded, even now unable to make herself say the word aloud. "But I trust you, and things between us…well, they got…intense and personal."

"How personal?" He didn't look at her. "A little personal or really personal?"

"Really personal." She swallowed down a boulder that seemed to have wedged in her throat. God, this was hard. Much harder than she had imagined it would be, and that had been pretty bad. "Later, I found out you weren't you and I felt as if I'd betrayed you. And I felt betrayed."

"You felt pissed off," he countered, still not meeting her gaze.

She didn't know whether or not to be grateful, but it felt like a merciful thing. "That, too," she admitted with a little shrug. There was little sense in denying the obvious. "I finally trust a man, and he isn't the man I think he is. He's someone pretending to be the man I trust. Yeah, you bet I was pissed. But I was…other things, too."

"I can imagine." He worried at his inner lip with his teeth for a long moment, then stuffed his hands in his pockets. "You were embarrassed because you'd been fooled and manipulated."

"Yes." She definitely had been.

He went on. "You were furious because you hadn't been able to tell the difference between him and me, and outraged because you'd finally let your guard down to a man and he deceived and used you."

She blew out a sharp breath that puffed her cheeks. "All of that, too."

He stopped on the road and turned to face her. "But most of all, I think you were scared of what might have happened to me, or what was happening to me. Am I right about that?"

She searched his eyes, her own heart, and knew that hiding her emotions and locking them in her internal safe was part of her past, not her future. "Yes, you're most right about that."

He clasped her shoulders, the night breeze ruffling his hair, blowing cool on her heated face. "I understand, Amanda," he said softly. "All of it."

The backs of her eyes burned. He couldn't *know* or *understand*. "You don't," she insisted, determined to get this out in the open. If they were going to go anywhere in this relationship, they had to start with a foundation based on truth.

"I do," he insisted. "Honestly."

"You can't, damn it." A hot rush of agony pierced her chest. "I slept with him, Mark. I—I thought he was you—but—oh, hell, Mark. I slept with him."

Mark looked deeply into her eyes and then calmly stroked her face with such tenderness that tears welled. She blinked hard to keep them from falling, not willing to suffer yet another humiliation in this. "I know, honey."

He kissed her soundly, proving he did know and that he did understand. But how could he? Guilt settled over her, streamed through her, weighing her down. "How can you accept something so awful so easily? I don't get it. If it were you, I don't know if I'd be able to get past it. I hope I would, but I can't stand here and say with authority that I know I would—not without lying to you. I—"

"Amanda, hush." He caressed her face, cupping it in both his hands and rubbed gently with the pads of his thumbs. "You thought you were with me. I know that. Don't you see, Amanda? In your mind, you were with me, not him. You wanted me. You let me into your life and your heart."

He pulled her close, rubbed her shoulders. "Listen, at first I admit I was jealous as hell when I thought of him being with you. I was hurt and angry. But then I realized I was being crazy. Even he thought he was me. Being jealous was like being jealous of myself." He buried his chin in her neck and pecked a kiss to her hair. "You really care about me. How can I not understand that, Amanda? After everything you've been through, you took the risks and let me in. You care about me."

Her heart swelled, too big for her chest. She sniffed, hugged him hard. "Peanut puns aside, I really am nuts about you, Cross."

"I know." He gave her a squeeze and then stole her canteen again and swallowed down a long tug. "It has me questioning your judgment."

She chuckled. "Glad to hear it. Maybe there's hope for you yet." She wrapped her arm around his waist, and they walked onto the plane.

Mark had slight tremors from dehydration, so Amanda took the pilot's seat. When they were airborne, she radioed Colonel Drake and advised the colonel to have their drop-zone friends retrieve Reese's body from the cemetery.

"I have reliable intel on Kunz's location," she finished.

"Amanda, I now have three separate confirmations that Kunz is dead," the colonel replied. "One is for the old Kunz, the two are for the new Kunz."

"He's alive, ma'am."

Colonel Drake said softly, "So if the real Kunz isn't dead then where the hell is he?"

"Kunz is in Texas," Amanda told her. "There's a network of tunnels and bunkers under the compound."

"Stand by."

The radio went silent. Colonel Drake was no doubt seeking intel on what they'd found at the explosion site to back up Amanda's claim. Soon, she returned to the radio.

"Field reports deny any findings to substantiate your intel, Captain."

"Ma'am. I was in there. I know the bunker exists." When she'd been blindfolded on Hangar Row and taken to Kunz's office, it must have been down in the bunkers or there would have been no reason to blindfold her to take her there. Kunz hadn't wanted her to know about the bunkers.

"Then get your ass down there and point them out to SAIC Mac McDonald."

The Special Agent in Charge obviously hadn't welcomed Colonel Drake's inquiry or responded well to her claim that the corpse wasn't that of Thomas Kunz. "In the appropriated aircraft, ma'am?" Amanda asked.

"Affirmative, Captain." A man's voice sounded through the radio. "I'm elevating this to a Code Two Special Project." The order was clear and succinct: do what you need to do to get the job done quickly. "How's your fuel?"

Amanda looked at Mark. "Who the hell is this guy?"

"Secretary Reynolds."

"Oh." She reeled in her tone, chastising herself for not recognizing his voice right away. Just proved how distracted she was by Mark. Being distracted at the wrong time could get her killed. Her heart rebelled against that thought. It'd wear off. Short-term, being with him would up her risks, but it wouldn't last. "Fuel's getting low, sir."

"Drake, arrange refueling and get them whatever else they need," Reynolds said. "I want this bastard Kunz, and I want him now. I want Reese, too."

"Reese is dead, sir," Amanda informed the secretary.

"Have you verified that firsthand, Captain? There's a lot of verified corpses turning up alive around here right now."

"I killed him myself, sir," she said.

"That's the kind of verification I like best, Captain." Reynolds turned his attention to the colonel. "Drake, give the order to move on Kunz."

"Yes, sir." Colonel Drake then spoke to Amanda and Mark. "We'll arrange refueling. What else do you need?"

About two weeks of sleep. A hot bath and a warm meal.

To make love with Mark. She looked over at him, raised an eyebrow in question. He pointed at her. Her heart gave a little quiver and she smiled. "Nothing at this time, ma'am. Except for some food and water for Captain Cross." *But later, watch out.*

Shortly after four o'clock in the afternoon, Amanda landed the plane on the Texas compound's airstrip. Running on adrenaline that was fizzling out and a few precious catnaps, she looked around, stunned by the amount of damage Kunz had caused to his own assets.

The compound looked as if it had been pulverized by a hurricane. Debris from the explosion littered the ground and trash and remnants of everything from equipment to clothes clung to bushes and trees. The scent of explosives clung to the humid air.

"Wow. He really fired it up, didn't he?" Mark stepped off the plane and set foot on the ground. "Kate couldn't have done better."

A lieutenant drove over in a golf cart. "Captains West and Cross?" he asked, his hair tousled from the wind, his face red from the heat.

"Yes," they said in unison.

"Hop in. SAIC MacDonald is expecting you."

Amanda got strange flutters in her stomach on getting into the cart. The whole experience was too reminiscent of the time she'd spent captive here. From Mark's somber expression, he was sharing the same feelings.

When they had circled the golf course and neared what had been the main building and was now a heap of burnt-out rubbish, the lieutenant stopped the cart.

A man pushing forty with graying temples and a sallow complexion on a face shaped like a pit bull's walked over to them. "West? Cross?"

"SAIC MacDonald?" Mark extended his hand.

Amanda didn't. He looked cranky enough to bite it off.

"Mac," he said. "Listen, I've had everyone on-site looking for some kind of entrance to this bunker system since Drake contacted us. We've found nothing." Skepticism filled his face and voice. "You sure your intel is solid?"

"As a rock," Amanda said. "I was in the bunker."

"Then how the hell did you get there?" He looked relieved that she knew where the ingress was located and irritated that his people hadn't been able to locate it on their own.

"I don't know exactly," she admitted through clenched teeth. This wouldn't go over well, but facts were facts. "I was blindfolded."

"Then how do you know you were in a bunker?"

"The lack of outside noises, the smell of recycled air, the absence of windows, any moving wind or natural scents. We were definitely underground, Mac."

Her answer must have satisfied him because he didn't dispute her. "Take the cart," he suggested, motioning for the lieutenant to evacuate it. "Look around and see if you can find the entrance. So far, we've tapped out."

"Sure." Amanda got into the passenger's side.

"We need a radio—to keep in touch," Mark said, getting in behind the wheel.

"Lieutenant, handle it." Mac turned from the young man back to Mark. "Anything else?"

"Water. Water would be nice."

Amanda's chest clutched. He'd emptied her canteen, and the refill from the emergency run she'd made to the artesian well near the cemetery to get him hydrated enough to make the hike back to the plane. He'd also emptied the water supply on the plane, and an additional gallon of water they had picked up during refueling.

Still, she knew that camel-like thirst. It would take days to quench it, and a lifetime to forget it.

The lieutenant returned with a radio and six bottles of water. "Sorry it's not cold, sir. We're primitive."

"Not a problem. Thanks." Mark took the items, cranked a top off one bottle, swallowed long and deep, and then took off. "Where do we go first?" he asked Amanda.

"Hangar Row," she said, weary to the bone. "I know we weren't far from there when they blindfolded me. Were you taken to Kunz's office?"

"No, I wasn't," he said, swerving to the opposite side of the road to bypass the twisted remains of something metal and no longer identifiable. "I was in a cabin some but they had me in a holding tank mostly. All-white padded cell. Empty, except for the cameras at the ceilings in the corners." He grunted. "A lot like the tomb except it was never dark."

Sensory deprivation and constant light induced a type of dementia. People lost track of day and night and time, and the disorientation played with their minds, weakened their ability to resist interrogation or input. She reached over and clasped his hand, grounding him in the now so he could let go of the then.

It was a small gesture, but it made all the difference in this situation. Appreciation and warmth shone in Mark's eyes. He lifted her hand and kissed her swollen knuckles. "Reese?"

She nodded, knowing the bruises on her face said far more than any words. "You should see the other guy." Her record remained intact.

"I did." He let out a low whistle. "Remind me to never piss you off when you have a weapon in your hand."

Cruising down the road between the hangars, she grunted. "Baby, don't you remember survival school? *Anything* can be a weapon."

"Yeah, I remember, and I won't forget it again when dealing with you." He smiled. "See anything?"

"Not yet." They rode from the hangers in all four directions, and then repeated the process a second time. And then a third, but still she saw nothing that she could pinpoint.

"You look so tired," Mark said.

"It's been a long—" she went blank "—hell, however long it's been. I've lost track."

"Too damn long," Mark said, glancing out over the debris. "Don't worry. I'll be your calendar."

"You're so good to me." The charred smells of burnt plastic and wood hung heavy in the air.

"That's the plan. Integrate and make myself indispensable." He sent her a speculative look. "Unless you have any objections?"

She worked at not melting into a humiliating puddle at his feet. He already had become indispensable to her. "Not if you meet one condition."

"What's that?" He didn't look worried, only curious.

She loved him for that. "Remember those little computer games you invented that all the college kids play? The ones that made you rich enough to own a view of the water that a house and deck came with, a boat and a Hummer?"

"Dirty Side Down," he said. "Yes."

"That is where all your money comes from—the games—right?"

"Yes. From them, my captain's salary and investments." He looked a little embarrassed. "But what does that have to do with your condition? Do you need money, Amanda?"

"No, I don't need any money." So different from her father. So giving and caring. Men really could be good to women. Some men, anyway. Mark's kind of man. "I want to win."

"The game?" he asked, his jaw dropping loose. "You play?"

She nodded. "Often—with Kate. We both have come close, but neither of us has ever won the damn thing." She shrugged. "I want to win."

He let out a little laugh. "You got it."

"There's one more condition."

"Greedy little thing, aren't you?" He kissed her wrist to take the sting out of his comment.

"Yeah."

"Well, what is it?"

"We sit on your deck and fish until sundown together as often as our crazy schedules allow us to. In the last year, it's the only place on the planet where I've felt mellow and at peace."

"It's the view."

It was the company *and* the view, but she wouldn't mention it. "Right."

"That works for me." He spared her a glance. "Now it's my turn."

His conditions. A little bubble of fear burst in her stomach. "Go ahead."

"Hand me another bottle of water."

She passed the water to him. "Is that it?"

"That's it."

"You're so easy, Mark." She smiled and let her head droop onto his shoulder—and noticed an odd little building. Its shape reminded her of the buildings leading into the bunkers in Afghanistan. "Stop." She bolted straight up in her seat. "Mark, stop."

He hit the brakes. "What?"

"There." She pointed to the wooden shack. "We need to look there."

He stopped alongside the shack and they opened the door. "It's a toolshed."

All the paraphernalia needed for maintaining the golf

course. But something was off. Seriously off. The warning prickled at her at the instinctive level. "If it's just a toolshed, why is it still standing when everything around it is rubble?"

"Good question." Mark pulled out his gun and a flashlight.

Amanda did as well, and they began examining the walls, ceiling and floor.

"It's too shallow," Mark said. "The outer shell is at least six feet deeper."

"False wall?" Amanda moved to the rear of the building.

Finally they found it—a panel hidden behind a rake hanging on the wall. Mark pushed it and Amanda took a defensive stance, aiming her weapon straight ahead.

A wood-faced, thick metal door swung open.

"Radio Mac," Amanda whispered.

Mark did. "Mac, we found it."

"Where?"

"Hangar Row. A wooden toolshed." He gave further, more explicit directions.

"Wait for backup before going down," Mac said. "We're on the way."

Mark looked over at Amanda, who gave him a negative shake of her head. "Mac, say again. You're breaking up."

"Don't pull that crap on me, Cross," Mac shouted, obviously onto Mark and Amanda's plans. "I said wait for backup."

Mark turned the radio off, hefted his .45 Colt and followed Amanda into the tunnel.

# Chapter 19

They moved carefully along the tunnel's single corridor, weapons drawn, senses wide open, instincts on high alert.

Amanda swept and scanned. White walls, ceiling and floor. Empty. Unadorned. No photographs of the alias Thomas Kunz hung here as they had every six feet in the aboveground buildings. And no security-monitor cameras or obvious sensors were mounted near the ceiling or ankle-high on the walls. The floor felt a little spongy; it could be pressure-sensor embedded. But if it was, they'd just have to deal with it because the corridor was too wide for her or even Mark to walk the walls and stay off the floor.

About twenty meters in, they came to a double fork. The air smelled stale and recycled and tinged with the burnt scents so prevalent aboveground, but no guards appeared. Not one. Amanda had an odd feeling that wasn't because she and Mark had entered undetected. Unsure what to make of it, she maintained stern discipline and moved with even more caution. Recalling her blindfolded walk into Kunz's office, she whispered to Mark, "It was a hundred twenty-seven steps from smelling fresh air to his office with a right turn along the way. We've gone sixty-three."

He acknowledged hearing her with a hand signal, and motioned to the right-most tunnel. The lighting in it was dim, but too bright for night-vision gear to be effective. Kunz had played that one perfectly.

Only Amanda's and Mark's shadows rippled on the ceiling, floor and walls; this corridor was also empty. They passed three openings to rooms that stood empty—training rooms, judging by the overhead projectors, film screens and audio equipment—and stopped when the corridor came to a dead end. Mark examined the back wall. Amanda took the left then the right. No panels, no triggers for secret openings. The corridor had truly come to a dead end.

"Nothing else here," Mark confirmed her assessment and turned around.

They backtracked to the fork and took the next tunnel, moving systematically. Again, they encountered no one. The place looked and felt empty. Spotting a large opening at the end of the tunnel, they approached with elevated caution. It was an operations center. Monitors lined two walls and back-lit maps covered the others. Desks littered with computers and phones, three fax machines, a megaduty copier, and in a little anteroom, vaults. A second alcove room had a table and chairs, coffeepot, sink and refrigerator. The cabinets were stocked with food and the fridge was full of cold drinks. The computers were on, everything was working, but there were no people manning the desks or computers. It was as if they'd been working one second and had just gotten up and left the next—which well might be exactly what had happened.

And which raised a vitally important question: *Where did they go?*

"Hopefully, we'll find out who's been doubled." Mark looked pointedly at the computers and then at the vaults.

It looked promising, she had to admit, but they couldn't afford to forget whom they were dealing with here. "I wouldn't bank on it." Amanda took a closer look at the computers. "No hard drives." She didn't check—leave it to the experts. "I'll bet they've wiped the RAM, too, and there's nothing recoverable on any of them."

"Maybe investigators will have better luck with the vault."

"You think?" Amanda looked over at Mark.

He frowned. "No. Not really."

"Your judgment might be okay after all, Cross."

"I have excellent taste in women. That should count for something."

"Oh, it does." She backed out of the room and into the tunneled corridor. "Kunz wouldn't lead us to what we want. It's not his style. He loves the game. Playing with our heads."

"I wish I could disagree." Mark followed her down the tunnel. "But the truth is, anything we find here will be only what he wants us to find."

Back at the fork, they took the next corridor. "Has to be it," Mark said, looking down the corridor. "Otherwise you would have made a left turn."

Amanda's stomach fluttered, and she double-checked her weapon. For a second, she thought she might be overreacting, but then she saw Mark do the same thing, and his shoulders tense in a way they hadn't moments ago. She felt more confident in her gut-level reaction.

She led the way down the corridor. This one was even more dimly lit than the others. So far, she saw nothing, but her instincts shouted that, unlike the others, this corridor wasn't empty. She moved cautiously, slowly, hyperalert to any sounds, smells or sensory perceptions.

They passed an empty room—stark and barren, not so

much as a scrap of paper littered the floor. "He kept the records here," she said, knowing it as well as she knew she needed to draw her next breath to live.

"Looks that way." Mark backed up. "He had to have pulled them out before you escaped from here."

"Yeah. Probably on the same flight as the detainees, though I'll bet my ass those records are not and never were at the Middle Eastern compound."

"He's got a place no one—not even Reese—knows about, Amanda. His retreat. That's where the records are."

"Do you know this for a fact?"

"No, but it's what you or I would do in his position. We'd have a sanctuary, and we'd go to it."

She thought about it and agreed. "It's frustrating. I have no idea where Kunz's sanctuary would be."

"Neither do I. But something, somewhere will lead us to it."

"In this lifetime?" The world was a big place for one man to hide. Especially when damn few people recognized that man as himself.

Mark thought about it, and didn't answer. He had his doubts about routing out Kunz, too.

Amanda moved on down the corridor. Two more empty rooms, and then a chill crept up her backbone. The next doorway would be at a hundred twenty-seven steps. Her mouth suddenly went dust dry. She licked her lips, paused just before the slightly ajar door, looked inside and saw the edge of a desk.

*Kunz's office.*

She stopped, lifted a finger to signal Mark that this was it, and motioned to him with the barrel of her gun.

He nodded and moved in front of her.

A man's voice sounded from within. "Come in, Captain West. I've been expecting you."

*Kunz.* She nodded to verify it to Mark.

"No need for concern. I'm not going to resist." His elevated voice ended in a wistful sigh. "There's little sense in it now."

Amanda touched Mark's arm, signaling him to step aside. He frowned, clearly opposed to doing it, but she insisted with a stronger nudge.

She crouched low, rolled into the room and landed on her feet behind the leather chair she once had sat in. "Hands up, Thomas."

He raised them. In one, he held a glass filled with ice, and if the smell proved right, bourbon. "I said I have no intention of resisting, Captain."

"This seems a bit too easy, Thomas. Us just walking in and finding you unprotected."

"Ah, isn't that what you're always looking for, Amanda? A break? Again, I'm not resisting. You've won." His placating smile didn't reach his eyes. "You can lower your weapon now."

"Lower my weapon? I'm going to kill you, you twisted son of a bitch." She took a two-handed stance and aimed at his forehead, right between his eyes. "You've done too much harm to too many for me to ever let you walk out of here alive."

He sipped from his drink, again raised his hand. "I permitted Paul to rape the good doctor in front of her husband. That's your primary challenge with me."

Amanda shook with fury. "It ranks right up there on the list with stealing other people's lives."

"Don't shoot, Amanda," Mark said from behind her. "He's more valuable to us alive than dead."

Surprise widened Kunz's eyes and the ice tapped his glass; his hand shook. He hadn't expected her to have to fight for discipline. She reveled in knowing he had underestimated her and he was afraid. And yet her training began intruding; the discipline he expected was, and should be, second nature.

"He deserves to die, Mark," she insisted, eager to shoot him and watch him die the way he'd watched so many others. She'd be merciful. She wouldn't torture. She wouldn't remove skin or bones or sew mouths shut or blind people just to watch them writhe in pain and suffer and then kill them. She wasn't sadistic, but she'd gladly provide humanity a service by just shooting his sorry ass and having justice done.

"Yes, he deserves to die," Mark agreed, his voice calm and reasonable. "But not before we use him to save the others."

Her hands shook violently, her finger twitching on the trigger. She battled the demon inside her that wanted to throw logic out the window, the outraged woman who had been hurt and used and abused by this man after swearing to never be hurt or used or abused by any man again. "We'll find what we need without him."

Mark stepped to her side, touched her arm and gently lowered the barrel of the gun. "No, we won't. And even if we could, we can't do this."

"I think I could."

"Please, don't. Not this way. This is his way, honey, not yours or mine. If he dies now, it's over for him while we chase shadows, looking for his demented doubles and the detainees he's put on ice. If he lives, he'll be a prisoner for life—just like he made others prisoners."

"You don't understand," she said from between clenched teeth. "You don't know everything he's done."

"Tell me."

Amanda glared at him. "He didn't just let Reese rape Joan in front of Simon. He made Jeremy watch." Anguish flooded her voice.

"Then you owe it to Joan to give her the chance to regain her dignity. Joan should have dibs," Mark spoke softly. "She knows how to make Kunz talk. She knows how to make *any-*

*one* talk. Let her make him talk and tell us how to find the others. Give Joan control over his destiny."

That "control" resonated with Amanda, but still she fought the battle of wills between right and wrong and justice and vengeance and good and evil. It was an intense battle that carried her back to her youth, to her father and that damn box, and scarred from the effort, she fought to remember not the child she had been, but the woman she had become.

Strength took root in her, temperance and the lessons she'd learned in life added to it, and she grew stronger and stronger, overtaking the red haze that had nearly made her like Kunz and her father.

Battle-worn and scarred, the woman she had forged by will and choice emerged, and she claimed her victory. "You'll never set foot outside prison again, Thomas. I swear it."

He gave her a look of mild interest, as if it were all that the situation warranted or all that he could be bothered to invest. "Never is a very long time. Soon, other matters will occupy your time, Captain."

Before she could respond, Mark interceded. "If anyone ever opens that cell door, Amanda, we'll kill him. I swear it. I swear it to him, and to you."

His promise had the desired effect. She dipped the barrel of her gun to the floor. "I'm going to hold you to that promise."

"You won't have to work at it," Mark assured her.

Kunz feigned a yawn.

Tempted to shoot him just for that, Amanda tensed. Footsteps sounded in the corridor.

"Ah, it appears the cavalry has arrived." Kunz smiled. "The choice of whether I live or die is apparently no longer yours to make, Captain West."

"Don't count on it," Mac spoke up from the doorway. "Captain West, if you want to kill him, now's the time. Otherwise, we're coming in."

Fear flashed through Kunz's eyes. Fear that gave Amanda an enormous sense of satisfaction, which, she was sure, had been Mac's intention. She waited a long moment, as if wrestling with whether or not to put a bullet in him, her gaze locked with his. The fear in him deepened, solidified, and he dropped the glass he'd held midair.

It shattered on the floor, and he nearly jumped out of his skin.

Amanda smiled. "Come in, Mac. There's no one in here worth a bullet."

A team of five men entered the office and arrested Thomas Kunz. The lieutenant read him his rights, and Amanda and Mark stood back and watched, immensely satisfied.

When they led Kunz out and he passed Amanda, he smiled, and an odd chill coursed through her chest. His eyes were empty, with no sign of remorse. "You've been amusing, Captain."

*Amusing.* He'd said that she would be amusing when she'd first seen him in that warehouse. It seemed like years ago. Amazing how much evil one person can cram into a short period of time. Refusing to let him get to her, she let out a little sigh. "I wish I could say the same, Thomas. But the truth is, you've been mundane and ordinary—almost boringly predictable. And Reese..." She paused for effect. "Why did you take on an arrogant, self-centered liability like Reese?" Giving her head a little shake, she grunted. "Huge mistake. Huge."

If looks could kill, Kunz's glare would have murdered her right where she stood. Enormously satisfied at having pricked his ego, she added, "You *will* tell us everything, Thomas, including the locations of the detainees and doubles and the other compounds. And seeing you screw yourself will be very amusing to me." She turned her back on him, signaling him as he once had her, that she didn't feel threatened by him.

"The FBI will take it from here." Kunz's footsteps echoed down the corridor. Mark swung an arm around Amanda's shoulder. "Let's go home, honey."

S.A.S.S. remained covert and unmentioned. The FBI would handle all the information made public. "Yours or mine?" She looped an arm around his waist and led him out of the office.

Mischief danced in his eyes. "Does it matter?"

"Not to me, but it could to Colonel Drake."

"Mine, then," Mark said. "Since she's at Providence."

Amanda stretched up to kiss him on the chin. "I'm seeing sunset and a fishing rod in my immediate future."

"And lots of water," Mark added with a lopsided grin. "I've got a promise to keep, too. About winning a computer game."

"Yes, you do." She smiled up at him and they walked down the corridor to the fork. "Do you have a laptop?"

"Yeah, why?" He clearly wasn't tracking her train of thought.

"It's portable," she said, giving him a wisp of a wink. "Multitasking is a valuable tool, Mark."

His gaze heated, glazed with a sensual fog. "You want to take it to the dock?"

He was playing dumb to tease her, and after all the tension, being playful was a welcome respite. Switching gears from life-threatening danger to a normal life was a lot easier with him than it ever had been alone. Wanting him to realize that, too, she tossed the playful tone right back at him, answering with a mysterious Mona Lisa smile. "Not exactly."

They walked out into the sun.

"Captains?" The lieutenant who had given up his golf cart on their arrival met them at the mouth of the shed. "Colonel Drake's ordered you back to Providence ASAP."

Amanda tried not to resent passion being postponed, and

nodded, hoping she could conjure up at least a little more energy to hold her over until they had resolved whatever new
crisis had arisen. "Thanks, Lieutenant. Can you give us a lift
to the airstrip?"

"Sure thing, ma'am."

"I wonder what this is about?" Mark asked, sliding onto
the back ledge of the golf cart.

"I don't know." Amanda sat down beside him and wedged
her hip between his and the wall of the cart. "But the way our
luck's been running, I'd say it's a sure thing that whatever it
is isn't good."

# Chapter 20

Mac provided a pilot to fly Amanda and Mark back to Florida.

.They sprawled out in the cabin and slept like the dead, not waking until the pilot awakened them after he'd landed the C-5. Bleary-eyed, Amanda glanced at her watch. It was just before 2:00 a.m.

When they had taxied in and parked, the pilot opened the hatch, and she and Mark moved to leave the aircraft. "Thanks for bailing us out, Captain," she told the pilot.

"No problem, ma'am. You two look pretty beat."

An understatement if ever one had been uttered. Amanda walked out onto the steps and looked down. Kate stood at the edge of the flight line, waiting for them. "I told you it wasn't going to be good," Amanda muttered to Mark.

He didn't bother to answer, just took a drink of water out of a fresh bottle and sighed, which said all that needed saying about both of them and their physical condition. They walked side-by-side over to where Kate stood.

"Tell me there's not another crisis," Amanda said. "I'm dead on my feet and Mark really needs a substantial meal." He'd been munching on emergency rations since they'd left the cemetery, but she remembered the feel, and his stomach had to resemble a hollow pit.

"No new crisis," Kate said, pointing to the car they were to get in.

Amanda walked toward it with Mark striding at her side at a good clip.

"Unfortunately, we're still working on the old ones." Kate tugged at her uniform skirt, cueing Amanda that she had run out of slacks, which was the only time, when given a choice, Kate ever opted for a skirt and the heels that went with it. The heels had her struggling to keep pace with Amanda and Mark. "This whole thing is so damn complex. It has more legs than a damn millipede."

Mark looked as puzzled as Amanda. "Then what prompted the ASAP summons to return here?" he asked.

"You can thank Colonel Gray for that." Kate frowned. "God, but that man's a real piece of work."

"What did he do now?" Amanda slid into the sedan's passenger seat, then shut the door behind her.

Mark usurped the driver's seat, leaving the back seat open for Kate.

She crawled inside, slammed the door and reached for her safety belt. "He petitioned Secretary Reynolds to reassign Mark as a liaison to the FBI to clear out the clutter in Texas and Kunz's other compounds."

"Texas?" Amanda shuddered. The compound was a heap of rubble in a barren desert. The only things moving around there were rattlesnakes and tumbleweed.

"Damn. He wants a finger in the operation, and I'm the

knuckle." Mark cranked the engine, knocked the stick into Drive and hit the gas. "I don't want to move again already—especially not to that hellhole."

"He wants to punish you for hooking up with Amanda and siding with Drake against him, the petty bastard."

Kate leaned forward and gave Mark a consoling tap on the shoulder. "But you're not going to have to move. At least, not if Colonel Drake has her way."

Amanda looked back at her. "What are you saying, Kate?"

"When Colonel Drake heard what Gray had done, she went to Secretary Reynolds, too. She said since Gray was willing to cut Mark loose anyway, she could really use his expertise in the S.A.S.S., which is where he belonged—with his own, not with the FBI. They wouldn't utilize Mark's special skills anyway, because he's not one of them. His being there will just make everything a turf war over jurisdiction." Kate grabbed a breath then continued. "Anyway, Secretary Reynolds talked with SAIC Mac about it, and then called back Colonel Drake."

"Reynolds agreed to bring me to the S.A.S.S.?" Mark checked Kate out in the rearview mirror. "Just like that?"

"He's considering it for twenty-four hours," Kate said. "Until then, at Colonel Drake's recommendation, he's restricted you both to quarters."

Amanda and Mark exchanged a glance and had to bite smiles off their faces. "Why?" Amanda asked because she was supposed to and not because she objected. She couldn't be more pleased.

"Colonel Drake convinced him it would be in the best interests of the United States—integrity of the mission—to not have you two interact with anyone until you've had time to rest and then do a full debriefing. After that, she says, you can be informed of new intelligence gathered from the compounds and/or prisoners. Keep the chain of evidence clear and clean and not contaminate your statements."

Mark looked at Amanda. "She's giving us time alone to celebrate?"

Amanda nodded.

"Celebrate what?" Kate asked, her blue eyes dancing with curiosity.

"Surviving," Amanda said, her voice deadpan flat.

"Right." Clearly disappointed at being shut out of the inside loop, Kate sniffed. "Swing by headquarters and drop me off, Mark."

Mark again sought Kate's eyes in the rearview mirror. "Don't we have to report to Drake?"

"No, that's why she sent me. She doesn't want either of you at headquarters, on base, or even checking your voice mail until 10:00 a.m., day after tomorrow. You're on isolated restriction to your quarters."

He pulled up in front of the building housing headquarters and stopped near a concrete barrier. "God, I think I love that woman."

"She has her moments." Kate let out a little laugh and got out of the car. "Ten a.m. day after tomorrow. No phones, no news, no interaction with the outside world," Kate reminded them. "Isolated restriction to quarters."

"No problem." Amanda promised.

"None at all." Mark glanced over. When Kate shut the door and turned for the building, he looked back at Amanda and added, "I think you'll probably sleep straight through until then."

She slid closer to him on the seat and nuzzled his neck. "I wouldn't count on it."

Amanda didn't make it out of the car much less to the bedroom.

It had been days since she'd really slept, and more days since that sleep consisted of more than stolen naps. But on the short ride from the base to Mark's house, Amanda had given in to her body and relaxed.

It was flattering, Mark thought, lifting her out of the car and carrying her into the house. She grunted twice but didn't bat an eyelash. He'd bet he was the first man in her life she'd trusted enough to sleep the sound sleep she was indulging in now. Just as he'd bet she was the first woman with whom he'd sleep that sound sleep. It was born in trust. And until now, and with each other, neither of them had had people, much less lovers, they felt they could trust enough to be totally vulnerable around.

He carried her into the room he'd given her upon her first arrival, fully intending to share the bed with her. Not because he intended to make love with her anytime in the next few hours, though the idea certainly held appeal, but because he wasn't ready to let go of her just yet. He thought he'd lost her.

In the tomb, through dark and empty hours, he thought he would never again see her alive. It had rattled him then, and it rattled him now. He didn't need sex any more than she did at the moment.

There wasn't a bone in his weary body that didn't ache, or a muscle that wasn't dancing with cramps, or a gray cell in his brain that didn't beg for sleep. Yet as much as he needed relief from all those things, he needed something else more. He needed to hold her. To just hold her and let it sink in that she was safe, and they were together.

The truth bolted through him with such force if he hadn't been holding her in his arms, he'd have fallen on his ass. He was in love with her. Totally and completely, head over heels, have-you-lost-your-ever-loving-mind-you-Delta-Force-idiot in love with her.

He didn't have to like loving her—he knew for damn sure she wouldn't like it—but he did have to accept it. He had avoided entanglements his whole life, particularly since joining Delta Force. That's when he'd first invoked the six-date-limit rule. But the first time he had seen Amanda he had known that there was no way he could keep himself from her. She was going to take him down.

She had, and she'd been damn quick about doing it, too. But he seriously doubted she would ever love him back.

*Like him?* Yes. *Care about him?* Yes. *Make love with him?* Well, she already had…more or less—and he'd spent a fair share of time in the tomb imagining how they'd been together. In his mind, he had been there with her. His double hadn't been involved.

That she'd had the courage to tell him about the double meant even more to Mark. Trust. Respect. Integrity. He admired her for that. But did she love him? Could she ever love him?

He scrunched the pillow, moving it out of the way, and watched the steady rise and fall of her chest. He wouldn't bet a nickel on it. Her father had destroyed the odds of her ever loving any man long before she'd even hit puberty.

Mark understood that, and made a conscious decision to never ask her for more than she could give him. He pulled back the covers and put her down on the bed, stripped off her shoes and clothes, down to her underwear, then removed his own, showered, and finally climbed into bed beside her.

As soon as the mattress sank under his weight, she scooted over, seeking him. He wrapped her in his arms and dropped a kiss to the crown of her head. She inhaled, let out a breathy little sigh he took to mean he smelled like himself so she could relax, and slung her leg over his, her head and hand on his chest, over his heart.

His throat felt like sandpaper. He craved a glass of water, but not enough to leave her arms to get one. Sighing his contentment, he closed his eyes…

Sometime later, Amanda fought to awaken. It was daylight

outside. The blinds at the windows were closed, keeping the room in near darkness, but fingers of light edged in between the slats. She didn't know where she was, but she felt a man's weight in bed beside her. *Mark.*

If they'd made love and she'd slept through it, she was really going to be ticked off. She smiled at her own absurdity. There was no way she could have slept through making love with Mark Cross—not with the fire between them.

He smelled good, fresh and clean. He'd showered—and obviously she hadn't. Tilting her head, she looked into his face. Sleeping soundly.

She eased out of bed and into the bathroom, used the facilities and took a long, steamy hot shower. The soap and water stung her cuts and she had more than a few bruises, including a real winner along her jaw where Paul Reese had knocked her senseless. The water rippled over her body and pinged against the shower-stall floor. The moist heat felt fabulous on her sore muscles and between her stiff shoulders.

Seeing a bottle of shampoo on the ledge, she smiled. It was her brand. She soaked her hair and lathered it up, then rinsed and soaped it again. Arms up, she worked the shampoo through her hair when she heard Mark outside the shower stall. "Need anything?"

"I'm fine," she said. "I thought you were sleeping."

"I missed you."

Her heart warmed. "Really?"

He opened the glass door and stuck his head in the shower. "Yeah, really."

She opened her arms. "Then come here."

He joined her, then closed the door behind him and turned on the dual showerhead. They stood facing each other, the warm water massaging the muscles on their backs. Amanda smiled up at him, lifted a hand to his jaw, caressed him. "Did I miss anything while I was sleeping?"

The devil danced in Mark's eyes and he teased her, "Only the best sex of your life."

"Figures." Teasing him back, she feigned a sigh. "Oh, well. It's back to hot baths, good books and chocolate for me."

He stepped closer. "There is an alternative."

"Oh?" She moved toward him until their stomachs touched, her breasts rubbed against his chest. "What do you have in mind?"

"A second round."

"Mmm." She pretended to consider it, letting her hands drift down his chest to his sides, and couldn't resist the urge to taunt him with an outright lie. "Hard to get enthusiastic when I have no recollection of the first round."

"Right." He gave her a killer smile that said he knew she wanted reminding of that imaginary first round, then bent to lay a row of butterfly kisses on her neck and throat. "Sometimes we only think we've forgotten," he said, playing along with her. "The smallest thing can trigger total recall."

"Smallest thing?" Her breath hitched and she sucked in deep.

"Mmm, a kiss." He kissed her right below the clavicle, the nested valley between her breasts. "A nibble." He straightened and caught her bottom lip, raked it suggestively with his teeth. "A look." He lifted his head, his gaze on her brazenly hungry and smoldering.

"Enough playing," she said on a hitched sigh. "Kiss me, Mark."

"Gladly." He closed his arms around her, pulled her to him and kissed her long and deep.

No tender exploration, this. This was a kiss steeped in passion, drenched in the desire to cut loose and satisfy or be consumed whole. His hands explored, his mouth plundered, and the combination sent her tumbling into a world of sensation that stacked layer upon layer of feelings and bared emotions she never before had dared to let loose, never before been tempted to let loose.

Rioting on their own, these emotions rose up from hidden places inside her and expanded one upon another, and another, and yet upon another until logic and thought ceased and only raw emotion and acute awareness of everything about him remained.

They came together first in mind and then in body, seeking to pleasure, to be pleasured, holding nothing back, giving without thought to protections and shields and repercussions.

This was a time for celebration, for the sheer joy of living and loving and being loved, and together, they reveled in it until spent.

Twilight found them on the end of the dock, sitting in low-slung chairs, rocked back, downing huge quantities of water and dipping fishing lines into the bay. Amanda couldn't remember ever in her life feeling this relaxed or satisfied.

It'd been a day of lovemaking, sleeping and eating—not necessarily in that order. And each time they had come together, it had been with the passion and urgency of the first time. That sense of total union. Amanda had never before felt it and brought it up to Mark. It was new to him, too, and they discussed and analyzed, put forth hypotheses and speculated, but neither was ready to admit out loud that what made their lovemaking so different from any other in their experience was love.

That would come with time. For now, they were content to give love and receive love without speaking of it.

Both had heard enough empty words in their lifetimes. They would never hear them from each other.

When the sun sank beneath the horizon, they returned to the house, made dinner—fish and salad and fresh greens with apple pie for dessert. They ate too much, and then tidied up the kitchen grumbling because they were stuffed.

When they were done, Amanda turned out the light and asked Mark about his laptop. "Are you ready to show me the secret path to winning Dirty Side Down?"

"Sure, but why the laptop?" he asked. "There's a desktop in the computer room."

"Is there a bed in the computer room?"

He smiled. "No, actually there isn't."

"There you are then." She lifted a hand and walked out of the kitchen and back to the bedroom.

Mark snagged a couple bottles of water from the fridge and his laptop from the computer room, then followed her. Amazing, but with all the hell they'd both been through, he could never remember a time in his life when he'd been happier.

And that struck him hard. Ordinarily, he'd just pull back. Not say a word and dive into avoidance. But this was Amanda. And he had no intentions of avoiding her. "Are you happy?"

"Reasonably." She sat up in bed. The sheet slid down her chest to her waist.

"I mean with me." He didn't move. Hell, he couldn't breathe.

"Oh, yeah." She smiled and tapped the mattress beside her. "Very."

"Good." He walked over, set the water bottles on the nightstand and passed her the laptop. "Because I'm really happy with you."

Her smile lit up his world. "I'm glad. Saves us both the trouble of getting testy."

He went to open the laptop, but Amanda lifted herself, shoved the computer out of the way and straddled him. "Later. Right now, I'm happy and I want to be happy with you."

"You're killing me, woman."

He didn't look like a man dying. They rarely smiled. "You complaining?"

"No. Absolutely not." He reached for her. "Make love with me, Amanda."

She growled low and deep, close to his ear. "For how long? Six dates?"

He stroked her hair, pushed it behind her ear. "For as long as it takes."

"For as long as *what* takes?" Her forehead wrinkled in confusion.

"For as long as it takes for you to realize you'll always want to make love with me—in and out of bed."

She glared down at him, half startled, half confused. "Are you talking about sex or sharing a life?"

"Making love consists of both, don't you think?" He smiled at her twisted mouth, all primed to blast him. "Great sex, great life, love in and out of bed. I was kind of hoping it was all a package deal."

Inside, her spirits soared. "It is a package deal."

"For how long?"

"For as long as it takes," she said, throwing his words back at him and punctuating them with a nip to his chest.

"For what?"

She rolled her gaze ceilingward and held it so he wouldn't miss it. "To see if we're as good together when there's peace as we are in crises."

He looped his arms around her shoulders, let his hands glide over her back and up underneath her bunched T-shirt. "Honey, I hate to point this out—in fact, I'm thinking I'm a damn fool to do it, especially when you're looking at me like you could devour me." He tilted his head on the pillow. "Have I mentioned that you're incredibly sexy, Amanda?"

"No, I don't believe you have." She captured his hands and cupped them on her breasts.

His Adam's apple bobbed hard in his throat. "Well, you are."

"You know, your judgment is looking better all the time." She smiled and rewarded him, rubbing their noses. "What do you hate to point out?"

"Um?" He hesitated, obviously having difficulty holding on to his thoughts.

"You said 'Honey, I hate to point this out, but—'"

He had to dig for it, but finally he grasped the thought. "But in our jobs, we're seldom at peace and we're nearly always in crisis."

"I know that, but still it seems like sound judgment." She gave a little shrug and his T-shirt slipped off her shoulder.

"Logical." He kissed her exposed skin, then grunted and kissed it again. "Completely."

As if any of it really mattered. They'd taken the fall and that was that. It was just a question of how long they'd both fight the inevitable. Hell, from the looks of things the fight was over before it had begun. It was the admitting it that was holding out. "Good." She smiled against his mouth. "Now show me how to win this game, and I'll forgive you for out-fishing me today." She stretched to reach for the computer.

"Forgive me later." He pulled her back, until she half-draped his body. "Love me now."

She sank against him, eager to grant his wish.

# Chapter 21

Promptly at 10:00 a.m. Amanda and Mark entered headquarters. For the past two hours they had been discussing the challenges of long-distance relationships and how they could avoid them. The thing was, as best either of them could tell, there were no real solutions. The challenges were facts and they could only be endured.

Headquarters was wild: phones hopping, people running from desk to desk information sharing, updating each other in informal briefings. A task force was operational and pulling simultaneous arrests on known Kunz doubles, and three OSI agents had been assigned responsibility for tracking and maintaining the umbrella: keeping tabs on the big picture of what was going on where and with whom at all times. They would issue all future Compilation, Assimilation and Assessment Reports.

"Looks chaotic, but it's actually pretty well organized already." Kate slid off her seat and walked around the edge of her desk to where Amanda and Mark stood observing. "Colonels Drake and Gray are waiting in the conference room. We have a 10:10 teleconference with Secretary Reynolds."

"General status briefing?" Mark asked. "Or is Reynolds going to announce his decision on my reassignment?"

"I wasn't informed, but I don't think it's general." Kate dropped her voice, checked for extra ears within hearing distance. Assured there were none, she added, "Whatever it is has a briar up Colonel Drake's ass and a feather up Colonel Gray's. It's the first time I've seen him smile since we've been here."

"He never smiles unless someone else is in pain," Mark warned Amanda. "Prepare for anything."

They walked into the conference room and took their seats. The colonels were the only other people present and, as warned, Colonel Drake looked as if her face had been carved out of rock and Gray looked as giddy as a circus clown. If they got out of the briefing without Drake decking him, Amanda would consider the meeting a resounding success. "Morning," she said.

"Morning." Colonel Drake nodded for them to sit down.

Amanda wasn't slow. Whatever this was about, it was part of the pissing contest between the two commanding officers. She motioned to Mark, and they sat down on Colonel Drake's side of the table. So did Kate. The move earned Mark a glare from Colonel Gray that would shatter steel, which Mark resolutely ignored. Clearly, he felt no obligation for loyalty to a commander who had sold him out to the FBI, where he'd be kept at arm's length because he was an outsider. The different branches of security and defense were extremely territorial, and Colonel Gray certainly knew it. That added insult to injury for Mark, and for Amanda and Kate.

The conference link came through at exactly 10:10, and Secretary Reynolds's face appeared on the computer screen. "Morning, everyone."

"Good morning, sir," they all replied pretty much in unison.

"Thanks for joining me," he said. "I've just been updated by Intel, who consulted with the task forces there and in Afghanistan, and with the FBI at the compound down in Texas. Across the board, they're convinced GRID has been severely crippled with Paul Reese dead and Thomas Kunz in custody. I'm assured we have enough hard evidence to keep Kunz in jail for the rest of his natural life. Dr. Joan Foster has delivered extensive reports detailing some of the duplicates. The SAIC in Texas reports locating a small cache more."

*From where?* Amanda slid a look at Mark. He'd seen the empty records room, too, and his puzzled expression mirrored Amanda's.

"Apparently Gaston," Secretary Reynolds went on, "one of the detainees you rescued, had been responsible for hand-carrying this cache to the Middle Eastern compound when they were evacuated. He buried them instead."

Ah, Amanda relaxed. Now it made sense.

"There's no way to determine how many doubles are operational at this point. Intel has proof of nearly ninety."

"Sir?" Drake interrupted. "I'm told Thomas Kunz literally laughed at that number, which has interrogators certain there are far more of them currently installed and operational in sensitive positions within our ranks."

"That's the report I've gotten, too, Sally."

"S.A.S.S. will eventually get them all, sir," Colonel Drake said. "GRID leadership and the doubles."

"I have every confidence it will," he said. "Which is one of the reasons I'm transferring Captain Cross to the S.A.S.S. to assist you. I'm impressed with the work he and Captain West have done together. Have his security clearance reinstated right away."

"Yes, sir."

Everyone at the table, including apparently Colonel Drake, knew that Mark's clearance had never actually been downgraded. But no one so much as blinked. The order was for show, and to get it on record in case the subject ever arose in this room, in the unit, or outside it.

"Good." He looked as if he had mixed emotions on what he was to say next. "The president feels it would be wise to move the S.A.S.S. out of Washington. Intel, the FBI and the CIA have all advised him that it would be best to distance the S.A.S.S. from easy access by interested congressional parties, if you know what I mean."

And diminish deliberate leaks, Amanda thought, as well as interference.

"Where are we relocating, sir?"

"Providence," he said. "Colonel Gray has been kind enough to offer facilities north of the actual base. You and the S.A.S.S. will have total autonomy." He looked at Gray from the screen. "I'm sure you'll be a gracious host."

"Of course, sir."

*Of course, sir?* Gray would be a freaking nightmare. But this did explain why he was so happy. He would have control over S.A.S.S.'s facilities and well-being, if not control of its missions.

"Make it effective immediately, Colonel." The secretary sighed. "I know it's a pain to face the upheaval of relocating during an ongoing mission, but there's always an ongoing mission with the S.A.S.S. Do the best you can to make it painless, Sally."

"Yes, sir," Colonel Drake said through gritted teeth.

"Dismissed," Reynolds said, then the screen went blank.

Mark spoke up. "Colonel Gray, what quarters are available to the north of the base?"

"The abandoned bombing range." Gray openly smiled, folded his arms over his chest.

Colonel Drake frowned but held her temper. Kate and Amanda kept their mouths shut. This was not a time to get in the middle of anything.

"But there's nothing out there," Mark protested. "No facilities, nothing but an abandoned water well and a dilapidated shack."

"I'm sure Colonel Drake has served in more primitive conditions, and it won't affect the mission—unless you think it'll be a problem, Colonel."

"It'll be fine." Drake stood up. "If you'll excuse us, Colonel Gray, I need to confer with my staff."

"I'm sure you do." He sauntered to the door and as he closed it, he laughed out loud.

Drake turned to Mark. "Is it that bad?"

"I'm afraid so, ma'am." He couldn't lie to her. "But give me a week. You all have things to settle in D.C. before setting up shop here, right?"

"Yes, we do."

"Then do that this week, Colonel, and leave Regret to me."

"Regret?"

"The range," Mark said, his jaw tight. "If Gray thinks he's going to give us a rash by pulling this stunt, he's going to regret it. We won't oblige him."

"I like your style, Mark." Colonel Drake smiled. "But Gray's never going to authorize funds for a building, much less for the electronics we need."

"We have the electronics. Hell, we have all the equipment," Kate reminded her. "We just don't have a place to put it once we get it here."

"You will." Mark shook his head. "You know, sometimes it's hard to remember that bastard is on our side."

"Amen." Colonel Drake smiled again.

"Colonel," Amanda interjected, uneasy about discussing this but knowing it was the right thing to do. "You need to know that Mark and I are exploring a personal relationship. I don't expect it to adversely affect my work, and I'm sure Mark doesn't either, but, well, you should know it."

"I'm aware of it, Captain." The look in Drake's eyes softened. "I'd about given up hope on you ever letting a man get close, Amanda." Her eyes sparkling, she walked out of the room. "Come on, Kate. Let's give them a minute or two."

As soon as the door closed, Amanda stepped into Mark's arms. "I'm going to miss you, honey," he said.

"Me, too." A little wisp of doubt clouded her eyes. "This is going to work out for you—us working together, right?"

"Absolutely." He let his fingertips slide down her face. "You know, Kunz's successor has likely already taken the helm. It could take a long, long time for us to run down all the doubles and demolish GRID's organization. Actually, it could take a lifetime." He looked very pleased with that prospect.

And so was she. A lifetime with Mark might just be long enough to satisfy her. A day less, and she'd be left wanting. "I could live with that."

"In plain sight?"

"Oh, yeah." She looped her arms around his neck and smiled into his eyes. "In plain sight."

\* \* \* \* \*

*Don't miss the next book in Vicki Hinze's thrilling* WAR GAMES *trilogy,* DOUBLE VISION, *coming soon from Silhouette Bombshell!*

*Available wherever Silhouette books are sold.*

## Books by Vicki Hinze

Silhouette Bombshell

*Body Double* #12

## Writing as Victoria Cole

Silhouette Intimate Moments

*Mind Reader* #510

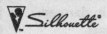